I0788211

The Deaths

Amanda Sandoval

The novel is fiction, except for the parts that aren't.

Contents

Chapter 1

It's peculiar to me the things you remember when you're watching someone die. It's always the good memories that creep back in, never the bad. I kept thinking of Mother singing Patsy Cline while rolling pink-sponge curlers in my hair for church the next morning; the way she spoke so elegantly to the ladies at her Garden Club brunches; the way she would contort her face to glue on her signature bold eyelashes and apply her coral lipstick; pruning her rose bushes with shears in one hand and a burning Pall Mall in the other, one of the very ones that killed her.

I've sat at her bedside and remembered her laugh; the exact art of it. Every syllable. Every sound. The lines that used to encapsulate that smile were hidden now by her oxygen cannula. Nothing was left of her eyelashes now but scattered bits of old glue that wouldn't come off and drove me insane and made her look like someone else's mother. Her black, beauty parlor hair was now soft, wilted against her thin, pale face.

Most of the time, my mind would be stuck in the past; I had nothing to do but remember. I would think of something suddenly, something simple – like her gardenia perfume, and it would overwhelm me to the point of insanity; make me want to grab her by the shoulders and shake her hard; make her wake up so she could laugh again or yell at me or call me names.

Fight back. Fight death.

But I already knew that there was no fighting death. That fact was what made me old before I had a chance to be young. Death: no one was safe from it; the undefeated force of endings. God's final taking.

At this point, I've lost everyone; my hands were tied by death again, and all I could do was wait. Was it all just bad luck? A family curse? The Deaths had come and shifted my focus from light to dark and covered me in a cloak of fear. That fear haunts me at night and chokes me in my sleep. It grabs me by the nape of my neck to whisper ugly truths in my ear. I don't know why I was so surprised when Dr. Rance gave us the grim report on her last trip to the ER. It's not like I didn't know how bad it was; I just couldn't seem to prepare myself for it. I guess denial does that – it makes people confused. A little fucked up. Denial does that, death does that, and life does that, too.

The house on Seminary Street will need to be emptied and cleaned out now that Mother is never coming back. I don't know why Mother kept so much of Daddy's things; more clutter, more punch-drunk memories of times gone by that I wished never had. More shit to discard with the guilt of generations of people who, at one point, were alive and well. Things they wore that held their smell; personal belongings that spark memories of the last time you saw them hold it. But, then again, thinking back, I do know why she kept it.

She kept it because it's too damn hard to let go.

I'd done the same thing when I lost my daughter. Saved heartbreaking mementos because that's just what you do when someone dies. Put a flower from their casket in your bible. Say a prayer. I saved a clipping of her thick, brown hair and the blanket she was wrapped in when she passed.

What sounded best to me was walking into that old house and pouring gasoline along the baseboards. Spraying it over the grass and in the rosebushes and striking a match. Watch it burn down to nothing and bury the ashes. Spend a whole evening staring at the flames; maybe even walk inside that burning house and go, too. Offer my own life instead of having it taken: catch the Reaper off-guard for once.

I'm delusional now, and I know it. Nothing seems to make much sense anymore. And I am so tired. It's exhausting, waiting for death.

The night Mother died, I dreamed I was in the dining room on Seminary Street.

Everyone I knew was gathered around for some kind of

celebration. There were pink balloons everywhere; pink and white crepe paper swirls strung across the ceiling; pink-wrapped gifts and bags with pointy tissue paper tips lined the table around the cake and other food on the table. Silver Mylar balloons bobbed and bounced behind me, tied to my chair. The celebration was for me; it was a baby girl, just what I wanted. Then, the chair I sat in became recognizable as Mother's old rocking chair from the back porch. Mother, dressed in royal purple so deep and majestic I could hardly look at her. She had on all her fancy jewelry, her hair was perfect, and her eyelashes were flawless. She was smiling bigger than I'd ever seen her. Absolutely beaming at me as she walked over and handed me my baby, swaddled snugly in a pink blanket. I took the baby, smiling back at Mother with tears in my eyes and accepting excitement from my guests, who were crowding closer and closer to see the little one.

Mother stood in front of me, and Daddy was standing near the stove. He was dressed for work with a beer in one hand and a cigarette in the other. He didn't seem to be interested in the party but was more focused on Gary, my Mother's first love – my biological father – who was standing by Grandma and Grandpa Rose beside the baby's crib. Gary, whom I hadn't seen since I was two aside from photos, looked smug and suspicious. He peered around the room like he was waiting for something to happen: a bomb to drop, a hurricane to swipe through. Something. When our eyes met, I smiled at him, but he did not smile back. Though I'd always been told I had my father's eyes, his were not big and blue; they were black and beady. Mischievous. Demonic. Then he fixated on Mother.

Michael walked into the room wearing red corduroy overalls and holding a yellow racecar. His smile was infectious; he was thrilled at all of the people and excitement. Then, the baby started squirming in my arms. I looked down and moved her blanket and saw that it wasn't my baby at all – I had never seen this child before in my life. Or had I? The closer I looked, the more familiar she became. I began to slowly recognize and marvel at my own infant self in my arms, fresh from the womb, wide-eyed and pink as a ham.

"Time's up," Mother said. She walked over to me, took my infant self out of my arms, and walked back over to the crib where Gary was standing – nervously, of course.

Then, suddenly, alarms sounded. It was the loudest sound I had ever heard. Everyone scrambled clumsily around and cupped their ears from the sound, but there was no escaping it.

When I opened my eyes, Mother was surrounded by chattering nurses, her flatline screaming loudly throughout the room.

It took almost an hour for Bob, the undertaker at Burgess Funeral Home, to get there. Until then, I sat and waited, alone with her body, with nothing but tears to shed. When Bob came in with the gurney, he stopped when he saw me, walked over, and came in for a hug. "I'm so sorry, Drue. Please let me know if I can help in any way. I'll be in touch this afternoon or tomorrow morning at the latest. I'll need her clothes and any accessories as soon as you feel ready. Again, my deepest condolences."

I walked away from Mother's hospital room holding a plastic biohazard bag from the nurse of all I had left of her: the clothes she wore when she was admitted, her watch, and rings. Her fucking shoes. That fucking inhaler that never helped. I took the jewelry out, put it in my pocket, and shoved the bag down the garbage can on my way out the sliding glass doors of the hospital.

It was raining, still, and had been for days. Spring was here, but instead of sunshine and flowers when I needed it, I got thunderstorms and a muddy graveyard ready for my mother's body.

I walked out to the lot and started up the Civic. I didn't want to go home; I didn't want to see her things, to feel the emptiness. I had never felt so alone in my life. While I was shifting into reverse, I caught sight of Mother's purse on the passenger side floorboard, right where she left it. "Drucilla, go get my purse and put my lashes on," she'd said when she still could. "Don't ever let anyone see me without my lashes. Don't forget that," she'd said, breathlessly. "And make sure I've got both kinds of glue in there."

"Jesus Christ, Mother. I've got it all, just go inside and check in while I park." I had said through gritted teeth.

I was a nervous wreck, and her lips were already turning blue while she spoke. My nerves were shot, and so were her lungs. We walked through those sliding glass doors that night for the last time.

Eloise, my boss at the flower shop, says that the things that make you weak during someone's illness are what give you strength after their death.

I remember the day she told me that: we had been up all night at the ER with Mother about six or eight months after she got sick. At that time, we were having to go once or twice a week, minimum. Both time and nerves were getting shorter and thinner. When I went to work the next morning, and Eloise told me that crap, I couldn't even comprehend what she was saying – but – later on, I got it. The hospital visits; the pain she was in; watching her struggle to breathe; watching her wither away before me – those things were supposed to make her death seem more logical. Or more tolerable. At least she's not hurting anymore. At least she's at peace. At least she's finally healed.

Well fuck all that shit! I wanted my mother, and I didn't care how I had her. I would take her to the ER every damn day, told myself to move in there if I had to. I would try to get her to the best doctors, maybe the Mayo Clinic, where they're trained better and could have done more to heal her. I would move somewhere with better air conditions to help her breathing. Something. I would do anything. Everything. I needed my Mother back. I know her, and she's not resting in peace. There's too much left unsaid.

I picked up the purse from the floorboard and held it against my chest. It was the little blue velvet one she used for casual occasions. I unzipped the top and dumped it out in the passenger seat. The inside contained three different inhalers, pill bottles, her wallet, lipstick, and eyelash glue. Both kinds. I picked up the wallet and unsnapped the button. When I opened it, I saw Mother's driver's license – an (at least) ten-year-old photo of her that punched me so hard in the heart that I found myself sitting there for a really long time, just looking at her, unable to process that the person in the picture was the same one I'd just lost.

Finally, I started up the engine and drove over to Seminary Street alone, with no other place to really go.

***

Opening the front door was like opening a portal to the past. Even though I'd just been there the day before to shower and change clothes, it was somehow different now that she was dead. The smells of meals cooked long ago mixed with mulberry potpourri lingered around like old ghosts and made me nauseous. The vast emptiness of energy in the house felt unnatural: Death was all around, stale and thick like smoke in that old house. I flipped on the television to help cut the sharp loneliness, then muted the infomercial guy's cheerful attempt to sell waterproof tape. The answering machine was blinking like crazy, so I clicked the play button and fell into the couch cushions in sheer exhaustion from death and love. Grief: the gift that keeps on giving.

Beep. "Mrs. Myers, Drue, it's Bob down at Burgess Memorial. I've set up an appointment to meet with you tomorrow morning at nine. Let me know if that's too soon. Again, I am so sorry for your loss."

Yeah, me too, Bob. Me fucking, too.

I tried to call Michael at Duane's but got no answer. Jackie, Duane's wife and the wrecker of our former home, politely greeted me with her voice on their machine. You've reached the Myer's residence… She's the reason I never went back to my maiden name, just to piss her off. I left a message for Michael to call me back. I had more calls to make, a lot actually, only I couldn't make myself dial the numbers. My Aunt Diane would need to know. The church, the garden club ladies, Mrs. Lamb next door. I'd take care of the flowers with Eloise at work. I need to cancel her *Meals on Wheels* lunch. If I see one of their styrofoam boxes out on the porch, I'll kill myself with the plastic spork they send with it.

I'd got stuck inside myself again, where it's always dark and raining fear – where the sun is always covered up by ghosts. I'd prayed like Noah for the floods to cease, but my dove never came back with any sign of safety ahead. The storm wasn't over yet, and I could either ride it out or die trying. I'd already grown bitter; had become dark-natured and morose, shoveling away old memories that stung like bees. I was still no closer to understanding death than I was when my daughter died; when my father died; when Mac died.

When everybody died.

I couldn't help but wonder if I was missing something; like, if I dug deeper through all that old bullshit, I might stumble across a light of hope from somewhere, the missing piece to the puzzle. A gem, perhaps. An oracle to lead me up and out of the valley of the shadow of death. But mostly, I was scared I was next. It was either me or Michael. I'd grown weary and eventually dead inside running from it, but I never made it very far. By the time Mother died, I didn't have the strength to find any oracle. I saw no light. I didn't even have the will to think about the future. I was done. Burnt toast.

I lay there on the couch in muted silence and tried to process my newly tattooed pain. The loneliness felt almost unbearable; there was no one but Mother that I wanted to talk to and sit with at that moment. The loneliness was inevitable – part of the play. That's all that is ever really left behind. My mind kept drifting to the dream I had with Gary in it, the one I had during Mother's end. Would he want to know? Should I call and invite him to the funeral? Would he even care? I baulked at the last minute and decided against it. I had enough to deal with without my walkout, absentee father coming in at the last minute. Forty years too late.

The entire house was still bathed in her presence: her stack of morning newspapers on the coffee table, red reading glasses on top; a single, coral-lipstick stained coffee mug in the sink; her royal purple robe draped across her dressing chair, and her house shoes in the corner waiting for a day that would never come. The longer I stood there holding that robe, the more I realized that even objects seemed to have souls, however, I had already started questioning the existence of my own. I felt like I had died, too. But, if I was the only one left, who was really dead? Only my body remained here, broken and useless, breathing unnecessary air I wish I could have given to my mother.

I took a scalding hot shower and tried to wash away permanent pain unsuccessfully. I cried until I vomited the acidic bile that boiled in my nauseous stomach all day, every day, in worry and fear. I took two of Mother's Valium and passed out wrapped in her robe that had, just days before, kept her body warm.

***

The next morning, I woke up too early, and time stood still. I sat at the table and tried to drink coffee but couldn't manage to choke anything down. Made some dry toast to try and settle my stomach, but didn't eat it. The phone still hadn't rung. Mother was still dead.

I remember the drive over to Burgess Memorial: the streets were busy with weekday morning deliveries and workday commutes. I found it appalling that people could be going on so nonchalantly about their day, smiling and enjoying themselves while my mother was dead. Even in the early morning hours, the springtime sun flooded the streets and beamed off the windows of the shops downtown, creating what I can only describe as the most confusing energy, considering that death had come and stolen from me all sources of light. Even the sun couldn't warm me.

I'd picked out a navy dress for Mother to wear: black seemed morbid, and anything with color seemed tacky and wrong. I put her jewelry, shoes, undergarments and makeup bag in a small tote and hung it over the hook of the hanger. Patsy's last look: Her final ensemble. No more costume changes. I included her driver's license inside a sealed zip lock bag and stuck it inside the makeup bag so the undertaker could see what she really looks like. *Looked* like.

I pulled into the parking lot of the funeral home; it was as empty as I felt. The only other car was the hearse parked under the awning with a subliminal sneer that only I could see. At the front of the entrance, the green bulb was burning. I'd been delivering flowers to the funeral home since the day I started and had learned from Eloise that that meant there was a body inside, to be respectful of the dead. Seeing it glow for Mother was a slap in the face. I stubbed my cigarette against the brick wall and rang the bell. Bob appeared almost instantly.

"Drue, come on in, dear," he said, taking the dress and bag from me. "Let's go down to my office. How are you holding up? Are you doing okay? You look a little pale, dear." Bob was always doing that, calling me *Dear* and acting like we were friends just because of work and the incident at Daddy's funeral, which left a wound I was still tending to.

Or hiding from, whichever.

In his office, I sat in the same old mauve chairs I'd sat in before; looked at the same cheap-looking motel art hanging on the walls; looked at the same blue Kleenex boxes and smelled the same floral stink of funerals. Bob cleared his throat.

"Drue, I was wondering if you knew that Patsy had taken care of most of the details, there's just a few signatures I need, and any personal eulogies and an obit. My wife, Maureen, helps with those if you need it. It can be difficult, as you know, to write one." He looked up from his paperwork and peered over at me from behind his reading glasses, waiting for my reply.

"She planned her funeral?" I asked, baffled. "I couldn't even get her to talk about it."

He smiled a polite smile. "That's not uncommon. That's what I'm here for. She was pretty adamant about the arrangements: no viewing, just graveside service, with an open casket… Wanted Pastor Clarke from First Methodist presiding; I've already contacted him. He is available tomorrow and the next; we can do ten-thirty or two o'clock on each of those days."

I couldn't seem to make a decision, couldn't pick a time to let her go. I just sat there, thinking all the wrong things, until finally, Bob interrupted my warped thinking. "If you don't mind my suggestion, there's a call for rain Thursday morning, but the afternoon looks great. How's Thursday at two?"

"Fine."

"Alrighty, now what about that obituary?" he asked.

"No obit."

"No? Are you sure? We will have to put out a death notice, but you don't want to include any obituary at all?" he said, looking at me sideways.

"Did I stutter? No fucking obituary." I fired back. "Waste of time."

"She will be ready this evening," he said. He put his hand on mine and patted sympathetically, like a grandpa would. "Drue, I really can't express enough how sorry I am that you're going through this again." I ignored his sentiment and stared at my free hand, which I had just begun to notice was starting to look like Mother's. Where did the years go? How are the days so endlessly long, but the years so immeasurably short?

It is questions like these we often ask ourselves during the course of our lives. Unfortunately, they forever remain unanswered.

Chapter 2

Back outside in my car, I could breathe again. I drove back home and pulled into the driveway behind Mother's gray Oldsmobile, which sat staring at me like some sad statue. A monument – a relic of the past. A little burst of nauseating nostalgia took over – it felt like smelling her goddamned perfume. I left the engine running and ran inside to check the machine. There were three messages, one from Eloise and two from church ladies wanting to deliver casseroles that nobody would ever eat.

No word from Michael, nothing from Duane.

I picked up the receiver and dialed Duane's number. When his answering machine gave me the go, I made my announcement at top volume, like I was speaking into a megaphone: "To whom it may concern: My mother is dead. Graveside service tomorrow at two pm. Surely you can find it."

Click. I got back in the car, unable to sit alone in the house, and made my way down Old Sandbanks Road to the cemetery and parked in front of Daddy.

Gerald Vincent Rose

January 12, 1944 - April 7, 1992

Patsy Lyn Rose

The Deaths

I forgot to ask Bob about adding Mother's death date to the stone. Add that to my list of shit to do. Daddy adopted me when I was only three after Gary had split and Mother moved on and settled. To the left was Uncle Bill, Daddy's brother, who died three weeks (to the day) of the same condition: a heart attack. Both of them in their forties. Bam. Bam. Like two gunshot wounds to the family.

On the right was my baby daughter, Samantha…

It still stung to read her name and dates. On her stone was a laser-etched teddy bear with a ribbon around its neck: A noose. The words *Walk softly, my baby sleeps here* were underneath her dates. I remember choosing it in a blur of tears out of a thick plastic binder of options. It was the only thing that seemed fitting. All of my grandparents were there, as were aunts, uncles, and cousins, most of whom I never knew.

The longer I sat there, the lonelier and morose I became. It was hard to believe the way things had turned out; it was hard to swallow the truth. What the hell was I supposed to do now? I have no identity anymore. The Deaths didn't kill me, but a part of me died each time I buried someone I loved.

***

I stopped by the shop to make sure Eloise ordered enough of the orange crush roses for the casket spray, which she did, and then had to listen to her scold me for ten solid minutes for *not calling her to drive me to the funeral home.* "I'll close the doors of this shop and be right there. You are not in this alone," she kept saying, but she was wrong. I was alone. She was working on a string of arrangements, mostly all for Mother, with cards of sentiments that didn't matter, attached to flowers you can't send to heaven.

With nowhere else to really go, I went back home and rolled a joint the size of a baseball bat. I sat at the dining room table, smoking in silence, thinking about new triggers. The only sound? The flatline hum of the fridge.

In the months leading up to Mother's death, I can think of only one good memory to speak of. Surrounded by mounds of chaos, coughing and cancer, life and death, there was that one little nugget of gold that I'll always cherish, and I had to constantly remind myself that one nugget of gold is worth a whole heap of silver.

It was a Saturday afternoon, and I'd brought Mother a salad from the deli she loved and a few groceries. We made small talk; she poked around at the salad but never ate a bite. After a little while, we retreated to the living room to watch television, which Mother kept blaring at thunderous volumes on the all-news channel. I listened to a plastic-haired man talk for what seemed like eternity about a pileup on the interstate just outside Indianapolis. Mother was as shaky and nervous as always, arms folded in fear, legs crossed with one foot shaking like a tremor. Irritated and nervous myself, I sneaked into the kitchen and slipped out the back door for a smoke break.

I lit the little pinner joint I'd brought to settle my own stomach, my own fears, about everything. I had questions swimming around my chest like hungry goldfish looking for words that only Mother could say, but wouldn't. Things I needed to know before it was too late.

Of course, Mother hated shit like that – questions. Vulnerability. She wore a thick mask and didn't believe in things like feelings.

I'd baulked every time I tried to ask questions about Gary, or about Daddy, or about anything from my past because I knew that she'd locked her secrets up long ago, and she would probably take it all to the grave. Though, maybe that was best. Maybe she was saving me from learning something else I'd have to recover from. Maybe it really is best to just let things be, to never learn your truth.

After the joint was gone, I lit a cigarette to try to change the smell of the smoke. But even still, when I sat back down on the couch with, Mother she made several audible sniffing sounds to let me know that I wasn't fooling anyone. Then she stared back at the talking man on screen, images from the accident flashing beside his face, lighting her face up with a bluish hue.

"Does it really help?" she said, making her question seem more like a statement.

"Does what really help, Mother?"

"Marijuana," she said casually, as if it hadn't been a blowup topic since my teenage years. As if smoking the occasional joint hadn't labeled me a drug addict during my formative years.

"Yup, it sure does," I said, still sticking to my guns. "Don't start your shit, Mother. I'll leave, I swear to God."

"I'd like to try it," she said, interrupting me. "I know I can't smoke it, but I can eat it. I did grow up in the sixties, you know. If it kills me, then so be it."

I couldn't help but laugh. Was I delirious? What was happening? "It won't kill you, Mother. It's not like that," I said, trying to reassure her.

"Well, you know what I mean, Drucilla. And we both know I'm certainly not the expert here," she sneered. I tried to picture Mother back in the sixties with a short miniskirt and gogo boots, puffing on a joint, but couldn't bring it forth. That was when I still lived in my little house on Apple Street, the one that stayed empty and abandoned ninety-five percent of the time. I drove over, grabbed my bag and a carton of eggs from the fridge, and headed back over to Mother's. I was euphoric, almost giddy with excitement. I had no idea what was going to happen, but I knew that pot was safer than cancer or chemo and that, at worst – she might eat and fall asleep – the two things I needed her to do the most.

Within the hour, the energy in the house had shifted from horror to high. We talked and laughed about stupid things: things I did when I was a kid, sneaking out as a teenager, and getting caught when the pillows under my blanket didn't get up in time for church. We talked about Daddy – only the good times – none of the times he made me want to kill myself. We joked about my persistence to marry Duane while big and pregnant at eighteen just to try to make it work, knowing full well that it would be a flaming disaster, but going for it, anyway. All or nothing, that was me, and only *she* had known.

We laughed about Daddy hacking the ass off the Easter ham to make a foldover just half an hour before the pastor and his wife arrived for lunch. We laughed about things Michael used to do and say when he was little before everyone either died or left. When people still smiled and talked about ordinary things like the weather or war – the kind fought overseas, not inside our homes. I remembered Michael saying "appy-douche" and "telehopter," and somersaulting all through the house in bursts of innocent laughter –

things I forgot and now miss.

After that, Mother started to talk again about Daddy. Her eyes were red and glassy from pot and tears of both laughter and pain. "I was so smitten," she said, addressing the flowers on the coffee table. "Gerald was so handsome and charming. And he loved me; he really did. And I loved him, too. I did." She was nodding her head as she spoke the words like she was trying to convince me of it, her foot still nervously shaking. She bit the inside of her cheek like she did when she was upset. Her brow wrinkled, and I could see her suddenly shift back into her sadness. Her happy tears ran dark again, and then suddenly – before my eyes – she'd reverted back to who she was now: miserable, trapped, hopeless. *Dying*.

We sat in silence for several moments, quietly letting our tears leak. Then I pulled her to me and hugged her close, which made us both cry harder. I held her fragile body like a child and tried to soak up her tears, her fear, and her grief. I cried with her and for her, furious and bitter with God and death and life and every damn thing in between. She fell asleep not long after, a still, eerie slumber that gave me a glimpse of what was coming.

I covered her in an afghan and sat nuzzled at her feet, thinking about the things she'd said that night. I marveled at how similar our feelings and our fears were. I found it devastating how many years were lost; so many beautiful possibilities had passed because of the masks we wore to get by. To survive. Death had come and taken from each of us, wrecked us all individually yet all together, leaving us grieving the same griefs in solitude.

I desperately wanted that night for Mother to talk about Gary, maybe give me a little insight as to who he was, why he left, and what he was like. I didn't know if they were in love, if they'd ever married, or anything. My father was just as much an enigmatic mystery to me as my mother. But, as usual, she never mentioned him. Only his replacement – who cheated on her and treated her daughter like trash.

It disturbed me to see Mother cry like that. Even after everything we'd been through, I'd never seen her cry so hard or be so vulnerable. Couldn't imagine her feeling *anything*, really. She had always been the best at hiding, something I tried to mimic all my life but never really could. No matter what was going on, Mother wore her mask and shone like a new penny in all circumstances. Maybe that's why Daddy's heart gave out and exploded in his forties. Repression.

When Bob called to tell me that Mother's body was ready, I panicked, suddenly paranoid and blind with fear of seeing her. Nothing I could escape, though. No way out. Numb with tears from painful memories, I drove over to see her.

At the funeral home, Bob guided me down that same dark

corridor, on the same blood-red carpet I'd walked before, and into a small room with flesh-colored incandescent lighting. In the air were soft hymns playing on a portable stereo I saw under a chair covered in baskets of flowers from people Mother probably didn't even like. It was a house of death, and in thinking that, I realized that that's exactly what I had grown up in over on Seminary Street: *a house of death*. It's all I had ever known: the suffrage from it, the bitterness, the resentment. I had no real safe place to return, no happy memories to cling to.

I, too, in many respects, had died myself.

The smell of the flowers was overpowering and sickly sweet. Yet the bright orange hue, the same color as her lipstick, beamed beautifully off of her champagne-colored casket. When Bob opened its lid, it creaked like the door of a haunted house. My knees buckled, and my heart tore out from my chest and escaped my body when I saw her. My soul: lost. At that moment, I was just as much of a shell as she was.

Aside from her pale, bloodless face, the most appalling thing was the work they had done on her hair and makeup… Hair flat and sprayed down flat against her face, pinkish lipstick, dark rouge. No eyelashes. The scattered bits of glue were still there, now covered by foundation but still visible, and there was mascara on the very few natural lashes she had left.

Drucilla, don't ever let anyone see me without my lashes.

She looked nothing like my mother. Bob stood beside me and put his hand on my shoulder. "She was a lovely woman, Drue."

Suddenly blind with rage, I shoved his hand away and looked him straight in the eyes.

"That's not even what she fucking looks like, Bob!" His eyes widened, and I could tell he was nervous. He was always nervous around me since Daddy died.

Don't ever let anyone see me without my lashes.

"Mrs. Myers, we really tried to recreate—"

I put my hand up to stop him. "Where's the makeup bag I gave you? Where is it?!" I was screaming before he could answer. Then, he disappeared momentarily and came back, holding the bag with shaky hands, which I snatched away from him too rigidly in my anger, without remorse.

"Get out."

"Mrs. Myers, I don't think that is—"

"Get out! Get out! Get out!" I shouted over and over until he slid the door closed and sealed me in there. Alone.

Don't ever let anyone see me without my lashes.

I grabbed the new set of lashes I had put in there and pulled out both kinds of glue. I remember she was cold, but her skin was still soft. I kissed her forehead and put on her left lash perfectly. On the right eye, a small drop of glue fell on her bony cheek. I remember apologizing out loud and then remembering that she was dead. I used the Kleenex provided to wipe off most of the rouge and changed her lipstick to her own signature hue. When I was done, she looked like Patsy Rose. The real one. And it destroyed me.

I cried and told her how sorry I was for her suffering and apologized for anything I added to it. I told her I wished she hadn't suffered so long in silence, that I was there and was suffering, too.

I remember vague, unreliable details about her funeral: the slow, monotoned reading from the book of Psalms; deeply painful hymns that strummed emotional chords within me like a grand-scale performance; the look on Michael's face when he said goodbye. During the service, I felt an odd sense of observing myself from afar, like I was watching my life play out before me from some alternate time or dimension where everything was dark and closed off, the air sucked dry by the sting of death. As the hymns droned on, I found myself thinking of Samantha; her paper-skinned hands; her lost, glassy eyes searching for nothing; that final moment while I held her and felt her soul slip through my hands like water.

My heart ached, broken into a million pieces that swam in a bloody river of rage and regret, withheld hugs and broken promises.

It was as if a million bricks lay upon my chest until my breathing became as short and erratic as Mother's had been near the end. My eyes were swollen and burning with tears, raw from grief. My entire being felt like pain. I was lost in some personal, tortuous void that was so deep now that I would grow weary trying to escape it.

Near the end of the service, the newspaper-grey sky broke open with a sudden burst of sunlight and lit up the earth again, a surprise I hadn't expected. An unappreciated gift. I saw a bird's shadow glide across the water-beaded grass as the pastor droned on and on about death. Reality would fade in and out and leave me with a sense that maybe this was all just a dream. But then, I would glance over and see Michael crying, and I would, in an instant, be pulled mercilessly back to the truth; to the darkness of our current reality.

It was a feeling I knew well, and each time I experienced it was even more dreadful and I would spend the remaining years of my own life haunted by ancient memories of The Deaths.

And this, then, is the story of how I died, too.

Chapter 3

The year I was ten, I got mono.

I was sick as a dog. Mother was a nervous wreck trying to figure out what to do with me because she had to be at City Hall for some irrelevant Junior League meeting, and Daddy had work.

After an endless-seeming battle, it was decided that Daddy would stay home from work to take me to see Dr. Lee.

***

"It's fifth disease," he said after he checked out my rash and looked at my throat with that big wooden stick pressed against my tongue. "It's common, nothing to worry about," he assured us. He handed Daddy copies of my two prescriptions and instructions on how to ease the discomfort from the rash.

On the ride over to Wright's Pharmacy, it took everything I had not to vomit on the floorboard. Queasy and overly warm from fever and the hot summer heat, I leaned my head against the door and closed my eyes, praying hard to feel better soon. But Daddy, seemingly oblivious to my disposition, was acting cheerful – almost giddy – and that was not at all his nature. He played the radio louder than I could stand and sang along to most of the songs, bopping his hands to the beat on the steering wheel. He wore his dark, sporty looking sunglasses like he did when we traveled. We seemed to be in two separate worlds.

After we dropped off my prescriptions at Wright's, Daddy drove over to Friendly's for chocolate malts, even though I made it very clear that I didn't want one. I sat in the passenger seat and watched him disappear into the shop and come out with two styrofoam cups in his hands. He handed me mine and pulled out the driver's side cup holder, put his malt in it, and grabbed some change from the ashtray. "I've got to make a call," he said. "Sit tight."

I watched him dial the number and rest his arm on the top of the payphone. He tapped his fingers for a minute, and then I saw him loosen up as he began talking. Suddenly, he was shifting around, lining the sidewalk with the tip of his shoe, smiling like he'd just scratched a winning lottery ticket. Daddy wasn't necessarily a happy person per se, so his smiling – to me – stuck out like a rusty nail.

My stomach was in knots, heaving from the few small sips I'd taken while Daddy talked. When he got back in the truck, I told him I didn't feel well and asked to go home.

"Goddammit, Drue," he said. "I've got shit to do. The world doesn't stop turning just because you're sick."

I was too sick to argue, but his comment played over and

over in my head while we drove all the way across town to the bank. He left the engine running, the radio still up way too high. *House of the Rising Sun* was playing. Every other time I'd gone to the bank with either Mother or Daddy, we always went through the drive-through, and they always gave me a lollipop with a loop handle on it. I turned the volume down on the radio and lay down in the seat. Quite a bit of time passed, enough so that I started to get scared.

I sat up and looked around, and everything seemed normal: an elderly couple walking to their car; a stray cat in the gas station parking lot next door; someone pumping gas with a smoldering cigarette like Daddy always did. I waited impatiently for him for several more minutes, and just when I was on the brink of tears, the sun caught the entrance door opening. Through the shaded glass door that stood ajar, I could see Daddy – or at least most of him – and I could see that he was talking to someone.

I slid over to the driver's side to get a better look and saw a lady with glasses lean in and kiss him quickly before he turned to walk outside the building.

He smiled all the way back to the truck. I remember being really confused, knowing what I'd just witnessed was something I wasn't supposed to. When he got in the truck, his cologne was pungent, and his demeanor was unlike his usual self. He checked his teeth in the mirror and smoothed his pilot hair before backing out.

"I need to go *home*, Daddy," I said, almost pleading now.

"After we pick up the damn medicine at the pharmacy. Do you want to get better or not? Why do you always have to complain? It's bad enough I have to miss a whole day of work for this shit."

This shit. He meant me. I had always been a sort of burden to him, and even as a child, I could feel it. I wasn't his real daughter, and it seemed he went to some measure to make sure I always remembered that. Acted like it was my fault that he was infertile and couldn't have his own kid.

"Daddy, why did we go to the bank?" I asked, secretly testing him after we came out of the pharmacy drive-through. He braked for no reason I could see – the car jerked to a halt. Then, he turned the radio down to a reasonable level.

"For money; what do you think? I had to pay for your medicine, didn't I? You think the world gives anything away for free? No, it doesn't. The cream alone was twenty-seven dollars, Drue. And that money I used to pay for it came from the bank. Got it?"

"Yup," I said, saying no more, pleased in some small way with having let him know I knew something he wouldn't want me to.

And after that, he was nice to me.

At home, he fluffed my pillow and gave me juice and my medicine. He even went as far as to give me a cold rag for my forehead and some saltines and iced ginger ale to settle my stomach. That's when I knew the secret I held wasn't a small one, and for the first time, I saw my Daddy act *weak*.

Later that same night, my fever spiked beyond a reasonable level, and Mother and Daddy had to take me to the Emergency Room. The nurses scrambled around me, poked me with needles for my IV, and ran test after test.

After the results came in, it was determined that I did not have fifth disease, but mono – undiagnosed and ravaging through my body.

I ended up spending the next few months recovering and fighting the illness inside a small hospital room. My temperature was sometimes uncontrollable, causing me to have hallucinations and some of the craziest dreams I'd ever had. Terrifying dreams consisting of conscious and unconscious material intertwined with delusion that would cause me to cry out and scream, my hospital gown clinging to me with my sweat.

When I was finally well enough to come home, I was so relieved to be back in my own bed; no needles in my arms or tubes in my nose or throat. Still shaken by the severity of my illness, Mother and Daddy both doted on me constantly. Nothing in our relationships was like it was before I was admitted to the hospital. Daddy would bring me candy home from work, and Mother would cook all my favorite things and brush my hair while she sang. Their constant care and concern, their sudden interest in my life and well-being, was the best feeling I had experienced so far. That was the only time in my life I felt like we might be a normal family after all. I had defeated death, and it shook them to their senses. And, before long, I'd grown a blind, naive affinity for their love.

It bothered me, though, knowing what Daddy did…

I mean, at first, I was just happy to be alive and fully recovered from my illness. Plus, the dynamic in the house had shifted so much that I thought for a while that maybe I hadn't seen anything at all – that it was just another delusional dream from sickness. But then, one day at the dinner table, we were all sitting there eating Mother's pot roast, which I hated. For some reason, it pissed her off that I didn't like brown gravy. I watched Daddy fork a carrot and wave it around while he talked to Mother about some bidding war he was in for the remodel of the courthouse. The memory of it came out of nowhere and slapped me right in the face, right while he bit into that carrot.

And after that, the secret stuck in my throat like broken glass.

Sometimes, Mother would be talking or even just sitting there reading a magazine and smoking her cigarettes, and I would look at her and wonder what she'd do if she knew. Daddy would be whistling in the bathroom in the mornings and I'd wonder what he'd do if I told.

***

I'd say we had a good nine months to a year of customary familial normalcy.

Then, one night around Christmastime, Daddy came home from working late smelling like perfume with lipstick on the collar of his shirt. Mother was in the kitchen cleaning up from dinner, and I was watching It's a Wonderful Life on TV. He opened the door and walked inside, unsteady on his feet and swaying, holding the knob of the door with both hands for support when he finally managed to get in. On his way through the living room to the kitchen, he caught his foot on the rug and tripped and fell face first into Mother's ficus tree in the corner…

I had never seen him drunk like that before. It was completely out of character. Daddy was a business owner, a pillar in our suburban community, and an elder at the Methodist church. He always wore his jeans and button-ups starched and crisp, his hair neatly hairsprayed and carefully styled. But, at that moment, he was sloppy drunk: shirt unbuttoned at the neck, slurred words, tone-deaf affect.

Mother came out of the kitchen with her hands on her hips. Her face looked like she'd just seen a ghost. "Drucilla," she called out. "Go to your room."

Inside my bedroom was no safer; I could hear every word, every piece of crockery crash, every accusation. I sat there stunned, unable to take in all that they were saying to each other and I wanted so badly just to slip out the back door and run away and forget anyone I ever knew.

But, there was no safe place for me to go; no comfort to find. Just when I had started crying and thought I couldn't take another second of it, I heard Daddy mention my name. I held my breath and listened. "Did Drucilla say something to you? That nosey little bitch." I got up and ran across my room and hid under the bed, all the way up against the baseboards, and didn't come out until morning.

***

Back in those days, divorce just wasn't ever something that was really ever on the table – especially if you were a prominent pillar of the community and represented the church.

I remember after their reconciliation – which was more like a sweep under the rug – Mother told me that at our church, in our circle of people we associated with, if you get a divorce, you might as well have lit an orphanage on fire on Christmas day, because you would be "shunned like the devil himself."

That always both confused and bothered me, how people would shun you from the church for divorcing a man who was unfaithful, dishonest, and harmful. That's when I started to really question the people who represented God in our community. Should she just take it and smile, like she did, or should she protect herself and have some damn dignity?

Regardless, what I thought didn't matter. She was way too vain to be a divorcee. A victim.

Things were different, though, after all that happened. Daddy won the bid on the courthouse and worked double the hours; eventually, that job won him a larger-scale clientele and kept him dressed more professionally and away from the house most of the time. But on the weekends when he had time off, we were all awkwardly together at home. He took up lifting weights on the weekends in the garage with a blue sweatband and black, fingerless gloves and drinking whiskey sodas all day long – even in the morning.

During his weightlifting breaks, he would drink his whiskey and smoke one Pall Mall after the other. Then, he'd get right back at it. Anything to avoid the confines of our house.

Despite the tightrope tension and lack of communication between the three of us, everyone seemed to be normal, playing appropriately. Mother dove head first into all of her social activities: Garden Club President, Junior League Secretary, head of the Methodist Church's women's ministry.

She did all but ignore me completely.

She started drinking red wine in the evenings, which bothered me because she would just sit there at the dining room table and chain-smoke while she drank, looking straight out at nothing, lost in the dark abyss of her thoughts, eyes drunk and glassy like she'd been crying.

The times I did see Daddy, I noticed that he would go out of his way to avoid me. If I walked into the kitchen when he was in there, he would walk right out, leaving the sandwich he was making or the cup of coffee he was stirring right on the counter. No subtlety. I wasn't even really sure why. Yes, I knew his secret, but I never told Mother.

Surely he knew that – surely Mother would have ensured that it was her friend Carlene who had told on him. He was calm but guarded, never had much to say, and wouldn't look me in the eyes, either. He just wanted to go to work and pump that iron.

That was it.

We didn't eat dinner at the table anymore, and we all kept our distance. He stopped asking about my day, and he stopped hugging me after school. Although it was something I thought would pass, it never really did. And, I was lonely. I was even starting to miss Mother's constant nagging; at least then, she was still acknowledging my presence.

She was starting to feel more like a stranger to me than my mother. And it scared me. It scared me like going out in the woods alone at night scares a child, like how fire is scared water will wipe it out, like how the day is scared of the spindly tendrils of the night taking over its light.

I was scared.

Chapter 4

Time marched on like a terminal walk through a dry, scorched desert, and when I was twelve, I decided to join the Burgess Middle School's twirling team.

Mrs. Craddock, my coach, had me on the front line during the halftime show by the first game. I was a natural talent; somehow, the baton rolled easily throughout my finger grips in an almost unreal fashion. I loved twirling – I loved everything about it: the halftime limelight, the green and silver sequined uniforms, and the feeling of being part of a team.

We practiced after school every day and had games on Friday nights, and the time spent away was certainly a step up from sitting at home doing chores, listening to Mother and Daddy's constant bickering. Mother would come for home games to watch, but Daddy never did. And, when Mother came, I'd catch a glimpse of her sitting disgusted up in the stands, looking through the crowd of fans instead of at me.

Over the course of the next few years, our team won the state twirling competition in Indianapolis, and I'd won a slew of personal awards at twirling camp in the summer. I made Homecoming Princess and studied hard to keep my grades up, so Mother wouldn't ride my ass about it.

And, for a while there, things were manageable.

You can't fight with someone you don't see. But, one night after twirling practice, I came home and heard yelling from the driveway. It was Daddy yelling, and then I heard Mother scream and something like glass breaking. Inside the house, I found them both in the kitchen, Mother sunken to her knees in the corner, her garden club trophy vase shattered across the floor, and another was in his hands, locked and loaded. He must not have heard me come in; he never turned around.

Which was the opportunity I needed.

I lunged at him, grabbed the crystal vase, and wrestled it from his hands. Then I used all the force I could muster and shoved it into his chest as I came violently toward him, eventually knocking him into the barstool and on the ground.

I held it over his head and almost brought it down to his head, but instead, the fear in his eyes disarmed me. He kicked me away and got up cursing, swiping his hands across the countertops, knocking plates of food to the floor, then walked out the back door and peeled out of the driveway, screeching down Seminary Street.

I tried to help Mother off the floor, but she pushed me away and managed to do it herself. Her house shoes crunched over the glass on her way to the bedroom. I got the broom and swept up the glass; it took two rolls of paper towels to clean up the boat of gravy that stained the upholstery on the dining room chairs. I grabbed Mother's half-empty glass of wine and chugged it, then poured myself another.

I sat on the edge of my bed in shock at what I'd seen. I had no idea what the hell could have caused a fight that bad, and in the past the only fights that escalated to those extremes was a reaction to *being caught cheating*.

That was the day that I'd lost enough respect for my parents to give up on a normal life. Things changed between us all; the discord between the three of us was unsettling and difficult to escape.

***

At that time in my life, I was dating Duane; we had already been seeing each other for a few months. I liked him all right; he was easy-natured and simple – vastly different from the direction my life was going at home at the time. He wasn't all that great looking, but I would have dated Herman Munster to get out of the house and away from Mother and Daddy for a while.

When I wasn't grounded for scaling by my math and history classes, Duane and I would spend our time driving around town with friends, drinking beer at the bluff when we could get it, and making out in Duane's parked truck out in the lot behind St. Mary's.

Since the big fight with the trophy vases, Daddy had deemed me a threat and punished me in small, petty ways that he thought were appropriate and well-deserved. When I turned sixteen, I was not allowed to drive any car that he paid for; when I missed curfew, I was grounded for ninety days (yes, he kept count, and yes, seconds mattered). I was only allowed to use the telephone in ten-minute increments; I was not allowed to stay over at a friend's house or to go to any parties, even innocent birthday parties chaperoned by parents. If I brought home a C on a test or any graded paper, I had to mow the lawn and wash his truck and Mother's car with a sponge and water hose, even in the blaring summer heat; and in the freezing Indiana winter, I shoveled snow.

He hated me, and I hated him, and that was the way we lived.

On one of those snowy winter days, we were on Christmas break from school, and I hadn't seen Duane in almost a week. I was grounded from failing my history test, and, according to Daddy's calendar on the fridge, I was only on day 62. I was miserable, had been locked up with Mother and Daddy for longer than I could take, I was starting to get depressed, and I missed Duane and my friends. While Daddy was at work and Mother was busy, I called Duane and made plans to meet him at our spot at midnight.

The Deaths

When midnight arrived, and Mother and Daddy were asleep, I crept slowly and quietly out of my bedroom window.

We spent our time parked at the bluff, drinking a few beers he'd brought and smoking a pack of stolen cigarettes from Mother. Buzzed from the beer and nicotine, we had sex for the first time. It was awkward, and we were both uncomfortable during and after, neither of us really knowing how to act or what to do.

Afterward, we talked about the holidays and my grounding and the weather, and then he drove me back home to Seminary Street, skidding on ice on the sidestreets. I kissed him goodbye and shut the door. I watched him drive away, his tail lights lighting up the snow with a bright pink hue.

The snow had silenced the town; the air was icy and painful against my face. The only sound came from the crunching under my feet, which made a dog bark nearby. That bitter feeling of loneliness came back in waves the closer I got to the house. I should have felt scared out there in the cold, but I didn't.

I stopped and looked up at the sky, saw the stars shining in brilliant glory against the velvet sky, and, for the first truly natural time, considered the existence of God.

My unconditional bliss was short-lived.

But when I crawled back through my bedroom window and

the lamp clinked on bright, I saw Daddy's angry face light up. In that instant – God and the stars were a far, distant memory.

We both stood silent for a moment. I held my breath and waited to see what he'd do. Then, like he'd been planning it for hours, he walked straight over to my closet, grabbed the armload of sequined uniforms, and slung them over his shoulder. Then he took my trophies. With all of my achievements in hand, he stormed out of my room and made his way into the living room, where I saw Mother sitting on the edge of her seat, pale and still as a corpse. He walked over to the fireplace, full of fresh logs and flames, piled everything on the floor in front of it, and tested me.

He picked up a jumpsuit from the pile, the one I wore my freshman year, and said, "What's it gonna take for you to learn, Drucilla?"

He threw the jumpsuit in, and after it ignited, he picked up another.

"I'm so sick of having to repeat myself. You don't listen for shit."

He threw in my letterman jacket and the suit I won state in that same year…

I stood and watched him, then looked at Mother, who wouldn't look back. I wanted to scream and cry and push Daddy into the wall, but instead, I just stood there and watched, my eyes stinging with tears I wouldn't release. I would not give him that pleasure.

"Do you think you're a grown-up now? Oh, you're a big girl now. You can make your own decisions no matter what the rules are, right? Right?" He threw in the trophies.

The more I resisted his bullying, the redder his face got, the angrier he became. When he was done berating me, there was nothing left but ashes. Mother was crying quietly – having said not a word throughout Daddy's performance. When Daddy left afterward, I faced Mother and looked her dead in the eyes. "Why can't you ever leave him? Why do we have to live like this?"

She took a sip of wine and sat her glass down slowly. Lighting a cigarette, she blew the smoke right in my face. "Don't you ever fucking question me," she said. "Do you understand me? Why can't you just follow his goddamned rules, Drucilla?"

The next morning, when I walked into the kitchen, Mother and Daddy sat having coffee and toast. Nothing had happened; it was all just a dream.

Only it wasn't.

And I wasn't as good at hiding it as they were.

***

I found out I was pregnant the same day I failed another history test in Mrs. Larson's class. Duane and I had been dating for almost a year; I had just turned seventeen. All week long, I'd been fighting off severe nausea and fatigue, and my period was already over a week late.

I sat in the second stall of the girls' bathroom at school for a solid ten minutes waiting for a group of freshmen to finish applying their lip gloss and fruity body sprays, and when I heard them finally exit in a roar of giggles, I opened the test stick's foil packaging and peed.

And I prayed.

Two positive, bright pink lines appeared before I said *amen*.

I wrapped the wand in almost an entire roll of the shitty one-ply toilet paper the school provided and shoved it deep down in the aluminum sanitary napkin receptacle. Then, as if on reflex, I vomited in the toilet.

I sat there with the door locked, sweating and scared shitless for I don't know how long; then I heard Missy's shrill voice coming through the door.

"Drue, you in here, still?" she asked.

"Yes," I managed.

"What did it say?" she asked. I opened the stall door and walked over to the sink and slashed cold water on my face. "Holy shit, dude," she said, smacking her pink bubblegum. "You are so screwed."

It was Missy who had gotten the test for me. Her sister worked down at Wright's Pharmacy and had easy, discreet access. "It's no biggie," she'd said when I asked her for the test. "She used to get them for me all the time before I got on the pill."

That was the thing – Missy was the promiscuous one. Yet she was safe. I tried to get on birth control when Missy did, and Mother acted like I'd asked for hard drugs. Told me I was way too young for all that business and that I'd better just keep my knees together. And then there we were, expecting the unexpected.

I spent the next week in private shock and horror, fully unable to grasp this new reality. Mother and Daddy were going to kill me. Things were bad enough as it was. I thought briefly about abortion. Just the thought of terminating the pregnancy made me think that it would terminate Duane from my life, too. However, going through with it was a life sentence neither of us was prepared to serve.

Duane remained clueless, high-fiving his buddies in the hallways at school and laughing at things that weren't funny. During the time I knew I was pregnant and he didn't, I saw him differently. I noticed how small and boyish he seemed, how immature he was with his friends, and how, both mentally and physically, he still had a lot of growing up to do. I'd seen him as a weekend escape, a night out of the house. Just a night – not my future.

I decided to tell Duane first before I could even think about telling Mother and Daddy. Homecoming was coming up the following weekend, and I decided that I'd tell him after the game on our way to the party his friend Donovan was having at his house. I was so sick and exhausted by that time that I almost couldn't make it. The pregnancy had sent me reeling with nausea to the bathroom at all hours, not just morning. Often, I would have to run the faucet or shower and vomit as quietly and discreetly as possible, then somehow make myself look like I was well and fine.

On homecoming night, after Mother and Daddy were sound asleep, I choked down a couple of saltines chased with Sprite and made my way down to the end of Seminary, corner of Rosebud – our usual meeting spot. He was already there, parked in his baby blue Isuzu under the burning orange streetlight. The bill of his cap shadowed his face.

"Hurry up," he called out. "We're missing the whole party."

The cab of the truck smelled like a brewery, and the malty smell made me want to puke. His breath came out in big, disgusting bursts while he talked about what was going on at the party before I got there. My initial plan was to tell him immediately, finally rid myself of the solitude of a secret, but I was a little surprised at how drunk he was already, and he wouldn't stop yapping about the damn game that I cared nothing about: punts and tackles; touchdowns and bad calls and kings and queens.

By the time we got there, my mind was numb; my stomach was retching in knots of acidic bile. The party was raging, and people were all around, spilling out of the house and into the yard. Green and white streamers and jerseys and cheerleaders and pom poms littered the backyard, where we sat in plastic lawn chairs with beer I would only pretend to drink. I was surrounded by loud, thumping music and flushed, drunk faces and laughter.

I wanted to die.

Duane stood up, "I'm getting a refill," he said. "Be right back." I watched him walk away and, for the millionth time, tried to find some good qualities to like forever if I had to. He was too skinny to be manly, and his thin face made his caps look too big and his ears bent over. He wasn't ugly at all, but he wasn't anything special either. He wasn't even funny, and he was pasty and frail, like a British person.

Over by the pool, I watched Amy Keeton funnel a beer in her purple dress and rhinestone-studded crown. I wanted to strangle her with her sash. Amy Keeton: Miss goody-two-shoes; Miss Burgess High; Miss All-American Teen Queen. She was a fake and a bitch, but she won everything that came her way effortlessly. Why hadn't life been like that for me? Where was my fucking crown? What made her so goddamn special?

Duane came back stumbling. So much for my ride home…

"Let's go out to the truck. I forgot my cigarettes," he said.

We walked through the house and out to the front, where it was quiet and separate from the raging party. The air was thick and humid, almost unbreathable from a storm that I'd been hearing the weatherman talk about every morning while Daddy drank his coffee.

I sat on the tailgate while Duane fumbled inside the truck, trying to get the windows rolled up before it started to rain. He came around to the back of the truck, and the smell of his burning cigarette made me so suddenly sick that I jumped off the tailgate and puked right there in the grass.

"What the fuck is wrong with you? How are you that buzzed, Drue? We just fuckin' got here."

I apologized repeatedly, embarrassed, wiping my mouth with the sleeve of my shirt. He just looked at me with a grossed-out, disgusted look on his face – but didn't offer a napkin or kind word. When a carload of girls pulled up on the opposite side of the yard,

Duane watched them all walk in like they were pieces of meat in a butcher's window.

It pissed me off to the core – enough that I blurted out the words like bullets. "I'm sick because I'm pregnant, you fucking moron."

If looks could kill, I would've been gone right then. But looks don't kill. They stay with you so you can remember the pain that comes with them.

"What?"

"I'm pregnant."

"No, you're not. Shut up, Drue. That's not funny."

"I'm not joking, Duane. I took a test and everything. Listen, we can…"

"Oh my God, are you fucking kidding me? What the fuck?" He threw his cap down and paced, running his fingers through his hair. "Oh my God, Oh my God, Oh my God," he kept saying.

Then the floods came.

The next day was the third Saturday of the month, which was the day for Mother's monthly Burgess Garden Club brunches at our house, where the women would dress up and sit around and gossip and drink mimosas and pretend to be part of something special. All week long, she'd been buzzing around the house like an angry bee, cleaning this or dusting that, pruning roses and polishing silverware, ordering Daddy and me to do our chores to make sure everything was just perfect.

When I woke up, Daddy was outside my window, weed-eating, wearing big, mad-scientist goggles. I could see Mother walking back toward the house with a handful of her prize-winning roses, the ones she always won those trophies for. She loved those vases more than me and Daddy both, and I know that was why he broke one during that fight when I almost nailed him with the next. Mother's proudest moments danced around those awards; he knew exactly what he was doing.

I sat down on the edge of my bed and looked out my other window that faced the street, the one I used to sneak out and get myself pregnant. Kids were playing kickball in the cul de sac, Mrs. Lamb was out on her porch in her rocking chair; somewhere close by, an ambulance screamed loudly.

Everything seemed to be going on as usual; everyone was normal but me.

I reasoned with myself that I would wait until after Mother's Garden Club performance to break the news; if I ruined the brunch, she might just kill me graveyard-dead. At least, then, I wouldn't have to deal with all this shit.

An alternate present and future weaved in and out of my

doom, teasing me like an oceanic mirage in a dry, scorched desert. I could have an abortion, just do it and get it over with – free us from this new reality and from each other. Take the second chance offering. But the thing about it was – I just couldn't make myself fucking do it.

I loitered around in the kitchen to try to see what kind of mood Mother was in. She was arranging the roses for the table setting. She was humming a song, a hymn. *His eye is on a sparrow, and I know He watches me.*

"Drucilla, don't you dare touch those cream puffs yet. Guests will be arriving within the hour. Go and get yourself cleaned up. I hung your dress on the closet door. Go. Now." I started to just say it and get it over with, but her eyes were serious, and I feared her much, much more than I did Duane Myers.

Inside a secret place in my heart, I wondered if it were a possibility for Duane and I to have the baby, maybe even get married and start a normal, American family. Would he eventually come around to the idea of it? I mean, I wouldn't necessarily have picked Duane as my life mate, but what if God had other plans? What if He knew we would love each other, and we just didn't know it yet?

Mother knocked on my door and interrupted my fantasy: her serious, three-rap knock. "Drucilla, five minutes," she called. Five minutes. You're on in five, Mrs. Minnelli. I looked at the dress hanging on my closet door, same as all the rest; itchy and uncomfortable, tight around the middle, my ass, hips, and gut – all sucked up neatly into my hosiery.

"Pain is beauty," Mother used to say when I complained about her yanking the pink sponge rollers from my hair on Sunday mornings before church. "And it only gets worse."

In the generalized miasma of guilt and shame I felt. I tucked away my feelings and hid behind my mask like Mother always did. As usual, I smiled and greeted guests and chatted with women I didn't like about things I didn't care about. I listened over and over about how grown up I was, how beautiful I'd become, and *oh, those eyes!* more times than I could count and answered a thousand questions about plans for after graduation. College and sororities and culture clubs, and all of the things I really hadn't had time to think about, but I managed to answer each question in a way I knew would please Mother, even though I was about to obliterate all of that with my new truth.

But, I managed. Wore the mask, played the part. This was my swan song; one final performance before I went out with a bang.

Finally, it came time to collect dues and listen to old and new business. Everyone sat around smiling, looking at Mother as she made the announcements and formal greeting. "And remember ladies," she said with her pencil pointed up. "Ugliness is so grim. A little beauty, something that is lovely, I think, can help create harmony, which will lessen tensions." The famous National Garden Club quote that I'd heard over and freaking over since Mother became chairman, a quote from Lady Bird Johnson, the famed NGC goddess by proxy. She looked beautiful up there speaking. She always stood out from all the other ladies. If the outside looks good, the inside must be spectacular. That was Mother's reasoning. She was stunning, and she knew it, and so did everyone else.

I think that's why she loved the garden club so damn much: because it had loved her back.

At long last, one o'clock rolled around, and everyone got up and grabbed their purses and peacoats and chatted more while heading out, wasting valuable time. While Mother herded them out like sheep, I went to my room and changed into my usual ripped jeans and t-shirt that Mother hated, but as soon as I saw my reflection in the mirror, I changed right back into my dress, hoping that my news would come off better coming from Drucilla, not Drue.

When the last of the lingerers had finally gone, I gave Mother a few minutes to have her cup of coffee while she counted the dues. As she sat quietly counting, I approached and sat down across from her at the table. "Did you see Carla Varvel? She looked like a potato in that dress. What was she thinking? You never wear horizontal stripes if you have a weight problem – even the tiniest one. You remember that, right?"

"Right. I know."

"Anyway, I think it went great, don't you?" she said. "Did I look okay?" She fluffed the back of her hair.

"Yes, Mother. You looked stunning. You always do." And I meant it. "Mother?" I said, gaining momentum.

For some reason… I had her attention.

"I fucked up. Really bad. I'm pregnant, and I don't know what to do." Tears came out in rivers. I couldn't hold them back anymore. I was choking on them and something else: fear. Mother's face was trembling. Her eyes widened in shock and horror. She put her hands on the table and stood up. Then she leaned over and slapped me hard across my cheek.

"Get out of my sight," she said. Then she screamed it so loud and close to me that I had to cup my ears on my way to my bedroom. "You just ruined your whole goddamned life!" she yelled after me.

***

Later, when Daddy came home, I could hear them mumbling through my bedroom door. I heard him react rather unfavorably for me. There was a lot of yelling and slamming that night. I lay there awake and alone for the rest of the night, Mother's words playing an ugly chord over and over through my head.

You just ruined your whole goddamned life.

Was that what I had done to her? Ruined her life? The questions and worries lingered throughout the night, making my nausea worse and stealing my sleep.

You just ruined your whole goddamned life.

Maybe I had.

Chapter 5

Six months later, the night before I married Duane at the Methodist church, Mother knocked on my bedroom door.

"Come in," I called.

She came in quietly and closed the door behind her. She looked tired. Defeated. Her eyes were red and swollen; her eyeliner was more like eraser smudges than her usual bold lines. She was holding a black velvet jewelry bag.

"Mother," I said, starting to offer some sort of apology or loving sentiment to make her not hate me, but she put her hand up to stop me – cleared her throat once, twice, three times before she could speak. Then she put her hand down and dabbed each teary eye with her balled-up tissue.

She was finally ready to look me dead in the eyes.

"Don't do it," she said, almost pleading. "You don't know what you're doing, Drucilla. Parenting is hard – the hardest thing you'll ever do. And if you marry the wrong person, it's even worse." She grabbed my hand and squeezed; her grip was icy cold. She was crying again. "You'll make sacrifices you don't want to, and you'll settle for things you don't want. You'll end up miserable, Drucilla, and by the time you figure it out, it'll be too late. It'll be too goddamned late. Jesus, I just hate this!"

The Deaths

She stood up and walked out, slamming the door, and leaving the velvet bag on the bed beside me. I picked it up and pulled out my mother's emerald earrings, the long ones I used to always say I wanted to wear when I got married… back when life was still make-believe and full of fairytale dreams.

She had remembered, and I hadn't.

Suddenly, I was overcome with the most intense feeling of filthy shame for having displeased my mother so much so soon.

I felt unclean, and unlike myself, things were getting too real, and Mother only threw gas on the fire. She hated that I was having a baby, hated Duane, hated Duane's family, too, and the fact that I'd decided to at least try to make things work with Duane despite her clear, utter disgust for it all. Daddy had other opinions: we had "responsibilities now," he said to us multiple times. "Both of you," he said coarsely, looking straight into Duane's frightened eyes.

Duane's family was vastly different from my own; not that it should have mattered – but it did. My father was one of the most successful businessmen in Burgess and ran the largest construction company in the county, and Duane's father worked on an oil rig. My mother was, well, *Mother*, and Duane's Mother was sedated and dysphoric from a nervous breakdown she'd had years ago but still suffered from. Duane's father was meek, kind, and humble: a man of few words. My daddy was a shrewd asshole who placed a lot of emphasis on the importance of clout. Since founding Richards Bros. Construction in '62, he'd built more homes and buildings in Burgess than I could count, and I hated it when he would point them out when we would go somewhere in the car. "I built that place, you know," he'd say through his tense, tight-lipped smile.

But despite all familial differences, we were all in the same boat now.

***

Duane and I married on June 1, 1982 – the weekend after our graduation commencement. It was a small, humiliating ceremony with only close family in attendance – Mother didn't allow Missy or any of Duane's friends to attend. No maid of honor; no best man.

Nothing.

I was so pregnant by then that I had to wear a maternity gown, which only pissed Mother off even more. She had worked diligently in her social circles to ensure that all came off the way she wanted it to appear: high school sweethearts marrying and starting a family without being able to wait for another second, so in love, that timing was irrelevant.

The entire ceremony was miserable.

The Deaths

Everyone dressed up with funeral faces instead of wedding smiles. Fake flowers, fake vows, fake happiness. Empty hearts and shattered dreams; impending doom ringing loudly in our ears above the music. Barbara and Gene sitting on the groom's side, looking tired and forlorn; Mother and Daddy on the opposite side looking even worse. The tension in the room was so tight that I could feel the ache in my bones; the air of bitter mistakes and stolen hope billowing through the pews like ice-bitten wind.

The icing on the cake? Duane wore a tux with a black bowtie and looked ridiculous, childish even, like a little boy dressed for church. Only his face was serious, reality-beaten (we both knew why), and pale as winter frost.

With money we borrowed from Mother and Daddy, we rented a small, two-bedroom shithole on Beech Street. Living with each other for the first time was agony, and there was no way to escape reality lingering throughout the house like poison.

Things were severely awkward between the two of us: we were just kids, barely eighteen. We honestly didn't even know each other that well; I didn't even know Duane's middle name until we filled out the forms to get our marriage license. Those nights sneaking out to drink lukewarm beer and have sex was a far cry from eating together. Sleeping together. Living together. Actually sleeping together, not sex.

On most days, the silence was like a fire alarm screaming between us, a subliminal siren that made me feel the need to run. But, as big and pregnant as I was, I wasn't running anywhere far.

I spent most of my time during our first week together unboxing and putting away wedding gifts without even bothering to show Duane. Then I'd watch old sitcom reruns until I fell asleep while Duane would sit out in the garage with the antique Harley Davidson his grandfather gifted him at graduation that needed restoring. Duane would come home from work, eat something, and head on out there. When I would peek through the blinds, I'd see him out there drinking beer with the game blaring on the portable radio, sitting on a milk crate nowhere near the bike.

I didn't know much about Duane Myers, but I knew he didn't know shit about motorcycles.

Thanks to Duane working with Gene at Atlantic Oil making decent money, I was fortunate enough to spend the end of my pregnancy nested on the couch alone with my daily ritual. Captain Crunch and cartoons in the morning (my biggest pregnancy craving; I ate it until the roof of my mouth was beat up and raw). Looney Tunes, Tom and Jerry, The Smurfs, and Scooby-Doo until ten; then I'd flip over to channel three for The Price Is Right.

After the morning, I had lunch – something substantial – while I watched my stories: Days of Our Lives, General Hospital,

Guiding Light. Then, if I felt like it, I'd straighten up and try to make dinner before Duane came home from work to ruin everything.

I hated cooking; didn't even know how to until after we married, and Mother made me learn from her how to make at least the basic meals: tacos, spaghetti, burgers. Then we moved onto casseroles and Sunday dinner-type meals like pot roast and beef stroganoff (which never came out right) and some quick things to make in a pinch.

The night I tried to make Mother's chicken and dumplings, I started having contractions.

And my heart stopped.

***

I couldn't get in touch with Duane at work, so I left a message with Barbara and called Mother to take me to the hospital. There was a bad storm going on outside. I had to run from the house to the car. The sky flashed white with lightning, and rain slapped in violent sheets against Mother's Oldsmobile on the way to St. Vincent's.

With Daddy in the waiting room and Mother by my side, I pushed my eight-pound, seven-ounce baby boy into existence…

Duane, Gene, and Barbara showed up a half hour late, holding a bouquet of red roses. When Duane held him, he smiled for the first time since the wedding.

Up until I held Michael in my arms, I'd felt mostly only fear about being a mother. Duane's behavior, Mother's advice and suggestions, and everyone's negative reaction had scared me up into a tree. I was starting to feel closed-in and trapped, like a caged animal Duane kept poking at with sticks. But when I held him and smelled him and touched his soft, brown hair, everything changed. *Everything.*

The night I gave birth to Michael Duane, I beamed while watching Mother cradle him in her arms and study him, laughing at his expression before passing him onto Daddy.

I held my breath momentarily, but my tensions eased when he seemed as happy as Mother, both of them whispering and smiling over him, and when Daddy caught me looking, I saw tears in his eyes. It was the only time I'd seen him cry happy tears for me. It was a brief moment, but I caught it. It was mine. It would be the only time I felt like I'd given him something besides grief.

Gene stood in the corner and looked uncomfortable in his dirty clothes and work boots. Barbara stood beside him in a glassy-eyed daze. On their way out to leave, Barbara surprised me and leaned in for a hug. "Let us know if you need anything, dear."

It was the closest she'd ever physically been to me. She smelled like chemical sweat and cigarettes – straight from the nuthouse.

Michael was such a good baby; a happy baby. He had thick, brown hair and light blue eyes like mine, and he had dimples on each cheek and one on his chin, like Duane. He was the most beautiful thing I'd ever seen. He was perfect.

But, nothing else really was.

My first year as a mother and wife was a mix of both pleasure and pain: toothless smiles and spaghetti-stained cheeks; bedtime splashes and lullabies combined with drunken fights with Duane; round-the-clock hours; extreme exhaustion; and the absolute worst, most haunting feeling of loneliness I'd ever felt.

I was isolated, and I hated it.

I ached for someone to talk to, someone I could trust. But, as it was, I had a disengaged husband who was becoming a career alcoholic and a child who took more from me than I thought I had to give.

Most nights during that first year, I would just sit there crying, rocking Michael and trying to get him to sleep with Duane's drunken snores ringing loudly in the background – not the kind of lullaby a baby wanted to hear.

The days were long, but the years were short. Dirty diapers, morning smiles, pancakes and cartoons. Dinosaurs and trucks and blocks and bathtime splashes and scraped knees. Midnight fevers, Santa smiles, and Halloween buckets filled to the brim. ABCs, visits to doctors, Easter baskets and bunnies. Life with Michael seemed to move so quickly that I could hardly grasp it all, and before I knew it, Michael was turning two, and I had seemingly aged twenty years more than him.

For his second birthday, I invited Mother and Daddy over for cake and presents. Duane showed up an hour late, drunk and stumbling, holding a brown puppy in his hands. I could have killed him with a stick of butter. While Michael played with the puppy on the kitchen floor, I sat horrified at the table while Duane talked Daddy's ear off about work, slurring every word that came out of his mouth.

I could see Mother watching his mouth, occasionally looking at me for a reaction. And when Duane belched loud enough in front of Mother to make the dog bark, I ushered them out of the house like it was on fire.

After they were gone, I had to listen to Duane try and convince me that the dog was a good purchase. Man's best friend, purebred, and the simple fact that Michael loved her were his top three points.

"Maybe it'll give you something to do while you sit at home all day," he told me, hoping I'd pop off and keep up the fight, but I didn't give him the satisfaction.

After that first night, Barkley went wherever Michael did.

***

On Halloween night, I dressed Michael in the green-felt Peter Pan costume that Mother had sewn from scratch. With his pointy hat and plastic sword, he would squeal in delight when someone dropped a piece of candy in his bucket.

Duane had to work late and couldn't make it to trick-or-treating, but instead of being pissed off, I felt relieved. The year before, we got in a fight in the street, and the whole neighborhood heard him tell me I was fat since I had the baby while Michael smiled and waved at passers-by in his stroller dressed as G.I. Joe.

When Michael got exhausted and fussy from the festivities, we drove back home to Beech Street.

Duane still wasn't home, and it was after nine.

The light on the answering machine was blinking with a message from him telling me there was a leak somewhere and he couldn't leave the job site until it was finished. I put Michael to bed and flipped on the television.

At a quarter till eleven, the phone rang. It was Missy asking if Duane and I were still a couple because she'd just seen him dancing with some blonde girl at the Electric Cowboy…

***

The parking lot of the Electric Cowboy was jam-packed.

With Michael asleep in the backseat, I drove up and down the rows of cars, looking. People in childish costumes with painted faces loitered around the parking lot like trash, and over by Freddy Kreuger kissing a bloody nun – I saw Duane's blue Isuzu parked behind a dumpster.

I was already near the entrance with Michael on my hip when I realized I was wearing my pink housecoat, the one Mother gave me after I gave birth. People whispered and stared at the only child in the building, and everyone in my path moved quickly out of my way.

And there he was, dressed as the Lone Ranger, dancing with a princess.

They were so into each other that I had to tap Duane on his shoulder to get his attention, but what I really wanted to do was punch him. When he turned around, Michael yelled, "Daddy!" at top volume. "Daddy, you're a cowboy!"

I looked at Duane but addressed her. "That's right," I said. "That's Daddy. Dear 'ol Dad. What a peach." I sneered.

She disappeared into the crowd of laughing onlookers.

Back at home, it was Duane who did most of the yelling. I had no right, he told me, to follow him around like a GD private detective. He rolled out insult after insult: the house was always messy; I was a bad cook and a bad mom; the baby weight I carried around disgusted him. I wouldn't perform oral sex. I remember trying to speak but not being able to.

But I had had it.

I looked over at the stove and saw the pan with bacon grease in it from that morning's breakfast. I picked it up and whacked him right in the side of the head. He faceplanted on the kitchen floor. I was sure I'd killed him.

In a panic, I rushed to the hallway phone to call 911, but before I got there, he tackled me from behind. We wrestled and fought and slapped and punched until I finally got a good angle on him, then I put my knee in his groin as hard as I could and bolted out the back door. I was in the car and on my way over to Gene and Barbara's within moments.

I was so scared, I don't even remember the drive over.

Gene answered the door in his underwear, bewildered and half asleep. After a brief rundown of events, he got dressed and followed me over to the house and wrangled Duane in his blood and anger and finally got him inside his truck and out of the driveway, where I sat hiding in the floorboard until I saw their tail lights disappear down Beech Street.

Back inside the house, Michael was still asleep, and the silence was eerie. I dumped out Michael's Halloween candy onto the table and filled the bucket with warm, soapy water. I scrubbed diligently and angrily, cleaning through my tears.

Finally, I just sat there and sobbed. I don't know how long I sat there shaking.

***

While Duane stayed at his parent's house after the fight, I noticed that when I picked Michel up to hold him, my breasts were tender. I had been a little nauseous, but I attributed that to nerves. I finally gave in to my panic and took a pregnancy test. I cried in the bathroom for over an hour, holding the positive stick in my hand. A stick of *dynamite*. Rather than try to contact Duane and tell him, I kept it a secret and used my time away from him to think about things.

A few days later, on a Friday night, Duane still wasn't back home. It had been six days total. Michael was down for the night, and I was sitting on the couch watching Unsolved Mysteries when I heard a horrible yelping coming from outside.

It just kept getting worse and worse, so I followed the sound out under the back porch where Barkley was having puppies. "Fixed" my ass. She was clearly in distress like something was wrong; I had no idea what to do. Mother and Daddy didn't pick up the phone, so I tried to call Duane at Gene and Barbara's, but Gene told me he wasn't there. I explained to him what was going on, and he was at the house within minutes, wearing a pair of gloves.

"Go in the house," he said. "Don't come out."

Inside, I cried for Barkley and wondered where the hell Duane was on a Friday night while I sat home knocked up and trapped again.

Barkley had eleven puppies that night. Eleven! I didn't even know that was possible.

Duane came home the next afternoon and acted like nothing had ever happened. When I tried to talk to him seriously about the dog situation and the fact that he'd lied about her being *fixed*, he laughed at me.

Like a hand-to-the-stomach, doubled over, can-hardly-breathe kind of laugh.

The harder he laughed at me, the angrier I became. I had to shut him up before I killed him. "And Barkley isn't the only one having babies. I'm pregnant." I said, bracing myself for the shift.

He stood up straight. His face was suddenly serious, his eyes wide as saucers. I had to back up because he kept walking toward me until I was backed up against the kitchen counter.

"If you're pregnant, it sure as hell ain't mine," he said. "That what you've been doing while I'm not here, Drue, whoring around?" Then he spat right in my face, grabbed his keys, and headed out the back door.

I chased him out, yelling things he didn't want to accept. "Fuck you, Drue!" he yelled. "That ain't my kid!" I saw Michael's tee ball bat lying in the yard, and I picked it up. I busted out his windshield first and beat the hood in as hard as I could. He backed out of the driveway, cursing me and leaving skid marks in the driveway.

Part of me thought that it was just another one of our fights, that he would eventually have to come home due to the fact that he had a wife and kid there.

But he didn't.

I waited and worried for a solid week for him to dry out and come to his senses before I drove over to Gene and Barbara's to see what was going on. By then, the pantry and fridge were bare, and the electric bill was past due. Michael needed diapers and milk. I scraped up some change from around the house and bought Michael a corn dog from the gas station on our way over there.

Gene was out on the front lawn mowing the grass. Duane's truck wasn't there. Gene shut the engine off on the mower and walked over. "He's not here," he said, still walking. "Haven't seen him in a few days."

"Well, tell him Michael needs food and diapers. He can't just disappear and escape all responsibility," I said. Gene looked uneasy. He pulled out his wallet and handed me two twenty-dollar bills. "Check Rio Vista Apartments," he said walking, back toward the mower. Then he turned around and looked at me. "But you didn't hear that from me. You hear me, girl?"

***

The Rio Vista Apartment Complex was made like an old, cheap motel with two identical floors. I found Duane's truck parked front and center, but I had no idea which apartment he was in. I parked behind the dumpster and waited while Michael napped in the backseat, finally full.

Over an hour later, I saw him come out of a downstairs apartment near his truck with his hand around the shoulder of the girl I'd busted him with at the Electric Cowboy.

Everything was happening too fast. I was hot with rage but also heartbroken and worried about my future. All the way back home, I cried myself sick knowing that I would have no choice but to go over to Seminary Street and sacrifice myself on the family cross.

A few days later, I finally made it over there.

Daddy's truck was gone, but Mother's grey Oldsmobile sat staring at me like a statue. I sat there for a minute or more, trying to get my bearings, while Michael squealed and shrieked in the backseat, wanting to go inside to see Nana and Papa.

I rang the bell and held my breath while Michael knocked with his tiny, balled-up fist. After a long wait, Mother came to the door looking as polished and pristine as usual; even in slacks and a blouse, she had some sort of quality that gave her an edge over other women.

"Drucilla," she said. "What brings you by so early? Michael!

Get over here and give me a hug!"

Michael ran to her, and she scooped him up and disappeared into the house in a trail of her gardenia perfume toward the kitchen.

"Cup of coffee?" she asked.

"Uh, sure. Thanks."

She grabbed a mug from the rack and sat it down, started pouring. "So how's Duane?" she said, even though it was well known that she hated Duane and didn't care.

"He's fine," I said.

"Great."

She turned around and sat the cup in front of me. Smiled an odd smile. Kept smiling while she cut banana slices for Michael. "Just say it Drucilla. Tell me whatever it is that you came here to say. We both know something is amiss."

"Duane left me, and I'm pregnant."

She stopped slicing, stopped the sarcastic smile. "I told you," she finally said, nodding her head back and forth, going back to her slicing. "I fucking told you."

Chapter 6

Living back home on Seminary Street was a chaotic mix of my current broken dreams mixed with childhood wounds and associations, and I found myself constantly picking apart the irony: I was different, but it wasn't.

My white wicker furniture was all still there, my mums and posters from high school were still hung by the mirror. I sat on the bed and stared out my bay window at Mother's roses like I always had, trying to decide what the fuck to do now. What I wanted to do was drive over to Gene and Barbara's and beat Duane with a baseball bat, but the pregnancy the second time around was so unbelievably debilitating that I hardly had the strength to get out of bed at all.

All day and night, I puked – from the second I woke up in the morning until I went to bed at night. I even woke up out of a dead sleep, dry heaving without warning.

After so many days of not being able to hold anything down, Mother would have to take me downtown to the ER for ice-cold IVs, anti-nausea shots in my ass, and cartons of chalky vanilla Ensure.

Every day was torture; every minute of it took its toll. It was a struggle to just get through the day, the hours.

"Let her drink and eat anything she wants," Dr. Raspberry

told Mother. "If she thinks she can keep it down at all, if anything sounds remotely appealing, give it to her," he said.

To this day, there are foods I can't eat, smells I cannot take, and even certain songs and TV shows I can't handle because they remind me of my sick days, lying there alone and miserable, sinking further and further down a deep hole.

I made a plan to live there just long enough for me to have the baby, then I could get a job and a place of my own, hopefully somewhere far away from Burgess and Mother and Daddy and Duane – away from all the bullshit.

I needed a fresh start. Needed to be able to *breathe* again.

Missy told me they were renting apartments at Timber Creek for three-fifty, all bills paid. I could hopefully swing that with child support from Duane, a battle I still had to fight as soon as I was well enough. Divorce his sorry ass; try to forget that I was married to such a fucking loser.

One day during that horrific time, Mother knocked on my bedroom door and woke me up from a sick-nap, saying someone was at the door for me. No, she didn't know who it was. No, they wouldn't just leave a message.

She helped me out of bed and to the door, where a handsome man was standing. He was wearing a white, long-sleeved button-up shirt and cowboy boots with navy slacks.

"Drucilla Myers?" he asked when I approached him, squinting and shielding my eyes from the sunlight.

"Yes."

"You've been served."

He handed me a manilla envelope he'd been holding behind his back like a weasel. Mother and Daddy read the papers for me: a petition for divorce. Daddy said we needed to hire a lawyer to read through the fine print and make sure custody and child support were square. When we did, he told us that Duane's petition included giving up parental rights to the unborn child upon determination of a paternity test.

"The way this reads is, he's giving up rights to the baby regardless of paternity," he said. "With the child you share together, he's agreed to pay two-seventy-five per month until the child turns eighteen."

"Can he do that?" Mother asked, exasperated.

"Oh, yes," he said. "Unfortunately, legally, *yes*, he can."

My mind was numb. I was horrified, humiliated, and sick as a fucking dog.

After that meeting was over, I drove over to Gene and Barbara's and beat on the door like I had a warrant. I knew he was there. His truck was parked out front in the street. He answered the door all cocky and sarcastic.

"You need to speak to me, you can go through my lawyer," he said. "I don't want to talk to you."

When I resisted and tried to tell him he was bastardizing his own blood, he slammed the door in my face. Through the closed door, he threatened to call the cops if I didn't leave.

***

A week later, three weeks before my due date, I began to swell. It wasn't chubby feet and cankles; my entire body was bloated. My stomach was bigger than ever, my arms and legs were big and tight from the swelling. My feet looked like two Christmas hams. Dr. Raspberry's smallish frame made him look like an action figure up against my big, swollen body. I felt like an orca getting medical attention at Seaworld.

He listened for the heartbeat, jotted down the heart rate. Took out a vinyl measuring tape and measured me all over several times. His face contorted awkwardly while he looked through my chart before speaking. "You have too much amniotic fluid," he said. "And your pressure's high. I'm writing you two prescriptions: one for swelling; one for your pressure. Bed rest only. See you back in a week."

Back at home, I stayed beached in front of the television in the living room while Michael ran Mother and Daddy ragged. Duane wouldn't answer any of my calls, and Gene and Barbara were no help. After four or five days on the medications, I was bigger than ever. The skin on my fingers and toes was burning; they looked like weenies about to bust open in the microwave. Mother called the doctor's office back and set an appointment for the next morning, but later that afternoon, I started having contractions.

Dr. Raspberry met us there and looked shocked when he saw me. I did my breathing exercises and pushed until I couldn't push any further. As soon as I felt her burst forth and release from my body, the energy in the room darkened, and Dr. Raspberry started calling codes. Nurses scrambled; more scrubbed-in doctors and nurses entered the room, all of them surrounding the plastic crib they'd just laid my baby in. Mother stood beside me, gripping my hand with the force of a thousand mothers as we watched, waited.

"What's going on?" I kept shouting. "What's happening?" But no one would answer me.

***

My daughter, Samantha Ann, survived her birth, but not entirely. She wasn't a normal, healthy baby like I'd expected. They kept her in the NICU and ran test after test after test.

Time stood still during that first week.

Samantha had to be hooked up to all sorts of machines; she had tubes in her nose and throat. The machines helped her with breathing and digestion, and the tests they were running on her would tell us why she was unable to do these things on her own.

"It's Anencephaly," Dr. Clarke, her specialist, told me in a grim report. "The top of her brain wasn't fully developed," he said. "That's what would control her five senses…"

I remember him speaking about her in past tense, like she was already dead, or at the very least, on borrowed time. He gave us the statistics on babies born with this defect and made sure before he left me that I knew very clearly that Samantha's prognosis was *death*.

"She will live on the machines until then," he said. "I'm sorry, Mrs. Myers."

***

When Samantha was a month old and still alive, we were assigned a team of at-home nurses to care for her around the clock. Every second of every day, there was a nurse in blue scrubs floating around her like a protective butterfly.

We made the den into a makeshift hospital room; Daddy brought Michael's crib down from the attic and assembled it in front of the windows that faced the street. Like he did at hospital visits, Michael marveled at her like a museum exhibit. "My baby," he called her. "My baby is sick," he'd tell the nurses, Mother and Daddy, and even strangers in the damned grocery store.

Duane never called or came by; he stuck with his desire to give up rights – even to a terminal infant. The paternity test came back positive, and I was sure he would stop the madness after that.

Only he didn't.

Our entire lives became Samantha: her stats, her progress or lack thereof. Her sad, tragic condition. Though she was quiet because of the tubes, she would move more and kick her legs a little when I sang to her. Even Johnnie, my favorite of all the nurses, said she saw it too, that when I engaged with her, she engaged back in her own, special way.

To me, that meant that some of her senses were working, that maybe she was developing out of death row, that maybe The Judge changed His mind and settled on a lighter sentence.

Johnnie worked the day shift, and I always felt better when she was there. She was a plump, kind, black woman with the soul of a thousand women before her. She told me stories of her great-great-grandmother, who believed that a tragic death in a family came with many spiritual responsibilities.

Of course, back then, they didn't think of things like we do now. They experienced death all the time. It was just a part of life to people in the beginning of cultural society.

"Then, when communities grew, and generations grew into bigger families, people felt like they had to put a name on what they believed in. Lump it all together whether they believed in it all or not. And that's how religion started. And don't even get me started on how they used to represent God, child; hell, or how they still do."

It would be years until I dove deep enough to understand what she meant by that.

Michael was quiet and mostly calm around her, without me even having to tell him. He knew inherently just how fragile her life was, and it broke my heart that he didn't get to spend a lot of quality time with her or play with her like a healthy baby. It wasn't hard to make him understand that she was sick; but it was hard to make him understand *why*.

Throughout those first few months, I blamed everyone for Samantha's condition – myself included. I could have made myself eat more; I could have tried to move around more or try harder to take the vitamins I kept vomiting up. Dr. Clarke assured me that the condition could not be helped and was in no way anyone's fault, that it was something due to environmental causes, but wasn't I responsible for the baby's environment? And Mother and Daddy? Could the stress from my crumbled divorce and stressful time back at Seminary Street have played a part? Did God just fucking hate me? Was there really a God that killed people's babies?

On Samantha's six-month mark, Dr. Clarke ordered all new scans and testing. Though nothing else about her gave any sign of hope, I clung to the fact that she responded to *me*. That was our saving grace. If nothing else, that was surely something. I waited several days, almost a week, for all of the tests to come back, and then Dr. Clarke's nurse called me to set up an appointment to go over the results the following day.

I didn't sleep that night; I was up tossing and turning and imagining the worst while trying to – needing to – remain hopeful at the same time. I needed her to *live*. If she died, I would die. There would be no way I could possibly go on without her. Michael would never understand; I would never understand. It would kill me, or I would kill myself.

The next morning at nine sharp, Mother and I sat in Dr. Clarke's sprawling mahogany office with walls covered in various degrees and accomplishments. There was a portrait of JFK by the window and a large rubber plant. His secretary served us flavored coffee – hazelnut or something nutty like that – while we waited for him to arrive from an emergency surgery he was finishing.

When he got there, he apologized for his being late and shook both of our hands. He picked up Samantha's thick chart and began leafing through a thick stack of newspapers. "She's not thriving," he said, sighing audibly. "The tests don't look good, not at all near what we would want to see." He went on to say that her weight was decreasing and her heart rate was abnormal now. Her oxygen levels were low, even on the maximum amount of oxygen for a baby her size.

It was, as he put it, only a matter of time.

I remember crying. I remember Mother squeezing my hand and crying, too. I remembered the stoic look on Dr. Clarke's face – like he'd done this a thousand times before. Killed many mothers with his words.

I told him how she kicked when I sang to her, how she showed excitement when I was in her presence, how she responded to Michael sometimes, too; I was still fighting. Why wouldn't I?

He leaned back in his leather chair with his arms on the rest, and his fingers steepled in wisdom. "Do you believe in God, Drucilla?"

His question shocked me; I had no words, no answer to give him.

"Those are gifts," he said. "Cherish them."

*****

Five weeks later, during Samantha's funeral, I found myself unable to stay focused on the present moment; my mind would jump from one random memory to the other: holding Samantha's still body while Mother wailed in the background, Daddy ushering Michael outside. I remember Johnnie opening a window "to let her spirit out."

During the preparations, I remember Mother trying to pick out hymns for the funeral, and asking for my suggestions. "No church songs," I told her. "Lullabies. The one her mobile plays."

Mrs. Jensen, my old Sunday School teacher and former seventh-grade English teacher, played the most haunting version of Braum's Lullaby I'd ever heard, and I remember locking eyes with her at one point during the song; we were both crying, and she looked at me with the saddest eyes I'd ever seen, and her pity only made me cry harder. Made me pity myself, too.

I remember the undertaker, Bob, reading from notecards and

looking at me sympathetically during his long, endless speech. I remember scanning the pews for Duane but not seeing him.

The days and weeks following her death were chaotic and uncomfortable: nurses disassembling machines and packing up useless survival gear; Mother cleaning and pacing around the house in nervous circles.

And Michael? Michael ran and laughed as if nothing had happened, playing ball outside with Daddy, completely oblivious to what it meant when we told him that Samantha had gone to heaven. Like most kids would think, he thought we could load up in the car and go visit her, or like it was when she was in the hospital, so he thought she would eventually come back home.

But when she didn't, and the den became a normal living space where Mother set up her sewing equipment, he started asking more questions. *Where's my baby? Is my baby still sick? Where is my baby's bed? Where did you put my baby's stuff, Nana?* He remembered Johnnie opening the window to let the spirit out, so eventually, he would go to the window and look for her; he would try to push it open with his little hands, calling her name.

I recall being drowned in flowers and plants; the entire house looked like a funeral home. While Mother stayed busy with Michael – setting up her sewing equipment in the den was her way of coping with the loss – Daddy went back to work, and all around, things began to go back to normal. Like it was when I was pregnant. Like she'd never even been born.

No one mentioned her besides Michael. No one cried anymore or acted sympathetically in any way – far from it. Things grew cold and awkward again, but this time, I wasn't focused on anything but my grief. I didn't care what anyone thought, did, or said. I had nothing to say to anyone, nothing to offer. Not even to my own son. Not even for him could I get up out of my gloom and face the world again.

Something made me feel I would betray little Samantha? Celebrating my son – alive and well – while she wasn't? That I wasn't mourning her.

Everything he did, every milestone, every cute saying or doing, became something entirely different to me: everything he said was something Samantha would never say. Everything he did became something Samantha would never do. Instead of making me happy, it would send me reeling in pain, so much so that I locked myself in my room and requested not to be disturbed for any reason.

Mother sewed new drapes for the entire house and new clothes for Michael. All day long, I could hear that damn sewing machine's bobbing. The squeak of its pedal.

It was *agony*.

The Deaths

***

One Sunday morning, while Mother, Daddy, and Michael were at church, a knock on the door startled me. I peeked out the front windows and saw a white van with the Abundant Life Church's logo on its side.

I opened the door expecting to receive more food from strangers but was surprised when I saw Joni Bingham, a girl who graduated a few years before me, standing at my door with a group of about six women who were all clutching bibles to their chests, tilting their heads at me sympathetically. It was Joni who spoke first.

"Drue! Hello, honey. I'm Joni. We went to school together… I don't know if you remember me..."

"I remember," I said.

"Good! Great. Well, we are here from Abundant Life, and we wanted to stop by and give our sincerest apologies for your loss. We were hoping that maybe we could give you some words of encouragement and love. Would that be okay with you?"

I was numb and defeated from everyone's *talks* already, but I recognized one of the ladies, Margie, from our church, so I let them in in a sacrificial effort to not embarrass Mother.

They filed in through the doorway like schoolchildren and made themselves comfortable on our living room furniture. Margie looked nervous, she kept fidgeting with the tassel on her brown, leather bible cover and staring down at the floor. They all sat there staring at me like I was a museum exhibit, wearing my housecoat with my eyes and face red and puffy from crying.

"Well," Joni began, "I guess we should start by praying."

Everyone joined hands; two strangers grabbed mine and squeezed.

"Heavenly Father," she began, "hallowed be thy name." During the prayer, my mind drifted back to who I remembered Joni to be: a high school dropout, a petty thief with a few mugshots, town slut. But now she sat before me praying for me and my dead daughter. She had married the pastor of Abundant Life and was now someone else.

When the prayer concluded, there were several awkward, silent moments. I was exhausted and annoyed, ready for them to leave so I could enjoy my last few minutes alone before everyone came home. "Is there anything else?" I finally said, hoping they'd take the hint and leave.

"Well, actually," Joni said, "we wanted to talk to you a little bit about your salvation – what it says about it in the book of Romans. Chapter six in particular. Have you read that before? Are you familiar with those scriptures?"

"No," I said. From my seat on the sofa, I saw Mother's car pull up. Saw Daddy get out of the driver's seat and stretch while Joni kept talking.

"Well, in that chapter, it talks about the things we've done before we knew about our true salvation. Before we were washed clean." Mother got Michael out of the back seat. He was holding his shoes in his hands.

"For example," she continued, "it asks in chapter six specifically, 'So what fruit was produced then from the things which you are now ashamed of? The outcome of those things is death.' This was a curse of sin upon you, Drue. By accepting Christ as your Lord and Savior, you can be free from sin. For our Lord hath defeated death and sin, both."

My eyes were fixed on Joni's as she looked at me for my reaction to the most hideous thing anyone had ever spoken to me in my life. Mother and Daddy walked through the door at that exact second, and Mother was in the living room looking annoyed but smiling at the uninvited, surprise visitors. She nodded at Margie, who nodded back with a smug look on her face.

"What the fuck did you just say?" I said to Joni. Her eyes widened, and I saw her hands tighten around her bible. I got up out of my seat and walked over to her, bent down, and met her gaze like she was a child and repeated myself. "What the *fuck* did you just say?"

"Excuse me?" Mother interrupted, holding her hands up to stop the talking. "What's going on here?"

Joni looked at the floor to avoid my face and Mother's, but she repeated, with unashamed audacity, exactly what she said…

Curse words and insults flew out of Mother's mouth like a Gatling gun. Daddy opened the door and ushered them all out of the house with Mother screaming behind them. "You goddamned hippie freaks! You should be ashamed! Everyone knows you're a tramp, Jonie. You're not fooling anyone with that bible!"

When Margie passed her and was heading toward the van, she turned around and shouted. "Old sins cast long shadows!"

Mother called out to her. "Margie, you slept with your brother-in-law! Who the fuck do you think you are! Get off my property! Shame on you, you whore! Go!"

And they did – they ran for their lives. They left skidmarks on the street… but also on my soul. My mind reeled in confusion.

Mother didn't come out of her room for the rest of the day, and Daddy stayed in the garage with Michael. I lay on the couch and cried until I fell asleep.

The Deaths

***

When March came, I had my final court date with Duane to dread.

So much had happened in such a short amount of time that when the day finally came, I could hardly imagine myself ever even married to Duane or *married* at all. Couldn't imagine ever having the energy to be who I used to be. How I could ever sleep one single night in that house on Beech Street, I knew not. I didn't even feel like the daughter of Mother and Daddy, didn't feel like Michael's mother…

I felt like nothing more than the girl with the dead baby.

The morning of court, Daddy had to work, so Mother had to stay home to watch Michael. I stood at my closet door for what seemed like an eternity, looking at a thick row of clothes I was still too big to wear. After multiple tries, I had to wear both a maternity shirt and pants. It felt morbid putting on clothes that I once shared with her, that once covered her still-beating heart. I shoved the thought out of my mind and drove to the courthouse in a teary daze. The sun was out and shining but offered no warmth. The city was still iced with snow.

Inside the room where our hearing was held, Duane and his

lawyer sat across a big wooden table from me and mine. The judge sat at the end like a king.

It was the first time I'd seen Duane since he shut the door in my face at Gene and Barbara's that day, and even though it was only months ago, it felt like it had been several, long years.

According to my attorney, Mr. Greer, all I had to do was sign my name and have it read and accepted by the judge. And while he read over the terms of our divorce, Duane kept looking down at his watch like he had better, more important shit to do. When he was finished, Duane's gel-haired lawyer asked to address the court.

"Your honor, the record should indicate that my client has formally given up rights to Mrs. Myers's deceased child, Samantha A. Myers. We would like the record to show that Mr. Myers be cleared of any monetary support accrued during the life of said child, medical or otherwise, including hospital bills, copays, or funeral costs."

I remember getting up out of my chair but not much else. The next thing I remember was my puny lawyer and the judge both restraining me until the bailiffs took over and dragged me to a holding cell. No charges were filed. I'm not sure if that was grace or not, but that's the way I took it.

Mother and Daddy scolded me all the way home for my behavior, not just that day but the past few months.

"You've let yourself go," Mother said sharply. "You need to get your goddamn shit together, Drucilla Rose. Life moves on; you can't just stop, no matter how much you may want to. You still have to keep moving forward. Still have to keep putting one foot in front of the other. You are embarrassing yourself," she said. "And us, for that matter!"

"Stop yelling at Drucilla!" Michael shouted, cutting her off. Drucilla. And with that, the car fell eerily silent.

***

A week later, I was sitting at the table eating cereal with Michael and reading the morning paper, and on the third page, I saw a 3x5 engagement photo of Duane and his girlfriend, Jackie, hugging on a bridge. The one at Burgess Park. The ring on her left hand, placed perfectly on his shoulder, could have sunk the Titanic.

I remember being completely struck by her plain, almost homely, looks: bleach-blonde hair cut into a bob with visible split ends; plain brown eyes; fake, too-cheerful smile. Tacky white sweater with gaudy rhinestones around the wrists.

Duane looked as despondent as usual. His eyes were lazy and his smile was crooked from the dip he always kept in his left cheek pocket that always disgusted me. *Worm dirt*, Michael used to call it when Duane would spit it all out to eat.

Normally, a blow like that would've clobbered me, would've sent me reeling in my anger, but at that point, I had nothing left to give. I felt nothing; nothing new, anyway. I was quite used to being both shocked and disappointed in Duane. He'd disappointed me in every situation so far, he'd never made a good decision in his life, and he somehow came out of our marriage unscathed.

I stared at that picture for hours that day, trying to understand what was different between them and us.

Although I received multiple calls from Missy, Johnnie, and a few others. I didn't take any of them. I didn't really feel like I had anything to say, and I know they didn't either, that it's just what you do when someone's grieving.

But I didn't want to do that. I just wanted to be left alone to try to sort through my hell.

I tried everything to distract myself from the truth: watching my favorite TV shows, ordering takeout I couldn't eat, taking long drives alone to clear my mind and make some sense of things.

But, the more I tried to distract myself, the heavier Samantha lay on my chest. I felt guilty for eating and nourishing my body; I felt guilty for smiling, even fake ones, for strangers passing by. I felt the need to withdraw and cover myself and emit no form of happiness whatsoever.

It sickened me to see Mother and Daddy and Michael all go on about their day, having normal thoughts and reactions to their everyday tasks and going on about life like the rug hadn't just been pulled out from under us. While Mother and Daddy tried to clean up the mess it had made, I felt the need to only crumble and wither away further into the chaos.

Mother had gotten into the habit of asking me to run errands for her. I couldn't decide if it was a ploy to get me up and out of the house or if she just needed help with Michael. Either way, I hated doing it. I had just lost my baby. I didn't feel like going to the grocery store or the goddamn post office or the pharmacy. I wanted to die.

On one of those splendid occasions, Mother called me out of my room to go to the store for a gallon of Michael's chocolate milk. He wouldn't drink white milk – not even with syrup in it. So I get dressed and put on my slippers, and Michael catches me on my way out and asks to go with me.

"No, it'll just take a second. I'll be right back," I said. He threw himself on the floor and cried like I'd burned him with a cigarette.

"Why don't you just take him?" Daddy said from behind his

newspaper. He flipped one half down and looked at me over his tortoise rims. "You never take him anywhere anymore."

Fuck you, I thought. You don't know shit about parenting.

Since the Vega was out of gas as usual, I put Michael in the back seat of Mother's car and drove to Murphy's, the little corner store closest to the house. We went inside and got the milk. Michael cried for a giant swirled lollipop that we ended up getting, and I stood in the checkout line like a zombie.

When I forfeited the twenty and got my change, I looked out the window and saw Duane pumping gas into the Isuzu. He had the windows down, and music – Sweet Home Alabama, to be exact – was pouring out at top volume. He was tapping his foot to the beat, blissfully unaware. Unaffected.

The bell on the door got his attention when we were leaving, and as soon as Michael saw Duane, he called out for him and started to run across the busy parking lot, so I had to catch his sleeve and pull him back. By the time I had Michael restrained and balanced him in my arms with the milk, Duane was in the truck and about to drive off. I ran as fast as I could and put Michael in the car, backed out, and chased him all the way down Magnolia toward Gene and Barbara's.

I followed the bastard closely, tailgated him with my high beams flashing, the horn of the Oldsmobile blaring like a fire engine.

I was so mad I was crying; anger was the first thing I'd felt in months. It felt sane, justified. When he stopped at a busy intersection, I didn't. I gassed it, revved the engine as hard as it would go, and drove him over and into a crosswalk sign, bending it straight over.

I could feel the crash of the car in my bones. I put the car in reverse, backed up, and hit him again. He got out, slung the door open, and then slammed it. He walked over to me, his face red and his eyes wild, but he looked more scared than angry.

"You crazy bitch!" he kept saying. "You crazy fucking bitch!"

Duane pressed charges on me, and I had to spend the night in jail. A judge and Duane's lawyer made sure I was responsible for the damages to Duane's truck and to the crosswalk sign. I got ticket after ticket and fine after fine, and Mother's car was almost totaled.

Daddy was so mad that night, madder than I'd ever seen him. He was so mad I thought he might hit me; it was *that* bad. Mother cried and acted like I was a mental patient. She had even mentioned to Daddy that I needed professional help when she thought I was out of earshot. Maybe they were right. Michael wasn't hurt in the incident, but he was definitely visibly traumatized.

Suddenly, I was the bad guy. Well, not suddenly, but still. Why the fuck was I always made out to be the bad guy? Where was the rest of Duane's penance? Why was I the only one still suffering? The weight of the world made it hard to breathe. Samantha's ghost felt heavy, lying on my chest. Everyone else seemed to be moving on, already forgetting. Everything forgotten. Why can't they seem to remember what I'll never forget?

When I refused to say that I was sorry for what I'd done, refused to admit fault on my part due to the nature of Duane's actions at the store, I had no choice from Mother and Daddy but to agree to see Dr. Carpenter about my mental state since the baby was born.

Duane ran from his own son. Peeled out and *ran* from him; hadn't seen him in months, not even when Samantha died. But I was the one seeking therapy… Getting help. What kind of sense does that make? Not even a dead baby could make him have normal, human feelings toward us? Just threw us away like trash – out of sight and out of mind.

Dr. Carpenter told me I had postpartum depression. It had been eight months since her death. He put me on two pills, an antidepressant and an anti-anxiety medication. I was to start the medication immediately and see him back in one month. "During that time," he said calmly through his grey mustache, "you should begin to feel much better."

Instead of balancing me as promised, the antidepressant

wound me up tighter than an eight-day clock. Sleep would not come no matter how hard I tried, no matter how much Xanax I took in retaliation. There was a war raging, and it was all taking place right inside the confines of my own mind. I was the battleground, and there was no escape.

Most nights, I would just lie there, my body physically exhausted but my mind awake and angry. My thoughts focused mostly on injustice – on how life had dealt me a hand I didn't know how to play. I questioned God, how could He kill little babies and leave their mothers in shambles? How could He allow Duane to live a good life while mine spiraled further and further down the toilet?

I became furious with Mother and Daddy, too; how they treated me like I was not Michael's mother but his big sister in need of scolding; how they seemed to push me away from them like I was a nuisance they had to tolerate for the sake of Michael: the golden child they never got to have.

Through natural means of survival and instinct, Michael had begun turning to Mother when he was hungry. He would ask for her or Daddy when he was sick or scraped his knee. Went to their bed to sleep when a thunderstorm came through during the night. It was as if I didn't exist most of the time, and when I did, it was an uninvited experience.

It was a horrid disposition – one I'll never forget – and after week two, I stopped all medication. Dr. Carpenter tried to switch me to something else, something with a more sedative effect, which I had to agree to try, only I didn't try them. There was no way I was going down another dark road in my psyche.

The day Mother found my full prescription bottles hidden in my underwear drawer, she accused me of not even trying to get better and told me something needed to change. *It was time to get a job and make a plan for the future.* "Life goes on," she was fond of saying, one of her favorites that made me want to slap her where she stood.

That day, she gave me an ultimatum: either get myself together and get a job – or get out. *Lying in bed all day wasn't doing me any good,* she told me. "Michael barely even knows you anymore!" she snapped when I baulked about her suggestions. "You've become a dark cloud in this house, Drucilla. I know you're upset, but it's been almost a year. It's past time for you to be back in the swing of things." She got up and walked out my bedroom door, slamming it hard behind her.

That night, while everyone was asleep, I packed a bag of clothes and just left. Had no clue where I was going or what I was going to do, but what I did know was that I couldn't stay another second in the House of Reminders.

I went to Murphy's and put a quarter in the payphone to call

Missy. She answered on the first ring and was shocked to hear me on the other end of the line. I hadn't seen or spoken to her since the funeral. I wouldn't take any calls; no visitors allowed – those were my grieving strategies.

But now, I needed her most; needed her to get me the fuck off Seminary Street until I could fucking breathe again. Do everyone a favor and just disappear.

Missy and Phil still lived at Timber Creek. So I drove over and parked beside Phil, who came out and unloaded my bags while Missy hugged me and scolded me for shutting her out.

"I've been worried as shit, haven't I baby?" she called to Phil from the other room. "Your mom was rude as hell," she said. "She's still the biggest bitch I know." Then she mocked her in a way that made me smile. She held a handphone to her ear with two pointed fingers. *"Drucilla asks for privacy during this difficult time,"* she said in Mother's fancy, practiced, speaking voice. *"And I'd appreciate it if you would respect that, young lady."*

I gave them a rundown of things, including what happened in court with Duane, as well as the *accident.*

"What a fucking asshole," Missy said. "You should've driven that car up his ass."

"Oh, I tried. Believe me." I said, and we both let out a laugh.

Phil said if he ever saw Duane again, he was gonna beat his ass, and told me he was sorry for what I'd been through.

It was weird talking to my old high school friends about death, and even harder to talk about one so fucking unbelievably horrible. When I told them all that had happened, I felt like I was describing some movie I'd just seen with all sorts of plot twists and a bad ending; I could hardly believe that this was my actual, *real* life.

When things got too heavy – and I could tell that Missy and Phil were baffled enough for the night – I asked them what they had been up to lately. Missy went on and on about her job at Claire's Boutique, and Phil talked about his new career in plumbing. Missy told me a story about a party they'd had the week before where someone took an actual shit on the balcony. "No idea who could've been fucked up enough to do that," she said. "But there was a lot of booze and other shit that night, so who knows. I paid Billy Pride ten dollars to clean it up, then he puked while doing it. It was a real fucking shitshow," she said, still laughing.

That night, trying to sleep on their cheap, fold-out couch, a bar behind my back, I marveled at the differences in the stories between me and my peers, the *insane* differences between us and our lives, and suddenly, I felt older. Old. Different. *Alone.*

The next day, I became paranoid that maybe Mother would

call the police and put out a missing persons report since I didn't even bother to leave a note. I started thinking she might try to have me locked up in a nuthouse or something. That's exactly how she'd been acting toward me.

I finally picked up the phone and called, and when I told her why I left, she didn't argue; she didn't berate me or lecture me; she didn't do anything. She didn't even ask when I was coming home. She simply told me that she hoped I would feel better – find a better path.

And that was that.

I muddled through two more nights of hearing Missy and Phil have sex through the apartment's paper-thin walls. Then while they were both at work one day, I finally broke down and called Johnnie.

Johnnie lived on the north side of Burgess. Though her house was big and old with chipped paint, it was clean, comfortable, and warm. I could smell food cooking from the driveway and Johnnie's head peeking out the blinds of the window facing the street. She was already standing in the doorway when I walked up the porch steps, and as soon as I saw her face, I broke down. Harder than ever, it was the most I'd cried since Samantha died, and at Mother and Daddy's, I always felt too angry to cry or too ashamed.

But then, alone with Johnnie, I became vulnerable, and

everything I'd been holding in came out in wails.

She held me and cried with me through the worst of it; tried her best to console me. I stood up and walked over to the sink and, splashed water on my face; blew my nose with a paper towel. When I turned around again, Johnnie was talking to a woman in purple scrubs, holding a clipboard. They were whispering about something.

"Hi," the nurse said, smiling. "I'm Gloria." I looked at Johnnie, and she smiled sadly at me. "Would you like to meet my mother?" she asked.

***

In the bedroom at the far end of the hall, I could hear voices and laughter from a television program playing loudly. The door was open and lit up with the blue light from the screen. Gloria stayed in the kitchen, and Bea led me down to the room. Inside, a small, frail woman lay on a hospital bed in the corner, her head and feet both elevated in an awkward position. "This is my mother, Bea. Well, Beatrice."

"Is she asleep?" I tried to confirm. "Don't wake her for me, Johnnie." Johnnie laughed.

"I wish I could wake her for you, Drucilla!" she said, still giggling. "No, honey, she can't be woken up. Had a stroke three, well, almost four years ago, now. Left her like this: a vegetable."

We walked up to her bedside. Her skin was so smooth and brown, her hair was in neat braids with colored beads. She looked completely healthy, *better* than me, even, but she was frozen that way. "Can she hear? Is she alive inside there?" I asked, genuinely curious.

"Nobody really knows," she said. "The doctors all say no, but then they have to give you the odds: some patients have a better chance than others, but no matter what the odds were, no matter how devastating, there is always that little chance that haunts me," she said, patting Bea's arm. "So I treat like she's right here listening, and laughing and raising hell, just like she used to. If there's even a slight chance, I'll take it."

I understood the sentiment.

My room at Johnnie's house had red, blue, and green plaid wallpaper that reminded me of Christmas. It was empty except for a small bureau and a full-sized bed. The walls were bare, the only personal item in the room was a framed picture sitting on top of the bureau.

It was Johnnie and Bea, an old, grainy shot of them sitting at a picnic table, both looking and laughing at the camera. Johnny looked exactly the same but with shorter hair, and Bea looked young and vivacious, full of life. Her smile was almost intoxicating; her braids hung down the side of her face and covered one eye. She still had the same buttery skin.

It was sad. It bothered me more and more throughout the night, seeing Bea in that picture and then knowing what she was now.

That's what could happen, though. In a snap, you could end up this far from where you thought you were going. I slid the photo into the top drawer and tried my best to sleep in my newfound silence.

***

My first few days there on my own were a mix of both pleasure and pain: there were moments where I reveled in my solitude and others when it made me feel guilty for leaving Michael in that house with Mother and Daddy, but deep down, I knew that before I even left, he'd been long gone. My freedom felt necessary, like bandaging an open wound.

In an effort to avoid my guilt, I reasoned with myself that it was only temporary, just until I felt better. Got my bearings. I knew I needed a new plan. I had scoured the classifieds for jobs that wouldn't put me in a too-social environment; I still had trouble faking happiness over my grief. Didn't want to have to yuck it up with customers or anything like that; I just wanted to keep my head down and quietly make a living somewhere.

Weeks went by with no calls for interviews except for jobs I knew I couldn't do. I let those interview days slip by without bothering to cancel; even a phone call for me was taxing. I got to know Gloria better since she was the only other conscious person in the house during the day when Johnnie was gone to work. She sat at the dining room table with a portable television in front of her while she did crossword puzzles or her knitting, which she tried unsuccessfully to teach me one day.

Gloria said that she'd been a hospice nurse for thirty-three years come December. She got her nursing degree while raising two of her own kids, plus her two little brothers. Her baby's father was a sorry son-of-a-bitch *who was going to hell one day, and he knew it*. Her favorite shows were soap operas, so from one o'clock to three, she barely moved. Just sat with the TV up close, her head tilted up, looking at the screen through her bifocals. There was a perfectly good normal television in the living room, but for some reason, she didn't like to use it.

She told me that she thought Bea could hear us. She said that if there was anything else she'd learned in her thirty-three years, it was that the human body is a miraculous thing, and much, much stranger things had happened on her watch. After that, I started to feel sorry for Bea, even more than I already had; I started to think about what it would feel like to be trapped inside yourself. I wondered if she would reach over and pull her own plug if she could. The very thought of it made me shudder.

One night, when I couldn't sleep, I went to the kitchen for something to drink and heard mumbling coming from Bea's room. The door was open, and the light was on, so I walked down the hallways and peeked my head inside. Johnnie was sitting at her bedside, singing and rubbing Bea's arms and hands with some kind of cream. She stopped singing when she saw me. "Drue, come on back in here," she said when I tried to creep back out to the kitchen.

"I didn't mean to disturb you," I said. "I couldn't sleep."

"Not at all," she said. "You never bother me, you know that."

"So that's what you use to make her skin so smooth?" I asked.

"Yup. Straight cocoa butter. 'Course Mama always had good skin, anyway. But I like to sit here and just be with her," she said. "Sometimes I talk, sometimes I sing. Sometimes, I just sit here and cry. Either way, I walk away feeling a little lighter."

She looked over and smiled at Bea, and put the lid on the

butter jar. "It's like she knows exactly what I need, just like she always did."

***

From that day forward, I spent hours of my life in Bea's room, talking. I first started by introducing myself, explaining to her how I knew Johnnie and how wonderful I thought she was for caring about me and for being there for me when I needed someone solid. From that, I began to tell her about Samantha and all of the details of her tragic little life. While I spoke, I couldn't help but look for any signs of life, any form of consciousness at all, just as I had done with Samantha, but there were none.

None that I could see, anyway.

I thought that maybe she was permanently in one of those awful dreams where you try so hard to scream or to run but can't. Some strange force is holding you back, running its scheming hands all over you, grabbing onto you from every direction.

Hands – so many hands. Try to grab you and keep you from escaping yourself.

Chapter 7

I talked about the weather, Desert Storm, Mother and Daddy. Michael. Duane. Life in general. My current state of weary disgust for both my past and my future. And Johnnie was right; I did feel better afterwards. Lighter; more relaxed. Validated.

Over the course of a couple weeks, I decided to write Mother a letter instead of calling. I gave her a brief update on my life, including where I was staying and why. I had gotten slightly more used to expressing myself after spilling my guts to Bea almost every night, so when I wrote the letter, I allowed myself to be vulnerable and tell Mother how I felt. Something I'd never really been allowed to do, something Mother *fucking* hated. It was scary… opening up to her. But, at the same time, it felt good, too.

It took over *three weeks* to get a reply.

The letter I sent was big and thick and heartfelt; I had to use extra stamps just to mail it. I guess, in a way, I expected the same thing back. Although, looking back, that's not at all what I expected – just something I desperately wanted.

Her letter was thin and light, with only one stamp. Shocker. Really.

When I opened it, there was one piece of Mother's floral stationary with her sprawling cursive penmanship. It was folded around a single photo: a candid pic of Michael wearing his red, corduroy overalls and smiling at the camera. He had a blue racecar in one hand and a lollipop in the other.

Seeing his face was like a gunshot wound to the chest, a blow I wasn't prepared for and couldn't fully recover from.

My eyes burned with tears while I began to read the note.

Drucilla.

You're emotional outbursts are not appreciated, nor will they be addressed as such. You need to get yourself together, and I mean get some real help. You still have responsibilities. It's time to grow up. We will consider a visitation with Michael once we are sure you can control yourself. You've become wreckless both as a mother and a woman, and I won't stand for it.

–P. Rose

It was then that I couldn't decide which was worse: having a Mother that couldn't speak or one that very much did.

I took a job cleaning motel rooms at Econolodge, right on the outskirts of town. In all my years in Burgess, I'd only driven past it a handful of times. It wasn't the greatest; it was pretty gross, actually. *Definitely* not somewhere Mother and Daddy would have ever paid to stay. A "roach motel," Daddy would call it.

Every day from 11-5, I rolled my squeaky cart from room to room, scrubbing toilets and stripping beds with cigarette burns on the bedspreads. My bosses, Don and Lorraine Masters, hired me on the spot. They told me they'd been looking for someone young and hardworking. The last girl, she said, had lead in her ass.

On my first day, I saw why the rooms rented for only 29.95. You'd be shocked at the things you find left behind in someone's room. Their integrity, or lack thereof, out on display for someone like me to clean up for chump change. Used condoms lying on the floor or nightstand, sometimes floating in the toilet that didn't flush. Human shit smeared across tiles; porno magazines and smelly old takeout containers; bloody sheets and towels.

That was the worst for me, all the bloody sheets and towels.

Jesus. For the life of me, I could not fathom what had transpired. I would always be terrified to continue cleaning, scared I would sling a shower curtain back and find someone's victim. That's exactly the type of place you'd see some shit like that – straight out of a horror movie.

Though the work was often horrid, I appreciated the very little interaction I had with the outside world. I worked quietly and diligently with little to no interruption. When I did interact socially, it was taking daily orders from Lorraine, a quick convo with Johnnie at home, or a midnight therapy session with Bea. I had no strength for any more than that.

And that's when I met Jimmy.

After I divorced Duane, I swore off men in general. Had no desire left, no sensual feelings whatsoever. Sex had repulsed me after it led to the birth of a dead baby. But, somehow, Jimmy managed to catch my attention, and he didn't let go easily.

I'd seen him a couple times at work but never paid much attention; I was always lost deep in my own thoughts, avoiding human interaction. Jimmy was Don and Lorraine's eldest son and did the maintenance work for the motel. When August came, and the sun was scorching the ground, Jimmy started painting the Econolodge's exterior from peeling white to pigeon grey, and through the windows, I could see him working from almost any room.

He was manly, *nothing* like Duane.

In the afternoons, he would work with his shirt off, and I marveled at the rolling through his muscles while he rolled on that fuming paint. His biceps were big and built; his back and stomach were like the guys I'd seen on MTV during spring break.

Before long, I caught myself staring through a slit in the drapes of the rooms I cleaned. Some days, I had to stay late because

I'd spent so much time gawking, imagining, daydreaming about what it might be like to be with a real man. A man that looks like a man and doesn't have a receding hairline in his twenties. One who might know how to treat a woman with respect, or at least one who is not insecure around her. One that would take me out on dates and hold my hand while we cuddle and watch old movies. One that would make me laugh when I was sad and would hold me when I cried. Someone who would actually listen when I spoke and appreciate my company. I guess I'd like someone to notice when I'm not around.

Love. Is that being in love?

One day, when the heat was burning in the triple digits, Jimmy stopped working early for the day and disappeared into the living quarters of the motel where Don and Lorraine lived at the time.

Once I was sure he was gone for the day, I walked down the sidewalk to the vending machine to buy a Diet Coke. My portable radio kept buzzing on my cart. The Eagles had just been singing *Peaceful Easy Feeling*, one of my very favorites. I was still humming the tune to myself while the quarters clunked down the slot, and I pulled my soda from the rack.

When I turned around, Jimmy was standing right behind me, smiling the kindest smile I had ever seen. Even his mischievous, brown eyes were kind. He had a dimple in each cheek. His bright demeanor was blinding like the sun.

"Drucilla, right?" he asked politely.

"Uh, *Drue*, actually," I said.

"Drue," he repeated. "I like that. I'm Jimmy, Jimmy Masters," he said, shaking my hand. "I work for my parents here, Don and Lorraine." He rocked back and forth on his feet, jingled change around in his pockets. "I've been seeing you around here cleaning," he said. "Was wondering if you might like to go out sometime? Maybe grab something to eat after work or something?"

I almost hyperventilated right there on the spot. It was a struggle to even speak. "Oh, I would love to, but I have a boyfriend. I'm sorry," I lied.

"No worries, don't apologize," he said, still smiling. "Just had to ask." He backed up and started to walk back toward the main quarters. But then, he turned out, and my heart skipped a beat.

"See you around, Drue."

I watched him walk away, and just before he was out of sight, he turned and looked at me – met my gaze. Smiled. Then, I went inside and closed the door.

On the drive home that day, I felt almost giddy. Excited. I never really thought I had a chance; I wasn't sure I even wanted one, no matter how much of my attention he stole. But it felt good – really fucking good – to be asked out by someone with those striking good looks. Since Samantha died, I had let myself go... I had stopped wearing makeup and fixing my hair. Wore whatever clothes were clean, whether they matched or not.

Surviving doesn't include good fashion sense, nor does it fucking care.

But regardless of what I'd looked like at work every day, I'd caught Jimmy's attention as much as he had mine, and there had to be something said for that, right? But, as soon as I pulled up in Johnnie's driveway, I was instantly shoved back down into reality.

There I was, living in my dead baby's nurse's house, trying to cope with life with another child back home who was alive and well that I'd quietly abandoned in grief.

I became overwhelmed with guilt. How could I even think about that? Having a relationship would include being vulnerable, too.

How could I explain my life so far? I was twenty-four with enough bad memories to fill the soul of a seventy-five-year-old grandma. When I asked Johnnie for her opinion that night after dinner, she told me I would be crazy if I didn't go out on a date with him.

"It's been a year and a half, Drue. I know the pain is still there, it always will be in some ways, but you have to cultivate a life outside of Samantha. And a date with a nice, handsome man sounds like a damn good way to start."

I thought about her words all night, like a record playing on a loop through my brain. *You've got to cultivate a life outside of Samantha.* When I asked her what she thought Bea would tell me to do, she laughed, bent completely over.

"Honey, my mama woulda done had you married by now!" I reasoned with myself in bed that night that if I didn't go out on the date, Samatha would still be gone. And if I did, she would also, *still* be gone.

The only difference was me. And I was long overdue for a distraction.

***

The following day, I stopped by Common Grounds and got two iced coffees to go. I got to work earlier than usual and used my extra time to darken my lashes with the tube of mascara I'd brought, and I applied a few dabs of my old lipstick. If I was going to eat crow and admit I'd lied, I thought it might come off better coming from someone who looked less devastating.

But Jimmy was late that day and didn't show up for several more hours. By then, the coffee I'd bought for him had melted in the garbage bin, covered up with bags of trash from the four rooms I cleaned while I waited, peeking through the drapes every two minutes to check for him.

When he cracked open a bucket of paint and began to pour, I made my way over to the courtyard. He smiled when he saw me walking toward him. "Drue," he said. "What a nice surprise."

I couldn't help but smile back at him. "Listen, I just wanted to tell you that I'm not really seeing anyone right now. I mean, I was, but not now." It felt a little awkward… suddenly declaring that I was in the market after only recently having told him I was not.

"Awesome," he said, easing the awkwardness. Just like that. "Does that mean I can take you to dinner tonight?"

"I'd like that," I said. I gave him Johnnie's address, and we agreed to six o'clock.

I wouldn't be lying if I said my heart pounded audibly until then.

***

Jimmy showed up at six-thirty, half an hour late. By then, I'd already accepted the fact that he wasn't coming. Heartbroken, I sat in Bea's room and ranted about what it costs a person to be vulnerable. Mid-sentence, the doorbell rang.

"I'm so sorry, I'm so sorry, Drue," he kept saying over and over again. "The AC went out in 120; Mom wouldn't let it wait even though there was no one in it. She can be like that sometimes. Well, I guess most of the time, actually," he laughed. *H* was still in his work clothes: white, paint-splattered t-shirt and faded Levis with the pant legs scrunched up around his work boots. Baseball cap. Immediately, I felt stupid and overdressed in the churchy, floral dress I borrowed from Johnnie.

Even though I told him over and again that it was fine and that it was no big deal, he continued to apologize. "I can't believe I ruined our first date!" he'd said at one point.

But that couldn't be farther from the truth.

We drove through Storm's and got greasy burgers and fries to go. Then, we rode all through the backroads behind Burgess, all the little winding roads where mostly farmers drove, eating and laughing with the radio playing.

Out there in the country, there was an odd peacefulness, almost otherworldly. I rolled my window down and let the warm wind flow through me while I listened to Jimmy tell me a story about a man who used to live in a house down that road who hung himself right in the front yard, only tree on the lot, when he found out his wife was cheating on him with his brother.

"They chopped the tree down after that," he said. "But the stump is still there, and people say if you are there at the stump at the exact time he died, you'll see his ghost sitting there on the stump, crying. 'Course, no one knows what time that really is, but some people say they saw him there."

The red-dirt roads behind Burgess were seemingly endless, one tree-lined road leading to another, the clear, Indiana sky giving way to the cosmos. It was magnificent. And we drove on.

When "Mainstreet," by Bob Seger, came on the radio. Jimmy slammed on the brakes, turned up the volume, threw the truck in park, and got out. The headlights blinked when he walked in front of them to my side, where he opened the door and took my hand.

There, we danced in the street like it was our wedding, and Jimmy held me close and sang softly as we swayed to the music. It was one of the best moments of my life so far. I felt safe, I think. Yes, at the beginning phases of my life with Jimmy, it was the first time I'd felt truly *safe*.

At the end of the date, in Johnnie's driveway, he kissed me. I felt weightless, vulnerable to even the slightest movement. But, back in my plaid bedroom, I was instantly reminded of who I was. What I'd been through. It was past midnight. The slipper was lost. Back to your old self, Cinderella.

The date had gone so well that for the next several days, all I could think about was Jimmy, mixed with imaginary awards of Mother's approval for having moved forward in life. It didn't occur to me at the time that I was basing my decision to date Jimmy on the approval of a woman who couldn't seem to pick a decent man any more than I could.

For our second date, Jimmy asked me to join him at his house for his niece's tenth birthday party.

I was anxious to see where he lived and what his house looked like. Who he was. We turned off Highway 177 onto a red dirt road crowded with trees on both sides. He made a sharp right and bounced again on another cattle guard that gated an enormous clearing, maybe five acres or so, with a shabby, white trailer house on a hill. Jimmy's truck bumped and rumbled all the way up the dirt path to the trailer and killed the engine.

Though I knew Don and Lorraine well from work, I wasn't too keen on spending the evening with them on my second date with their son. If things didn't work out, would they fire me? I was already trudging through the overgrown grass toward the house, so whatever was gonna' happen was already in motion.

The smell of a campfire filled the air around us, and muffled voices and music from the party at the back of the house swam alongside. The front of the house had been modest, slightly junky, and cluttered with broken-down cars and a string of several old lawnmowers rusted almost completely. But around the back of the house was an enormous metal awning covering an enormous outdoor patio with lounge chairs, picnic tables, large speakers playing music, and twinkly lights running along the ceiling. All it was missing was a stage.

There were several people in the corner playing cornhole and kids on the opposite side shooting hoops. There were tables set up with food galore; The Last Supper times fifty. And there were people everywhere, mingling and talking and laughing and eating. "Who are all these people," I whispered to Jimmy.

"What do you mean? This is my family."

***

We all sat around and ate from paper plates, everybody talking to everybody happily. When the conversation focus shifted to Jimmy's new date, they all began telling me childhood stories of him, cute things he used to do and say, how much of a troublemaker he was but too cute to ever be in too much trouble.

Their stories reminded me of Michael, and I found myself wondering what he was doing, what he looked like now, and if he missed me – or, more importantly – would he even remember me? I had another beer and asked Darla about her to avoid remembering.

When everyone was done eating, some of the ladies were cleaning up and Jimmy suddenly disappeared inside the house for a moment and came back holding a shiny black guitar.

"PARTY TIME!" Darla shouted.

Her husband, Billy, whooped along, too. I was truly amazed when he started playing. Everyone sang along and danced while Jimmy played song after song, from Aerosmith to Zeppelin. It was like an episode of the Partridge Family, but then, before I knew it, the beer had relaxed me, and I was singing, too.

I spent the night at Jimmy's that night and never left.

***

I made Jimmy fix the leaking roof and the rotting steps. We planted hydrangea bushes, my favorite, on each side of the new cedar porch. It wasn't perfect, but it was home.

Home for me had become wherever Jimmy was. When I was with him, I was somehow *new*, a completely different person who didn't always feel like dying or like she was already dead.

He proposed to me on that porch on our four-month anniversary. We were married at city hall on Halloween day, with a reception out behind our house, and danced the night away.

My mother would have been appalled by the whole thing. I knew that, but fortunately for her, she wasn't included on the damned guest list. But for some odd reason, I still felt myself wanting to share my happiness with her, to show her I could do right, but I knew that couldn't happen and that no matter what, she would still be disappointed.

In the evenings, when our time was our own, Jimmy and I would pile up on the couch and watch old movies or have supper up at Don and Lorraine's. Most weekends, Jimmy's friends would come over to drink beer and play guitar. Hardly a weekend passed that there wasn't a campfire circled with friends and laughter.

We were happy, I was happy.

For a while, I'd forgotten who I was: who I'd been before Jimmy Masters and his family breathed new life into me and showed me a way of living that, as of then, was far from my own. Though I hated living in that tiny trailer house, I was comforted that the rest of the family lived so close, and I had come to really love them as my own.

I think what I liked most about the Masters family was their humility. They were so humble it was almost unnatural. Though they ran their own business, I learned that most of the time, they didn't turn much of a profit and that the little money they did make seemed, oddly enough, to be good enough for them. No fancy houses, no fancy cars or hobbies. Just good, hard-working people with only love to give to each other.

My own experience with family and money had been quite different. There were much, much more vain concerns involved: who had the biggest house of all city council members (Daddy, us), who was president of the garden club and won the plaque for *nicest lawn*? (Mother, us), who had done the most charitable work for the Methodist church? (Mother and Daddy, ugh).

But the Masters were great.

Casually, one night after sex, Jimmy asked me if I ever thought about having any more children. My stomach turned at his words. He knew my situation with Michael, but I didn't mention Samantha. I don't know why, exactly, I withheld this crucial piece of my history from my husband. Maybe it was part of my plan to try to form a life outside of her death. Maybe it was because I just absolutely couldn't fucking talk about it? I don't know...

And that haunted me every single day of my marriage. I

pictured Michael, smiling in his red overalls, and then Samantha's mushroom-colored face in her coffin. Suddenly paranoid, I muttered, "Sometimes," and got out of bed and into a hot shower that couldn't wash away my shame.

That night, I dreamed of Samantha for the first time in months.

We are in the Baptist church sanctuary. The oak pews are filled with people, mourners, sniffling and crying.

I walk down the burgundy carpet aisle to her coffin. No one seems to notice my presence in the room. The focus is on Pastor Robbie behind the pulpit, talking about prayer.

"And this, then, is how you should pray..."

No one sees me.

I continue to walk to her. I had to see her one last time. I needed to see her.

"Our Father in heaven, hallowed be your name..."

As I finally approach her, she looks at me and smiles. She is pink and healthy, kicking and squirming in her yellow dress. She kicks hard and squeals when she sees my excitement. Her eyes are focused on me. They are not lost. She can see me. She knows exactly who I am. I can feel her love, her acknowledgement of my presence.

I pick her up and held her close, smell her smell. But just then, I feel a heaviness in my hands and in my chest, and I have a sense of fear that I remember very well. And then, in a rushed instant, she reverts back to death: her stiff, unnatural body cold against my skin.

***

The waiting room at Planned Parenthood was crowded with girls I pitied: young women with pregnant bellies and no clue; one with an infant climbing up her leg and one being rocked with her foot in a carrier on the floor; a young couple who looked scared enough to make me assume they were there for a pregnancy test, and a few strays who appeared oblivious to real life, smacking gum and reading Cosmo, waiting to get their birth control refilled. I was an odd mix of shit in comparison – I was there for birth control, sure. But not for pleasure-seeking purposes. I took it out of fear of what I knew could happen.

I suddenly recalled the "talk" Mother and I had had about sex when I was a girl. She made it very clear that sex was nothing more than a duty of the wife, that it was barbaric (which she also felt breastfeeding was), and that it was disgusting and stuff ran down your legs that you had to clean up.

A duty, an obligation. I was horrified; though, apparently not enough.

When I got my blue compacts for the next three months, I put them safely inside the lining of my leather purse where I kept them, accessible only by a tiny slit I'd made in the fabric. A secret I shared with no one, and one that at first had offered me a little peace, but that soon just turned into another reason for me to have to apologize to someone.

***

Every year on Michael's birthday, I sent him a card with a five-dollar bill inside. It would take me days to fill out the inside of the card and to write the names on the envelopes. To sign "Love, Mom," a sentiment I wasn't sure he understood anymore.

Maybe Daddy wasn't completely wrong after all…

So when Michael turned five, I decided, after weeks of self-torture, to include a letter to Mother asking for a visit. I didn't tell Jimmy; I just did it.

All that night, I couldn't sleep; I tossed and turned and watched the ceiling fan blades whirl in circles, knowing that my heart was now in the hands of the U.S. postal service, and there was no turning back.

I was scared I'd said too much or not enough. I avoided apologies and feelings and stuck to the facts. I asked about Michael, then her, and even Daddy. I told her I was feeling better, that I'd fallen in love and worked a steady job, and said all I could say to convince her that I was a normal person living a normal life, the same mask I wore for everyone. Jimmy was my disguise, my mask, with the moon the only witness to my madness.

Over three months passed before I received a response from Mother. Even though I'd bravely included my home phone number on the note, she had still chosen to write to me and not call. When the letter finally arrived, my hands were shaking so hard I could barely open it. My stomach heaved at Mother's sprawling, fancy penmanship:

Drucilla,

Our priority is to ensure that Michael is in a safe, stable environment. Consistently, not just for a little while. Re-making the same mistakes with a different man does not constitute change for the better on your part. We have not seen you in two years, so we cannot allow Michael to visit until a connection has been reestablished and supported by your father and me. When you are ready to do that, let us know.

A. A. Sandoval

Blessings,

Mother

Reading the letter felt like being shot in the chest at point-blank range. I crumpled the floral stationery into a small, tight ball and shoved it down to the bottom of the trash can – just like I did in the school bathroom all those years ago when I took that pregnancy test, and my world imploded.

Hide your sins, your shame. I was grateful I hadn't told Jimmy that I reached out, and now I knew why I made that decision. And then, all at once, a feeling of old came back up fiery and hot inside me, and suddenly, I realized why I'd resisted them until now – going back made me who I used to be. That letter instantly reverted me back to my old self on Seminary Street.

Ordinarily, a blow like that would've clobbered me in one way or another – either I'd cry and vomit and lie in bed for days, weeks even, wallowing in my feelings, or I'd completely lose my shit and burn their house down or something, but I felt oddly at peace the more I thought about it… Like I was owed that response. Like I had earned it and never really expected anything more and nothing less. It was a penance. I knew very well how cold my Mother could be. How uncaring Daddy was. It was all more of the same, merely extensions of the past that had come back to haunt me in different ways.

On Friday mornings, the soda vendor came to take the money and refill the machines. On that particular Friday, Carlos, the hot vendor, was the one on duty. I smoothed my hair in the mirror and walked out to sign for the order form from Carlos when that bright orange wig caught my eye against the gray, *January* gloom. The lady was getting on the passenger side of her small brown sedan, and there was a man getting in the driver's seat. That man was my daddy.

For a brief moment, my heart stopped. Then, my adrenaline kicked in, and it was as if I had the strength of a thousand men inside me.

I stood and watched, unable to move and amazed at his audacity, and at his situation, his being on the other side of shit. It was like a gift straight from God, not the God that took my baby daughter, but the one who brings justice to the real offenders and stands for what is right.

I watched Daddy back the car out from under the awning, knowing he was about to drive right past me. The motel was a circle; one entrance, one exit. Within seconds, I'd stepped out from behind Carlos' Coke truck, and Daddy almost ran me smooth over. He slammed on his brakes to avoid the hit, which missed me only by inches. Then, with my hands on the hood, I looked him dead in the eyes.

"Gotcha," I mouthed over the roar of the engine.

I backed away, expecting him to get out and defend himself, but he didn't. He shifted the car back into gear, grinding loudly and intrusively, and the car bucked and sped away in a thick, choking cloud of guilt. And for the first time in all my existence, I felt like I was in control.

I ran into the house and looked back at the books.

The lady's name was Rita. Rita Sanders. Rita with a Wilma Flinstone wig. Rita the woman having an affair with my father…

I didn't know exactly what to do. Would he come back? Call? Kill me? I knew he didn't just drive off into thin air; my guess is that he was trying to get rid of Rita. But the truth was this: now he could drive Rita to the moon if he wanted to. Leave her there for eternity. But her existence would remain inescapable inside of me.

Can't unsee things. You got caught with your pants down. *Busted.*

My mind was reeling with several guilt-ridden options. Each would end in his demise. And Mother would know that I had been right all along; she would have no choice but to admit it.

As I sat there in shock, weighing my options, the bell on the entrance door of the office chimed and startled me back to the present.

Then, Daddy was beating on the office door like he had a warrant.

I was terrified and hid in the bathroom with the door locked. But then it hit me – I wasn't the sinner here. It was Daddy in the hot seat this time. Not me. I jerked the door open so hard I startled him. His eyes were wide and panicked, his face white as a sheet.

"Drucilla," he began, breathless. Panicked. His eyes addressed the counter. "You know as well as I do that people make mistakes. C'mon now, we all know you do." He cleared his throat and coughed a bit. Ran one hand through his graying hair. "You open that mouth, and you know what'll happen. It's best to just let sleeping dogs lie."

The audacity!

"So you want me to show you mercy now? *Real* mercy, or the kind you showed me? I want to see my son." I responded, now angry.

He looked up at me accusingly, almost sarcastic. His beady eyes narrowed in on me. "You think I'll let Michael come to this roach motel? Or at your trailer trash house? With you? Over my dead body."

We both waited to see what I'd do. I screamed so loud that

Daddy cupped his ears. I called him every name in the book, spilled my entire being out through my throat, so loud and angrily that Daddy finally backed out the doorway and ran back to his pickup, his hands still muffling my words. By the time he was out of sight, I had grabbed my car keys and was starting up the Vega, locked and loaded.

Though he'd been just moments ahead of me, there was no sight of him on the way to Seminary Street, and his truck was not in the driveway when I pulled up. I'd expected him to be there, to continue our battle all the way up to Mother's face, but that hadn't happened. Now I sat on my newfound throne of knowledge, staring at the back end of Mother's grey Oldsmobile that I hadn't seen in years. A swingset was out back now, coated in winter frost. The only sign of life in that early morning hour was the light in the kitchen and steady puffs of smoke from the chimney.

I had convinced myself the whole ride over that I was doing the right thing, that I had a right to tell the truth and at least be on equal playing fields. They were no better than me, neither one of them, and now I had proof.

Suddenly alive with the fury of years of pent-up aggression, I rang the doorbell with a shaky hand. Held my breath. Mother answered the door, looking like she'd just gotten back from the beauty parlor. Helmet hair, coral lips. An emerald green dress I'd never seen with shiny golden earrings. The smell of bread or cookies baking flowed out from behind her and slapped me with memories of times gone by. She did not look happy to see me; tongue in one cheek and single eyebrow lift – her signature scowl – was in full swing.

"What are you doing here?" She looked around as if scared someone might see me, then ushered me inside and into the house.

"I need to talk to you," I said, sighing audibly. Knowing I was about to crush her with the truth.

"About what, exactly?"

She was wringing her hands in a blue and white dishcloth, looking at me nervously, when the oven timer chimed.

"Hold on," she said on her way to the kitchen, where I followed her. The large granite countertops were covered in lavish silver towers of quiche cups and finger sandwiches, crystal platters full of fresh pastries and bagels. Garden Club brunch, of course. She used the dish towel to remove a pan of cinnamon rolls from the oven.

"You should have called first, Drucilla, Jesus Christ. I've got company coming within the hour." She buzzed around the room, working on the food. "What do you need?"

"I don't *need* anything, Mother. I just thought you should know that Daddy is cheating on you. Again. And this time, I have proof. I saw them together. He's probably with her right now as we speak. I just saw him not five minutes ago."

She stopped cold and looked hard at me. Then put the pan down. She balled up the cup towel and tossed it aside, blinking rapidly several times. She narrowed her gaze on her way over to the dining table where I stood beside a tier of tea cakes.

"Excuse me?" she said sharply. "What did you just say?"

"He's *cheating* on you. I told you he was a piece of shit. You always sided with him, but he was the bad guy. Not me."

She slapped me hard across the face.

I stood confused, face stinging and eyes burning with tears, and then she spoke. "What goes on in my marriage is none of your goddamn business," she said. "And don't you ever, *ever*, question my decisions now or ever. You have no idea the sacrifices I've made for you, and you never could just let things go, you always just had to make everything worse than it already was."

At that, I slapped her right back, knocked her glasses off her face, and saw them slide across the spanish tile floor and wedge under the stove. I picked up a crystal plate and chucked it at the bay window. The sound of glass breaking and Mother's cries filled my ears. I swiped my arms across the table, sending the rest of the food to the floor, and then I took off. I ran as fast as I could out of the house and across the yard. I could still hear her yelling when I started up the Vega.

From that day forward, any correspondence I sent for Michael was sent back stamped "Return to Sender" in red, *evil* letters.

And so time slid out from under me in drifts; the days were so much alike that I hardly noticed them change. Weeks, then months, and finally years that passed with forlorn clouds of gloom that I couldn't seem to shake. I had never felt so alone in my life. No matter how many people were around me, in any given situation, I was still somehow far away from them.

I'm not sure exactly why I felt so worthless, tainted, and hopeless, but I did. I felt haunted, the ghosts of words left unsaid between me and my parents, goodbyes for Samantha still stuck in my throat, a long string of apologies to Michael for being gone. The lost narratives between us all hung over my shoulders like the weight of dead relationships and time, all bitterly lost in translation.

Over a year had passed – basically two – and I'd long since given up on my parental pursuits. No one wanted me around, reminding them of things they were ashamed of, of times gone by and hopefully forgotten. My presence, I felt, was only a reminder of all of the bad things we'd been through; every path seemed to strangely connect back to me. Nothing made sense anymore. Time had blurred things. I had gotten into the habit of forgetting; that was the only way I could move forward. If I looked back, even for a second, I would never go forward again.

I steered away from reminders of my past life; the one before the bottom fell out. And, against Jimmy's knowledge, I was indignant in the fact that I would never procreate again, and I wanted, yearned to even, leave this little antiqued town with sorrow in the bricks of every building I saw, and run far away somewhere magical and distant, a hidden community, with only new experiences and strangers in my path with the safety of my new anonymous existence.

Jimmy seemed oblivious to my emptiness. For him, to avoid pity, I became some sort of a skewed, dream-like version of myself- just a normal girl living a normal life. But on the inside, I had crumbled, shrank, shriveled up from my grievously tainted memories of everyone I'd ever known.

In public, I worked and cooked and laughed and smiled. In private, when something would trigger me, a memory – anything, and I would cry and choke and gag on tears and rocks of regret in my burning, nauseous stomach... My bitter, war-torn soul demanded my misery.

I spent each day scrubbing toilets, dusting dressers and television screens, and making bathroom mirrors streak-free. I stripped beds and washed sheets and vacuumed old, musty-smelling carpets and threw away takeout containers, and used condoms and cigarette butts. Then I'd come home, smile for Jimmy, make dinner, and watch television miserably with Jimmy beside me, laughing at some slapstick comedy that I was only pretending to be interested in, my eyes burning with exhaustion and my mind someplace else, separate from my being. Maybe Jimmy should just leave me and run: save himself from me, too…

Things between Jimmy and I became increasingly strained since the fallout with my family, mostly because I hadn't taken the heat so well, and I took out a lot of my frustrations on him for their mistakes.

They'd burned me at the stake for telling the truth, the only shred of honesty that had hit the surface of our family that I can remember, which was what I hated most about my parents, their secrets I had to eat just to survive my life with them – to make us seem perfect instead of flawed, all for the sake of vanity. The logic of that never made sense to me, mostly because there was no logic in it at all. It was hell, and we all knew it.

I thought, as a child and young adult, that I would never be like that, that my home would be open and honest and loving and kind. But the problem with that was that I was married to a man who knew nothing real about me. I'd stuffed my past inside a box in my soul, locked it up tight, and didn't share it with anyone. I tried to forget it all myself to make the days easier, which never seemed to work.

Now there I sat, beside a man I didn't know and who didn't know me, while trying to trudge forward through life. With every passing day, it became more and more clear to me that I had likely made a huge mistake marrying Jimmy, and I was now committed to a man and his own dreams that I had no energy for, a marriage that left me exhausted and stressed and pressured to do things I hated and didn't want in the first place.

When I first met him, I welcomed all of those meaningless conversations and long drives down dirt roads, the feel of someone sleeping safely beside you, the comfort of human interaction, and distractions from grief. But now, after all that's happened, I didn't feel like talking anymore about Jimmy's favorite bands or listening to him play their songs on his guitar. After Mother slapped me, I became disenchanted with anything that resembled love.

I felt shitty about it, too. Jimmy was a good man. His family was loving and welcoming and kind. Jimmy had come into this marriage innocently and lovingly but also blind to who stood before him at the altar. He had wanted nothing more than any normal person would want in a marriage: love, kids, companionship. Happiness.

And honestly, God knows, I should have been able to give that to him. I should have wanted that for myself, but I didn't. *Couldn't*. All of my thoughts ran along dark, suspicious, paranoid fault lines. I was unfocused, my moods erratic and filled with fear: fear I covered with a false mask of normal complacency.

I knew Jimmy had been ready to start a family since the night of our wedding. He'd asked to start trying that very night. Don and Lorraine talked about their excitement for more grandchildren the second I moved into the trailer, and after the wedding, I started to feel like I was on a set timer to conceive with a gun jabbed in my ribs.

But secretly, I had been taking my birth control pills from Planned Parenthood every morning at six AM on the dot like it was my damn job. I talked Jimmy into waiting until we were more financially secure to start building a family.

"That's just another excuse," he said. "Is this about Michael? Haven't we been over this?"

Then we'd have a blowup fight, and then the dust would eventually settle right back down into a pile of shit.

Most of our money went to pay Jimmy's loan payment for the land we lived on, so money was always tight. He was so proud to tell me he was a "landowner" while we were dating, but when we got married, I asked point blank. "So we both own this place now?"

He said, "As long as we keep paying on it, we sure do."

That was why I'd asked, he had me coughing up ninety percent of every paycheck, but we were eating canned soup and shit for dinner. And the less money the motel made in nightly rentals, the less our paychecks were. "Can't give you what I don't have," Don would say in defense on payday.

He would always get really defensive, too; like if I suggested that maybe we find more steady-pay jobs or at least one of us, he would act like I'd committed familial treason. *Off with her head!* I even suggested then that maybe Jimmy do some work outside of his scheduled work hours, some odd jobs or something, just for some extra money for bills and food, but he would have none of that. Not even an option.

The humble nature of Jimmy and his family reached new heights during the winter of our second year together when the pipes at the motel froze and then burst, causing us to shut down while staring at thousands of dollars in repair bills. The insurance Don and Lorraine had on the property was the bare minimum, not nearly enough to cover what we were going to be losing in nightly rentals, plus our own paychecks.

Because the insurance company hired a contractor to make the repairs, Jimmy wasn't able to help. We had no tenants, so I wasn't able to clean. By week three, we had no lights at home and had to live in one of the rooms with no running water. We had to go across the street to the gas station to use the restroom, even Don and Lorraine. It was humiliating. I had to go days without bathing; we fed ourselves with vending machine pastries and tiny bags of chips and cans of soda.

We were camped in that room for five solid days before Jimmy came up with enough money to pay the light bill. I think he borrowed it from a friend, I can't remember, but I do remember telling him I was done with the camping situation and using gas station bathrooms and that he had one day before I bailed.

Being back at home was bittersweet; it was a far cry from that motel room, but it was also a cold reminder of reality. The clocks on the microwave and stove were flashing, and the air smelled like the moldy, rotted food in the fridge. It took days, maybe weeks, to get that smell out of the rugs. I resented Jimmy from then on, didn't see him as being a good provider, and I shuddered to think what it would be like to raise a child in such cheap, wavering conditions – not that it was ever on the table (my table).

On our second or third night back home, the phone rang. I asked Jimmy to get it, thinking it would be either Don or Lorraine. He picked up the Caller ID box first and then examined it closely. "It's your parents," he said in a serious tone. He raised his eyebrows in disbelief. "Holy shit. You want me to answer?"

"Shut up, Jimmy," I said. "Get serious."

"I'm not fucking around, Drue," he said, waving the box like evidence. I got up and walked over, and sure enough, there it was, plain as day: Gerald Rose. I almost fainted.

"Oh my god," I said. "No, don't answer. Don't answer!" I yelled. "Oh my god, oh my god." We both looked at the answering machine at the same time it caught and clicked on it. Hangup call. No message. I paced and paced around the kitchen, nervous and curious. Then, the phone rang a second time.

"It's them again," Jimmy said. "Maybe you should answer. It could have something to do with Michael."

"Hello?"

"Drucilla, this is your mother. I have something urgent to tell you, and it's not good."

"What? What is it, what happened?"

"Your father died," she said.

"What? Gary?" I asked.

"No." I heard her voice change… *crack* a little. "Gerald." For several moments after that, time stood completely still. "I need you to come here," she continued. "Now, if possible. Please come now… If you can." I could hear her start to cry.

It was past eleven when I got there. The drive over was torturous: a chaotic, emotional mix of trying to process Daddy dying and seeing Mother and Michael for the first time in so long. What would Michael say? What did he think of me, or better yet, why does he think I'm away? There were no cars there besides Mother and Daddy's. I'd expected at least a couple of Mother's friends would be there to console her, but there was no one but me. The only light in all the darkness came from the single burning bulb in Mother's Tiffany lamp that sat in the front window, always glowing in its stained-glass glory.

I knocked lightly, held my breath, and waited. Mother answered the door, looking soggy and defeated. Her face was red and swollen from crying. She straightened up and took a deep breath when she saw me, trying to compose herself. Mother was never one to show much emotion, and it was almost painful to watch her try to hide her pain. "Come in, come in," she said. "Thanks for coming."

I sat at the kitchen table while Mother started a pot of coffee. The house was painfully quiet. "Where's Michael?" I blurted out. "Asleep? Is he okay?"

She sat the coffee can down and turned to look at me. "He's with Duane," she said. "Yes, he seems to be doing okay."

"Duane? He's with Duane? What the fuck is he doing with Duane?"

"Because that's his father," she said sharply. "And legally, I can't keep them apart. If that makes you upset, then you can take that up with Duane and his lawyer. Be mad at him. Or yourself, for that matter. But certainly not me. Meanwhile, your father has just died, so do we really need to get into that right now? Please don't start your shit, Drucilla Elizabeth. Not today."

I pulled my reins in, but I was furious. When I tried to speak, she put her hand up and cut me off. "When I got up this morning, Gerald was dead in that chair, right in there with the news blaring on the television." She put her face in her hands and cried hard, so hard she shook. I tried to touch her to console her, but she pushed my hand away and wiped her face angrily, sucking all of her emotions back up inside to shift back to her old, hard self.

Over the course of the next hour, she caught me up on what had been going on with Daddy, not feeling well and then being put on medication for his high blood pressure. "He wouldn't take the goddamn pills," she said. "All he had to do was take the goddamn pills!" I listened, horrified and shocked to my core, her words blurring my emotions and making me feel pity for her and Daddy both. "And poor Michael," she finally said through another string of tears, "He spends every weekend with Gerald. He's crushed, I know he is."

"Weekends? What do you mean weekends with Daddy?"

"Michael lives at Duane's. Has been for the past year. Well, almost a year. Things weren't great with Gerald and me, and you were gone; Duane asked for custody, and he got it. Simple as that… Again, I couldn't keep them apart, Drucilla. There are laws in place for that, and only you can fight them. But he will be here tomorrow. You'll see him then."

That was Mother. "Should we do a morning or afternoon service? What do you think?"

Chapter 8

It was almost 2 AM when I got home.

Jimmy had fallen asleep in bed watching TV instead of the couch, which I was grateful for. The last thing I wanted to do was talk. My mind was flooded with anger and sadness, my stomach was tied in a thousand different knots. Old, familiar feelings had begun to surface without warning. The living room was dark except for the dim lamp on the end table; the only sound the flatline hum of the fridge. I pulled my tray out from under the couch and got so high that I saw Jesus.

***

Mother called the next morning while I was out and left a message on the machine that she'd set the visitation for the following day, six sharp. "Wear a dress," she said in the message. Pissed me off. What else would I wear? A tee shirt and cutoffs? A fucking clown suit?

I spent the entire day trying to decide if I should go to Mother's or not, I wanted very badly to see Michael, but I was also terrified of the same thing. Did he have questions about me? Did he remember me? The thought made me anxious and uneasy. I felt raw. Exposed. I knew I wasn't good enough in my mother's eyes, I never had been, and I worried that Michael might have that same, inherited trait of disgust. I couldn't help but wonder if Mother had ever made Daddy feel as inadequate as she did me; or even Gary Berryman, for that matter. Was that why they either cheated or left her? Was that why Daddy was always so angry?

Since the last year with Jimmy, I'd come to carry around with me a new sense of shame – being poor. I was ashamed of who I'd been, who I'd become; was appalled at where I lived, and where I worked. Who I was married to. I felt small and weak, felt like disappearing. Prayed for it.

There was no way to explain to a child that I was sad, or *why*. No good way to explain that a great deal of people aren't able to handle someone who is just sad. No nice way to say what a horrid person Duane was on the inside, or that my mother never stood up for me, not even once. I had to swallow it all, gobble up all those secrets for Michael. For them. The only problem with that is that secrets turn out to be poisonous, and inside of me, they wreaked havoc. They demanded my remembrance; my acknowledgement. They jumped in front of every happy moment, in front of every smile that tried to come across my face.

Never in my life would I see Daddy alive again, and I found

that really hard, almost impossible to believe. And all the way over to Seminary Street, I was harshly reminded of our last exchange, his panicked, pale face and breathless words. His fear, both on his face and in his voice, would haunt me all the days of my life and played like a record on a loop through my mind.

Cars bled from the driveway out onto the street. I had to park over on Rosebud and walk, a path I knew well and hated, the one that had led me to Duane all those years ago. The yard had already started to bloom for Spring: bright red and pink roses all around, the air thick with their sweet, perfumy elixir. The hydrangea bushes were ripe and thick with their bursting, cotton-candy looking blooms. The sight and smell was an instant portal back to my past, and all I wanted to do was run. I stopped in front of the carport, still bathed in Daddy's presence.

Projects he'd been working on were scattered all about, as they always were. I don't remember him actually ever finishing anything, just starting and stopping little home projects to keep him out of Mother's hair on the weekends. His table saw set up and still plugged in, a stack of sweet-smelling lumber piled carelessly beside it with a pair of leather gloves that would never be used again. His truck was parked in its usual spot, staring back at me like his ghost. I opened the drivers side door and was instantly regretful: the smell of Old Spice and cigarette smoke strummed emotional chords I wasn't even aware that I had. A half-empty pack of Basics lay in the seat with a red Bic lighter tucked in the cellophane, the way he always kept it, ready for a day that would never come.

I closed the pickup door as quietly as possible, and headed around the carport to the front of the house. Nervous as a mouse, focusing on my feet as I walked and thinking of what I might say; questioning my ability to hold it together, I crept up the front steps and stopped, godsmacked, when I saw Michael sitting alone on the porch swing, holding a piece of pie in his lap. We saw each other at the exact same moment: and the second our eyes met, he smiled. It was one of the best moments of my life, one that I always cherish, his natural reaction to me had been a genuine smile. My most intense fears became quited to a dull roar. My heart began to beat normally again. I smiled back at him.

"Hi," I said, embarrassed. "Can I sit here?" I pointed to the spot beside him.

He blinked several times, nodded slowly. "Yes."

I sighed a little, not knowing exactly what to say… "I'm so sorry about Papa."

His lip began to quiver and he broke down in tears, the pie dropping to the floorboards. And I just embraced him and hugged him tighter than ever, we sat there hugging and crying together for several minutes. It was the saddest and happiest time of my life, all at once, right there on Mother's porch. When I looked up again, I saw Mother disappear behind the lace curtains of the front window, and then reappear at the front door to interrupt the moment.

"Drucilla, honey," she said walking towards me, Mrs. Callahan and Mrs. Gonzales from church were right behind her, tending to the new widow. She hugged me like she used to, quick and tight. Polite. "I'm so glad you're here. Michael honey, are you okay? C'mon inside let's get that cleaned up." She ushered him and me both inside the house, where people I both knew and didn't filled the house as word began to spread around town about Daddy.

I was a little taken aback that so many people were there so quickly, had made it to Mother's and settled in before I'd even made it over. I watched Mother take Michael to his room while Mrs. Gonzales kept asking questions about my faith and my "current church."

The following day, Jimmy called Don and had him cover his work orders to spend the day with me, and told them about Daddy's passing. So instead of spending my day preparing for Daddy's viewing at the funeral home that evening, I had to listen to Jimmy talk about stupid, meaningless shit that I didn't care about because he thought I needed a distraction. I did not.

All day long, he followed me around like a puppy, was handsy and sympathetic and clingy – all traits I despised – and by the end of the afternoon, my nerves were so shot that I no longer carried the ability to be nice for Jimmy's sake. When he started to get dressed for the viewing, which had been my primary focus all day long, I realized that I couldn't possibly take him with me, and there was no nice way of saying that. *Sorry, honey, but you're an embarrassment. My Mother wouldn't approve of you or your family. Thanks for all your love, but you are not invited.*

When it was time to get dressed, Jimmy put on an old brown sports coat that looked like it had just crawled out of the seventies. He had his hair gelled and slicked over to one side. He wore starched blue jeans that made an obscene amount of noise when he walked. And boots. Those fucking boots I hated. I sat on the end of the bed, putting on my pantyhose, wondering which was worse – seeing Daddy dead in a coffin or Mother meeting Jimmy.

At six sharp, Jimmy and I pulled up to the funeral home. There were so many cars… we barely found a spot to park. The more people I saw, the more nervous I became. I saw Mother's car parked near the front. Respectfully, Jimmy came around and opened the car door for me and ushered me out before I could change my mind. "C'mon babe, let's go," he said. "We're late."

We walked up the long sidewalk around the building where Mother stood smoking with my Aunt Diane under a big tree. She looked at me, then over at Jimmy. She eyed him up and down with the face she made when we saw panhandlers at a red light in the city, the turned her head quickly away in disgust, whispering something discreetly to Aunt Diane. It was a look I knew well, one she'd given many times.

I introduced the two of them as we walked up, and they politely shook hands and exchanged polite greetings. An awkward energy surrounded us, a feeling I remembered very well from my Mother – embarrassment. That's what it was. That's how I always felt around her. Embarrassed. Inadequate. Ashamed.

Where's Michael?" I asked her.

"At home. A funeral parlor is no place for a child." The statement cut like a knife, Samantha's face flashed like a neon sign in my mind's eye.

We made our way inside and Mother faded away into the crowd of mourners. The sanctuary of the funeral home was still raw and familiar: the blood-red carpet, polished oak pews, and thick floral stink. Hushed whispers from strangers, silent stares of sympathy and wonder, hugs and handshakes from the masses.

My focus shifted immediately from myself unto Daddy's grey casket at the front of the sanctuary, his hands folded across his chest and his nose were visible from the very back where we came in, and almost sent me back home – but somehow I managed to swallow my fear and sit, wishing it was me up there instead of him.

Dozens of people came up to me and gave their condolences; some I remembered, some I didn't. Aunts, uncles, and cousins I wasn't close to were there, too, adding to the chaotic energy. Daddy's parents died a long time ago, and other than Uncle Bill, Daddy had no use for the rest for reasons I wasn't really aware of. I guess I never really cared enough to question it; or perhaps I just assumed he treated them as poorly as he did everyone else. Typically, one doesn't question what they know as truth, or at least I don't.

Jimmy and I sat near the back and tried hard to blend in. Everywhere I looked there was someone or something that reminded me of Samantha's funeral: same people, same flowers, same place. I wanted to run so far away that no one would ever see me again. Say, whatever happened to that girl? Drucilla, something or other? Oh, I think she died a long time ago.

After two solid hours of the same torture, when the last of the lingerers were gathered outside smoking and saying goodbyes, Jimmy and I were on our way out to the car when I heard my name. It was Mother. "Drucilla, come here. I need to speak with you," she paused, looked over at Jimmy annoyingly. "Alone, please." She led me back inside, down the red aisle and all the way up to Daddy. She held my arm and addressed me seriously.

"I want whatever ill will that's been living in between us to be buried with your father. He was a good man who made mistakes, just like we all do. No sense in reliving the past over and over or speaking ill of the dead. It's time to make peace between the three of us so we can move forward."

"He is not my father," I said.

"Yes, he most certainly is," she argued. Her eyes were dark and piercing. She must have noticed that I couldn't look at his face.

"Look at him," she said sharply.

"No."

"Look at him!" she said, imploring me.

Ordinarily I would have fought her, causing a scene. Make my point, or try to. But I didn't. I turned my attention to him completely for the first time all evening and really looked at him, and was immediately disarmed by what I saw. None of his true character was visible in his face. His usual ham-pink complexion was muted down harshly by death, and he lay there stiff and waxy, pale as winter frost. Color of a dead man. I remember thinking how eerie his mouth was, somehow turned up at one side like a smirk. A smile. Unfamiliar.

"He did the best he could for you, and he was everything to Michael." She started to cry, walked over to the first pew and grabbed a tissue from the box in the seat. A lump the size of Georgia was lodged in my throat, my eyes were stinging with tears when suddenly I caught movement out of the corner of my eye. A thin stream of yellow liquid trickled down the corner of his mouth, rolled quickly down his cheek, and soaked into the satin pillow under his head.

I remember screaming, falling backwards into a tangle of several big sprays of flowers and plants. I remember Mother's voice, the shriek of terror. I remember Jimmy sitting beside me with a cold rag on my forehead. "Here she is," he said. "She's okay." I sat up, looked for Mother but couldn't see her. The undertaker kept apologizing to me over and over, kept saying something about temperatures and the two hour maximum while Jimmy tried to push him away and shut him up. The more he spoke the farther away I became, like I was drifting or succumbing to some sort of trance, or like I was in another dimension altogether, where everything was uncertain and unfamiliar, where the only true feeling that existed was a deep, dark fear that had swallowed me up whole, to which there was no escape.

I rode home in the passenger seat of Jimmy's truck with the windows rolled down for air, looking at the steady stream of blurry green trees passing by through my tears. The image of Daddy leaking in his casket was burned in my brain, a cross I would bear the rest of my life, another cross to drag through my desert.

All that week I lay in bed, sick and traumatized, reeling and spinning in fearful misery peppered with regret. I was tortured by memories both old and new, images of Daddy from the past superimposed with his death smile that sent me spiraling in the depths of death itself; the lack of peace that accompanies it and the tragic splinters that no one talks about. That lack of peace, eternally intertwined with such young and sudden deaths, seemed to be an invisible thread through the deaths I had experienced so far in my life: my grandparents in a tragic car wreck when I was eight, Uncle Bill with a 45 to his head, lungs full of his demise. Samantha pure and innocent, cold and alone somewhere without me, without anyone or anything, for no good reason I could see, the curse of death upon her before she even had the chance to be.

Though I was thoroughly unable to attend the funeral the next morning, Jimmy went for me. Sport coat, slicked hair, the works. And that's something about Jimmy Masters that I'll never forget, his going to my father's funeral. What a genuinely loving gesture, something I had experienced very few times in my life.

The Burgess United Methodist church believed that death was, overall, the ultimate healing. That's what the pastor spoke about during the service. I always had a lot of trouble with that, the logistics of it. It had been my experience that death was fast and unexpected, unreliable. Unrelenting. It was a force bigger than us all, the unstoppable black force of endings that could come at any time, ready or not. Young or old. Bleak and meaningless, chaotic and traumatic. Always inescapable, a cloud of truth we have to try to forget in order to live.

Months went by before I spoke to Mother again. We both knew why. During those months I slid even further down, there were too many emotions to feel at once, my mind was tangled and confused. There were days when I was so grief-stricken that I couldn't stand; re-imagining Daddy in his casket while trying to forget it. Thinking of the old days, when his spirit was still bright and full of hope, when he would take us on Sunday drives for ice cream and to look at all the buildings and homes he was currently working on, plus those he was currently bidding on. I thought of his face the moment he held Michael for the first time; the twitch of his face while my memories burned. I thought of his pilot hair, always perfect, not a strand out of place.

Other days I was angry, angry at Mother and Daddy both for having let Duane have Michael. After all he had done, he won. They let him fucking win. *He's a deacon of his church now, Drucilla. He coaches baseball. People change. Grow up. I had to do what was in Michael's best interest, you know that.* She didn't even know what my life was like, had no idea if I might be the one he should be with if they were having trouble. I had written her the letter, faked happiness for her benefit. Still didn't work, nothing ever did. Nothing I ever did was good enough for her and I can honestly say that's what I hate most about her, her complete unwillingness to break character and throw me a bone for being human, or for being Gary's daughter… It's not my fault I have my father's eyes.

I looked Duane up in the phone book and got his address: 101 Royal Oaks Drive. The house was nice; something Mother would have liked. Probably a house Daddy built. It was a big, sprawling ranch-style house with a big yard and chainlink fence. There were two yellow labs that occupied the yard and ran and played with the kids. I saw Michael swing on the swingset, and play fetch with the dogs, and I saw him throw a baseball back and forth to Duane in a blue baseball cap and matching shirt.

For the first few months after Daddy died, I drove by there several times a day, looking for clues. The more clues I found, the less frequently my drivebys became. He had gone on without me; everyone had swept me under the rug. There's no telling what Duane, or Daddy for that matter, had said about me. No telling what lies were told or what kind of bad behavior had been blamed on me.

Daddy haunted me, Samantha haunted me, and Michael haunted me, too. It was hardest to be haunted by someone who was still alive. As much as I would have liked to have been in a position to prove Mother wrong, to show her that I could give him everything Duane could and more – I couldn't.

One day, not long after Daddy's funeral, Jimmy had to go

help Don fix a leak late at night. I couldn't sleep, so I rolled myself a joint and sat on the couch in silence, smoking and thinking about all of the things Mother and Daddy – or Duane, even – would have used against me if I had fought for custody. I could see in my mind what Mother would say if she saw where Jimmy and I lived. I remember once she told me that "trailer houses" were for immigrants and FEMA victims. She would have told me I lived like trash. She would have told me that Jimmy was a simpleton. She would have told me that I wasn't capable of being a mother right now, that I was in no better position now than I was with Duane. She would say all of that while Daddy nodded along with his arms folded across his chest, right under his pounding heart.

Maybe she was right. Maybe she was right about everything. I'd assumed getting married would be the next right thing to do, something to help me to forget. But none of that worked. I hated my job, I hated our house, I hated the pressure from Jimmy and his family about having a baby. I hated Mother and Daddy. Hated Duane. And I hated myself and everything about me and my life.

Besides all that, there's an innocent little boy who would have to meet me all over again, with no telling what kind of stories in his head had already come from Duane. Probably told him I was crazy and that I ran off and married some guy instead of taking responsibility. But that would be real easy for Duane to say because he didn't have to grieve that loss; to him, Samantha never even existed. So yeah, Mother, I'm sure Duane is doing great. Because he never lost a child, much less two. The worst part, though, about Michael was that I knew, without a doubt, that our past was woven into my presence. I would be nothing but a shadow, a reminder of all the bad. Maybe that was why Mother treated me the way she did because I reminded her of everything she'd ever done wrong in her life. I was the only one who knew it all; either kill me or keep me away, right?

During that time, only rage lifted me. I couldn't make myself feel sad, couldn't feel any empathy whatsoever. Every emotion I had was all secondary to my rage. Jimmy and I fought constantly, and very quickly, life shifted from whatever it was to something different. I stopped being nice to Jimmy for his sake, and I stopped talking altogether for quite some time, scared I would blow up and hurt his feelings like usual, but somehow, I wanted it. Craved it. Wanted that release. And when Christmas time rolled around, the memories came back in waves: the time had come.

Since Samantha was born in December, every Christmas season was a long, grueling torture that was unbearable. The holidays, to me, were like drowning; completely submerged, but you just won't fucking die. The colors, the lights, Santa fucking Claus, I loathed it all. The worst for me was Christmas stockings. They are like a phobia to me; I hate them. For one reason nobody knows but me…

The Deaths

When I was having Samantha, during her actual delivery, my blood pressure was at stroke level. We didn't know anything was wrong with her except that she was not in position. She wasn't in the birth canal; she was all the way up in my ribcage. The doctors had to push and press all over my belly to get her into the birth canal. The pain was indescribable. I thought I wouldn't make it, didn't think I could push anymore.

While they were maneuvering her, one of the nurses, an older lady, took my hand and held it. Then she rubbed my sweaty forehead to get the hair out of my face, and she looked me dead in the eyes and said, "Did you know that at our hospital, every baby born in December gets to come to you in a Christmas stocking? Your baby will be in a Christmas stocking! Isn't that neat? There, there, I think they've got her now. You're doing great, sweetheart. Just keep thinking about that stocking!"

My baby did not get brought to me in a stocking.

Chapter 9

One day during early June, the Vega sputtered and struggled all the way to work. About a mile from the motel, right on Winchester Avenue, I broke down. Smoke was billowing away from underneath the hood. The car was old as shit, and I'd been begging Jimmy to let me trade it in for something better, but, of course, we couldn't afford it. I'd been having to spend more money on oil than anything, the leak clearly wasn't going to fix itself.

So the day the engine blew, so did I.

I cussed him out after having to walk a mile in the heat and be embarrassed at the same time. Maybe if he didn't have his head up his ass all the time, he would've been competent enough to fix the oil leak. He stayed at Don and Lorraine's for two nights and left me at the house without a ride. When he came back, he was driving a blue, two-tone Chevy Astro. A big van, a family vehicle, for an apology.

I didn't care how he got it, I didn't even ask. I accepted it, and I soon accidentally made it a new habit to take long, country road drives late at night to clear my mind. The Astro was huge. It felt like sailing a ship down those winding roads. I could've never done that in the Vega. It had been unreliable for years and would have definitely been stranded at some point. But the Astro, though several years old and used by a previous owner, was clean and solid. It became my new friend; the only thing in my life that I looked forward to was taking a drive.

The first time Jimmy complained about it, I felt so strongly defensive that I fought him – yelled right in his face. Screamed straight into his eyes, accusing him of trying to take away the one good thing I had left. He never brought it up again. Never addressed that I'd included him on the list of things that I hated.

I wasn't necessarily used to being loved; I didn't really know what to do with it. Jimmy had tried to love me, tried to be a husband and friend to me, but somehow, I couldn't accept it. I don't know if I just felt like I didn't deserve it or that his love was fraudulent in some way, the way he had come right when I had lost my mind at a time when I needed to be somewhere different, when I'd needed to feel different, somehow, immediately. And still, years later, I'm still a museum of things I want desperately to forget; I'm still haunted by a string of nightmares that feel oddly like what I imagined a curse would be like.

I wished so badly that I could shrug off all those old memories like the heavy coat they are, but sadly, most of them are sewn directly onto my skin. Death and grief had raised me in a cruel emptiness, and I slayed everything that tried to fill me. The worst thing about real love is that I remember it; the moment I held

Michael for the first time, the second he grabbed my finger with his tiny, newborn hand; the smell of Samantha's soft, fine hair, the softness of her skin; the look in her eyes that told me that she loved me, no matter what the doctors said. I had looked for my mother's love in all corners of the world and never found it, but I still knew what love felt like because I'd been a mother myself.

I felt there was no point in telling anyone what was going on inside me; no one would really understand – at least the way I needed someone to. I just wanted to drive those old dirt roads and not have to pretend to be someone I was not. The silence in the night were whispers of a life I had dreamed of long ago: a peaceful, cozy life with love and joy and hopes and dreams, not this life of cold misery and regret, too much time gone by without changing.

It was during one of those long, dark drives, watching the treeline darken against the purple sky, that I decided I couldn't be married to Jimmy anymore. I was sick of hiding from him, from myself. I needed some breathing room; I just wanted to be alone. My misery did not want company. All that week, Jimmy had been going on and on about taking me out on a date, saying he thought it would do me some good to get out, claiming that since Daddy died, I had become a "recluse." I didn't have a nice way of telling him I didn't fucking want to go, and his constantly bringing it up all week for little subliminal reminders pissed me off. I knew all too well what date night meant. Sex. And the very thought of it made me want to kill myself.

On date night, he had Lorraine cover the desk while we went to Murphy's for steak and wine. Jimmy drank a thick glass of red wine with his meal, then a second, then third. He was slurring his words by the time we left and had caused a scene when he tripped over his chair on our way out, laughing inappropriately about it while I made a beeline for the Vega, mortified.

Back at the house, as soon as Lorraine left to go home, he started pawing all over me, trying to kiss me and be passionate, and it took everything I had to get him off me. When I did, and he finally noticed the degree of my resistance, he asked me what the problem was. Accused me of cheating. Asked why I was always such a bitch, why I never wanted to have sex or even hold hands at the movies.

Then, soon, he confirmed my suspicions.

He started on the baby train: he wanted to have kids, and in order to do that, we would have to have sex... blah blah blah… I was so sick of hearing it, of thinking about it. Of looking at his stupid face and not understanding my position on the subject, just as no one else had. I'd had enough. I'd had a bad day (life) already, and suddenly, I snapped.

"I don't want any more kids," I said. He was sitting at the table eating from the styrofoam box of leftovers.

"What?" he asked, genuinely confused. "What do you mean you don't want more kids?"

He stared hard, suddenly sober-looking, waiting for my reply.

I picked up my purse, hanging from the dining room chair. Reached deep inside my secret abyss and pulled out the blue compact. Sat it down, slid it across the table. His fork clinked on the plate. He looked at the compact, then at me.

"You've been lying to me this whole time?" he said. I could see tears welling up in his eyes. His face was getting more and more flushed. I couldn't tell if he was about to cry or hit me. Then he slammed his fists down hard on the table, spilling drinks and food on the floor. Yelled and cursed me. I ran to the bedroom and pulled out the box in my closet, the one I kept hidden. I hadn't looked inside it in years.

Back in the kitchen, Jimmy was bracing himself on the table, looking down in defeat. I sat the box in front of him. "Here," I said.

"What the fuck is this?"

"Just open it. Look."

He sat down, took off the lid, and sifted through a collection of hospital bracelets, mine and hers, and a ziplock bag with the clipping of her thick, dark hair. Birth certificate. Death certificate.

The teddy bear Michael gave her was in there, too. It had a red ribbon tied around its neck: the metaphorical noose. Then there was the small white satin photo album, now yellowed with age, the one Grandma Rose gave me after the funeral, much too soon for me to have seen.

The first photo was Samantha's birth photo, the one that was taken at St Joseph's, after the initial transfer. She already had tubes in her nose and mouth, but aside from that, she looked pink and healthy. Perfect, even. Candids of Michael crouched down with me beside the crib when she'd gotten too sick to be held. Michael and I wearing fake plastic smiles while Samantha's eyes looked out at nothing. Mother and Daddy with serious, icy expressions. There was an awkward shot of Gene holding her and Barbara standing nearby with fear in her eyes, the only time Samantha touched anything truly paternal.

Jimmy's face fell flat when he reached the last picture: a post-mortem shot in her casket, wearing her yellow dress. Her eyes were closed and peaceful, and there were no tubes. No life. Porcelain and serene, like a doll.

"This is what I was scared of," I said. "This is why I can't do it again."

Jimmy closed the album, pushed it aside as he got up and walked over to the kitchen sink to vomit. I felt avenged, a shade of freedom pulsing through my veins, and even though I knew I hurt him, at least he knew it was because I'd been hurt too – only in ways that mattered.

Jimmy couldn't look at me, talk to me, or be around me at all. I can't say I blame him. I would have felt the same way – and in most respects – I was glad. Jimmy wouldn't officially end things; he was far too kind a person to do something like that, but he and I both knew it was over. I'd blown up and severed things for a reason, and the freedom that came with relieving myself of the tension was by far the greatest feeling I had felt so far, and I would spend a long ass time chasing that high.

I felt bad, but not enough to appease him or even fight. I loved Jimmy very much. He'd been there for me and stitched up emotional wounds from Samantha's death, even if they did keep coming back open again. He loved my frizzy perm days, my fat days, my skinny ones, all of my mistakes (almost) and all of my crazy, depressive episodes that would have scared most men off. And the worst part was – he had done so very lovingly, in such a pure and sincere manner that even though it was like medicine at the time, I was selfish to get into a relationship when all I could do was take.

I had nothing to offer Jimmy; I wasn't even someone he really knew, and I'd broken his heart to save my own. It had all just become too much to bear: the darkness surrounding Michael that reminded me of Daddy's judgmental glares made me anxious and uneasy. Jimmy's constant neediness and pressure about pregnancy were way too far off track from reality. All the darkness I'd been trying to shut out came roaring back so hard and forceful that it made it hard to breathe, like a million bricks lay upon my chest. My thoughts of unworthiness and shame crept back and tortured me with unpredictable, intersecting scenarios of panic mixed with pangs of reality, so much so that sometimes I had a hard time deciphering.

It was time to go. Past time. I didn't give him the big dramatic apology I knew he wanted, and I didn't try to make things worse. I'd said my piece, and I was done. I had no strength nor will left to appease anyone outside of myself at that point, nor had I ever been. I packed my clothes and walked out the front door, and never looked back. Jimmy was put on the list of things I had to let go of, and I never let anything go without leaving claw marks on it.

I withdrew the $761.00 we had in our bank account. I knew that money was for bills and shit, but I didn't care. The only thing I cared about was getting as far away as I could from everything I'd ever known or loved, especially things I loved.

With nowhere to really go, I did as I normally did. I drove. I drove all night long, watched the sun set and then rise again, the cool breeze from the windows still blowing through me. I drove until I couldn't hold my eyes open another second. I didn't know where I was going; I had no destination in mind. I assume I thought a plan would come to me down those dark country roads, but nothing ever did. If anything, all I really thought about were the people I couldn't call: Mother, for obvious reasons; and Johnnie, who didn't think I was ready to marry Jimmy in the first place; the only person I had to lean on I'd let go, had let her letters eventually go unanswered, until she was a mere ghost like all the rest. Never in my life had I been so alone, but there was an odd sort of freedom to it. No longer did I have to wear my mask, the one I wore to hide my shame and wretchedness that would eventually fill me to the brim.

I ended up on the same path Jimmy and I took on our first date: I passed the spot where we had danced on the road, and he made me feel like a real person again. I kept going, trying hard not to dwell on all of the pain I'd caused Jimmy. When I came to that old, abandoned house where the man supposedly hung himself, I pulled in and drove over weeds to that old stump. I pulled up right to it, my high beams illuminating the rings in the wood, the texture of its bark.

It was just an ordinary tree stump – no flowers, no marker or indication of memorium whatsoever. A man with a broken heart had taken his life on the branches of that tree, and they cut the tree down like it was the tree's fault? Why not at least let the goddamn tree live? But that's how most people like to remember: they don't. Hide all the evidence and stuff away your feelings. Pretend it never happened, like those people didn't exist, and like no one cares that they're gone. No one ever pays true homage to the dead. "It's just part of life," they all say. "It's all part of God's big plan. But when you ask them what God's big plan is, they can't tell you.

The abandoned house, you could tell, had not been lived in in decades. There were no other homes or signs of life for miles and miles. It was just a small, forgotten tragedy.

After too much driving and thinking, I decided to pull around to the back of the house, killed the engine, and slept right there beside that old house. Slept the sleep of the dead.

***

When I woke up, the vast emptiness of life in my surroundings was peaceful, but, at the same time, almost alarming and unnatural. So much so that I found myself getting anxious. I got out of the van and with a handful of paper napkins from the glovebox, surveyed the area, looking for a restroom. After that, I sat on the creaky wooden steps of the front porch, drawing pictures in the dirt with my toe, trying to decide what to do. If nothing else, I knew I needed food and drink, so I hesitantly went into town to get it. I needed a plan, but options for me simply did not exist. I would let myself die before I asked Mother for anything. I knew that for sure. But that was the only sure thing I knew at that point.

It was Monday morning, around nine or ten. The town was pretty dead; most everyone had already done their morning commutes and errands and were stuck somewhere else for the day. Normal people with normal lives. I had $761.00 to last indefinitely, so I had to be thrifty. I filled up with gas and drove over to Walmart, where I purchased items any homeless squatter would: An insulated cooler, ice, lunchmeat and bread, water by the gallon, matches and lighter fluid, and bullets for the 357 I'd taken from Jimmy's gun cabinet for protection.

After stocking the van with the essentials, I grabbed a newspaper from the machine to see if there were any job postings for someone with little to no skill set and a pocketful of grief. Before heading back out to the dead man's house, I drove down Old Sandbanks Road to tell Samantha that I loved her and still thought of her every day. I pulled over and picked a handful of wildflowers for her and made my way down the lane. Daddy's grave shocked me; someone had put a fresh bouquet of yellow roses on by his tombstone sometime recently. They still smelled strong and looked healthy. None of the other graves had flowers, only the one that had caused the most harm. I picked the roses up and tossed them into the passenger side seat of the van, and laid the wildflowers down for

Sam.

Back at "home" for the evening, I made a fire to keep me warm. A healthy, substantial bonfire that I was proud of, where I sat for hours, days, and then months, just trying to decide what to do next, and also, subconsciously trying to figure out just what the fuck "God" had planned for me, had my penance been enough? Had I suffered enough, or was there more? What was, if one might take the time to ask, the "purpose" of any of it?

There was an odd sort of comfort in camping out there all alone. I couldn't really put my finger on why, but nonetheless, I found some kind of solace in nature, scary as it was. Lonely as it was. Ordinarily, a situation like that would've been terrifying and probably impossible for me; but my desire to be alone at that point far superseded any fears I had about living in the backyard of an abandoned house in the middle of nowhere. If I'm being honest, never in my life had I felt more free. *Where's Drue?* someone could say. But no one would be able to answer.

Without any distractions, I sat on a log I'd dragged over and stared into the flames of the fire, burning orange and red, smoking and crackling and devouring the wood I kept having to gather. While I studied the fire's growing intensity, I suddenly remembered the roses in the Astro that I'd stolen from Daddy's grave. I walked over to the van, retrieved the flowers, and sat back down on my log. One by one, I plucked the heads off each one and tossed them in the fire, watching each one separately and completely burn before I tossed in the next. I watched them burn with an eerie satisfaction, the same as Daddy had when he burned my things that night. Only this time, I was burning him, not the other way around. When I'd burned them all, I tossed in the stems and spit in the ashes.

The classifieds were filled with jobs I didn't qualify for: teaching assistants, paralegals, customer service at First National, personable sales clerks with retail experience. I burned that in the fire, too.

It was on the third night, the night after I burned Daddy's roses, that I began to wonder again about my real father. Who was Gary Berryman? What was he like? Had he regretted leaving me, inadvertently signing me over to the father I never wanted? I decided that, with nothing to lose, I might reach out to him. Settle my questioning of his nature once and for all.

Later in the night, I heard leaves rustling and coyotes howling somewhere close by. I think the only thing that protected me was the fact that if they came and attacked me and tore me to absolute, unrecognizable shreds, I would be glad.

I fell asleep that night wondering still about Gary and if all I had been through had somehow magically led me back to him, to be suddenly released from all the sadness I had ever known.

Chapter 10

The next morning, as soon as the doors opened, I was inside the Burgess City Library to use their phone directory. It was the only place where I would have access to not only Burgess residents but for the surrounding counties as well. I had no idea where he lived now or where he ever lived, for that matter. I knew that Mother met him in Burgess, but who knew where he was now, all these years later… I'm sure he didn't stick around long enough to casually run into the daughter he abandoned while pumping gas or something. If I were him, I'd be gone.

Even at 9 AM, the library was packed. Not only were the patrons like students cramming for exams and leisurely readers with thick glasses and knowledgeable attitudes, but there were also homeless people, travelers, and vagabonds. Just outside the library was one of only two bus stops in Burgess, and it was, and always had been, a migrating place for those who always seemed to look like they don't belong, that they might be lost. It occurred to me at that moment that I was no better than them, that I was in no better position, and the very thought of the shame that came with that made me shake.

It took hours of sifting through ink-stained tissue pages to find him or possibilities of what could be. There were close to twenty or thirty Gary Berryman's in all of the directories combined, but only two showed the middle initial as T, and I knew from my birth certificate that Gary's middle name was Thomas. Neither address was in Burgess. One was in Indianapolis, on Amity Road, the other in Shelbyville, only thirty-five miles away. I decided to check Shelbyville first for obvious reasons. I wrote the addresses down on the back of a receipt and shoved it in my bag, bought a hamburger to cure my ham sandwich burnout, and made my way back out to the dead man's house. The only place on Earth where I felt remotely at home.

Overall, for me, the house stood out there like a museum of pain, of grief unsettled, of times that were probably once pleasant memories, that had, over time, rotted to nothing. Oddly enough, the pain in that old house comforted me, too: it was, in fact, all I had ever known in my own life. The difference, though, was that at the dead man's house, the pain that lurked within it wasn't mine.

I sat on the front steps of the house eating my burger, amazed at how isolated I was out there, fascinated at the brilliance of nature taking back over where man had once cleared. On one side of the porch, an old, rusty chain hung nailed for nothing. It looked like, at one time, a wind chime had been there, the empty breeze of the country playing elemental music for a miserable couple, for a man whose heart wondered why. Up against the side of the porch was faded, now colorless, ceramic frog wearing a bowtie. It imagined the whore, crouched down and tending to the garden, smiling happily at that frog while she thought of another man, why she ruined a man's whole life.

Almost out of nowhere, the wind started to pick up, and I could smell the grassy, earthy smell of rain. I covered my burger and got inside the Astro to stay dry. Within thirty minutes to an hour, the rain had turned into a full-blown storm. The wind grew and grew as hail pelted against the windshield. When the Astro started rocking violently back and forth, I had no choice but to seek shelter inside the house. I'd already been terrified to go in there, afraid for some reason of what I might find. But the storm insisted on it. The front and back doors were both locked, but a side window was open. With two bed pillows and a small blanket, thunder and hail roaring behind me, I crawled in and shut the window tight as fast as I could. Inside the house, instead of feeling scared, I felt safe.

I was shocked to see the inside of the house; it was nothing like I'd expected. I waited out the storm for well over an hour, cuddling with the blankets and pillows I'd brought inside. After the storm waned, I got up and looked around. All around were boards from the walls and old furniture that had been left to the elements. It was hard to really tell what anything was, it had all been reduced, by time, to rubble. Inside the bedrooms, graffiti covered the walls; broken beer bottles and cigarette butts littered the old wood floor.

One room was filled with ancient furniture, including a mattress, and that's when I decided to move in. The room was safe, the windows were secure, and there were three doors between the entrance and that bedroom. My bedroom. I brought in some of my belongings from the van, and rearranged the furniture, moving some Over in the corner so I could barr the room with it while I slept. In one end table, I found an electric bill in the name of Carl Baker. Carl. With a couple of candles lit and pillows and blankets on the mattress, it wasn't half bad. It was doable.

When I got everything arranged, I lay down on the mattress and lit a cigarette. Thought again about the dead man, Carl, and how I clearly envied him in some weird way. He accepted that what had happened to him had left a permanent scar, one he knew he could never heal from. I wondered if he ever reached out to God, and if he did, I wonder if he ever got an answer.

Obviously, he did not. I assumed all of his questions remained unanswered, just like mine.

Where were the answers? Were there any? Answers to the question of why God lets evil kill babies. Why He lets wars happen and poverty and murders and tsunamis and all of that horrible shit you see in the news every single day, the shit that fills the headlines. Horrible shit. Awful.

After Samantha died, I tried desperately to find answers in the church; pleaded for someone to explain to me how God could ever let this happen, and why was I the only one still suffering. Where was the justice or reason in any of that? And, the more each of those pastors from churches spoke to me about God and death, the more scared I became of it. The more of the bible I read and tried to understand, the more fearful I became of impending doom, which, essentially, is reality. I found great difficulty finding comfort in the fact that God would take innocent souls away from us and up to heaven just to worship Him for all eternity. I thought He was the Almighty God? The Supreme King? Why did the bible have such a narcissistic approach to the afterlife? Couldn't Samantha have at least stayed with me and lived a full life first? Why would he give her to me in the first place, for only seven months?

I'd received several interesting explanations for her death from various church elders and pastors. Some of them were friends with Daddy, who would laugh and discuss football statistics and chain-smoke with him in the kitchen after talking to me about God and His mysterious ways, praying over me, and filling me with fear. If I collected comparisons of the church leaders' explanations, which I did, there was only one conclusion that I came to, and that was that each and every one of them didn't know any more than I did and that they wrestled with the same questions I was asking them, without admitting it.

It made me nervous to sit across from them, asking questions about God while feeling their nervous energy, desperately flipping through scripture to piece together some sort of theory as to why Samantha had to die and why it was *all part of God's plan, whether you can accept it or not. Have faith, anyway. Hallelujah, anyway. Praise God, anyway.*

However… "It was an act of SATAN!" Pastor Chessir proclaimed to me. "The devil is to blame!"

I studied the bible after that, secretly late at night, away from Mother and Daddy. Nowhere in the bible could I find the one thing I wanted to know… Was any of this my fault? Had I not protected her from evil, saved her from sin and Satan? Did I do something wrong to have deserved such horror; had I somehow unknowingly allowed evil access to my child?

Those are the questions that kept me up at night. That swam in my heart like hungry goldfish.

Randall Bishop, a preacher from the Church of Christ, read to me from a yellow tablet of handwritten notes, some underlined and some marked out with big, red lines. I noticed hot pink post-its with addendums stuck in random places as he attempted a poorly versed monologue he'd created of the original fall of mankind.

I sat staring past him at an arrangement of sympathy flowers someone had just sent while he argued with himself that the Original Sin had actually been a blessing in disguise, that it was all intended for man's ultimate good – whatever that was. Before he left, he prayed over me like they all did. He asked God to deliver me from my sins. He must've thought it was my fault, too.

Another preacher, I cannot recall what church he reigned from, but he offered that without evil in this world, we would be unable to develop in any moral or spiritual sense. But this man went a step further than all the rest and gave his own insight into what God's Plan might actually be. His theory was that in the end, the devil would be redeemed and all evil abolished, being freed for his role in "the plan." Though I found some of his views interesting, I did not find solace in the fact that the devil would be redeemed for killing my daughter or that anyone should.

But, of course, none of this really explained to me what happened nor why, and it became increasingly unsettling that there was no explanation, that everyone in the world was just as lost as I was, no matter what they preached in their Sunday sermons.

Fucking frauds. Just like Mother and Daddy.

***

I still had Gary's info, now ink smeared from holding it constantly. I'd had the number memorized by then, but I held on to it anyway. I slept in my new room that night, and before bed, I resolved to meet my father, win him over, accept his apologies, and become the new addition to the Berryman family. A real family who loves you no matter what and doesn't hide behind masks.

I spent a large portion of the next day trying to decide what I would wear to meet my father for the first time in over two decades. Since it was still the chilly part of Spring, I would need to wear something warm in case of rain. My coat, my only coat, was worn like armor to keep me warm almost constantly. It was tired and smelled like campfire smoke, and that just wasn't going to cut it. The more I dug through the clothes I'd packed, only about a quarter of them, I realized that I had nothing at all appropriate for such an occasion.

Defeated, I decided to just say fuck it and spend money on a new outfit, even though I couldn't afford it. I reasoned seriously with myself that spending the money didn't really even matter because if things didn't work out with Gary for some reason, I was going to kill myself. Did I feel guilty for putting such pressure on an unsuspecting man? No, I did not.

Later on, at a Beall's department store, I tried on several outfits, mostly dresses, until finally settling on a casual pair of slacks and a blue silky blouse with a dark navy overcoat that looked expensive. Was expensive. The outfit would cost me at least one fifty, plus tax. I sat in the wood-paneled dressing room for a good fifteen minutes, trying to decide if I should make the purchase or not. If I did buy it, and Gary was a bust, I'd have to kill myself.

I decided at the last minute to buy the coat, and nothing else; at least the coat would cover whatever I wore underneath, even if it was dirty. Back out on the floor to hang up my unwanted items and grab a clean pack of socks, I noticed that though there were several shoppers, I had seen only one store clerk the entire time I was in there. Not one person came to ask if I needed help or if my items worked out. Nobody checked on me while I sat in the stall thinking about suicide and new clothes and runaway fathers.

I scanned the store several times, pretending to look at bras. The only clerk was spraying perfume samples for an old lady in a motorized wheelchair. I slithered back to the dressing room and tore off all of the price tags from the clothes I'd chosen, put the entire outfit on, and walked right out the front door without even a question, looking like a completely different Drue, ready to meet my father, may he please be someone good.

On the drive to Shelbyville, I thought about what Mother would say if she knew I'd just committed theft on my way to meet the man who had broken her heart long ago and left her alone with me.

***

There was no doorbell, so I knocked. Gave three good raps and waited. On the other side of the door, a dog barked. A small-dog bark. Sure enough, when the wooden door opened, an angry chihuahua barked at me through the screen. A middle-aged-looking woman with stringy brown hair and smoker's lines picked up the dog and yelled "Shut up, Paco!" about five or six times before even looking at me. "Who the hell are you," she finally said. The dog started barking again, and she popped him on the nose.

"Well, um… My name is Drue, and I'm looking for my father. Her eyes narrowed. "His name is Gary… Gary Berryman."

"Oh my GOD," she said. "Drucilla?" My heart fluttered with excitement. I smiled without even meaning to, letting my vulnerability show too soon.

"Yes, ma'am."

"Oh, hush with that ma'am business. I'm your Aunt June! Get in here. Let me get a look at you! My God, I never thought I'd ever see you again."

"Yeah," I said with a sort of fake laugh. "This is really awkward. I'm sorry. I know this is weird. I just wanted to meet him – and you, know, haha… I hope I'm not intruding. I just wanted to, well, see him, I guess."

"Intruding? No. Only to Paco here!" she laughed, nuzzling the angry little dog. "Gary should be home soon. Just went out for smokes. I'm surprised he's not already back," she said. "Fucker is slow as Christmas," she said, lighting a cigarette. "Always has been. "I call him Grandpa sometimes just to piss him off." Michael's face touched the surface. "Here, sit here and make yourself at home." She pointed me to a green velvet sofa covered in a thick antique quilt.

"I'm Gary's sister, June, but most people call me Junebug. I met you once when you were just a little thing. Precious, you were. You smiled at me. Took a liking to me for some reason." She took a long drag off her cigarette and blew out a thick stream of smoke. "And I never forgot that. Can I get you a beer?" Not wanting to be rude, I accepted, even though I hated beer because the smell of it reminded me of Duane.

While she was getting the beer, I scanned the room for clues to who Gary was but found very few personal effects in the house besides cigarettes and ashtrays and a few magazines on the end table beside the ugly orange chair that June sat in across from me. The house reminded me of a motel room, clean and plain, void of personality. A flash from the window caught my eye as a red and white Bronco pulled into the driveway, driving past my van parked in the street. My heart was pounding; blood banged inside my head. June came out and sat the beer on the table in front of me.

"There's Gary," she said, looking out. "Hey, sit tight, will ya? Gimme one sec."

"Yeah, of course. Go ahead," I told her. She met him at the driver's side door before he got out. I could hear them talking, but I couldn't make out the words, thanks to Paco's incessant barking. I held my breath and waited.

Moments later, Gary came walking through the front door, smiling politely and came in for a handshake instead of a hug. Looking into his eyes was like looking in a mirror. I saw the eyes my mother and Daddy hated seeing in me.

"Drucilla, how are you? My goodness, you sure do look like your mother," he said. He had long grey hair in a braided ponytail like Willie Nelson and big, white teeth. "It's so nice to meet you."

"It's so good to see you," I said. "I was telling June, I hope I'm not intruding. I just got your address from the phone book and decided to visit. I hope that's okay. I'm sorry." I don't know why I couldn't stop apologizing. Something about his presence made me suddenly inferior, weaker than usual.

"No need to apologize," Gary assured me. "Happy to have you." He reached into the pocket of his tee shirt and pulled out a pack of Camels; lit one. "So how's Patsy?" he said, with smoke falling out of each nostril as he spoke. "She still married to that slick-haired fella? Your dad?"

It was unsettling to hear Gary refer to Daddy that way. "Yes, well, she was. He died, actually. Not that long ago, couple years, maybe."

"Wow, I had no idea. I'm sorry to hear that."

"I'm sorry for your loss," June added with a sorrowful expression.

"Patsy taking everything alright?" he said, shocking me with such a personal question, one with concern for Mother. I struggled with my answer because the truth was, I didn't really know. Then, without warning, tears came and spilled out like a faucet. I could do nothing but cry for several minutes; I couldn't even make out words for a while. When I could, I apologized again. "I'm sorry," I said. "I've just had a really bad life, and I wanted to meet you."

His face was white as a sheet. June had come closer and put her arm around me, consoling as best she could. "Shhh… it's okay honey. It's okay…"

Gary was just sitting there, stunned and motionless, until June shouted his name, signaling him to intervene. He leaned over and patted my hand. "There, there, now. You're okay. You're all right." I looked down at his calloused hand and saw HATE tattooed across his knuckles.

Over the course of the next hour or so, I told them all about Duane, about Michael, about Samantha's life and death. About Daddy's death. All the shit I'd stuffed deep down. They both listened intently, June squeezing my hand and holding me through the hardest parts. I hadn't expected my first interaction with Gary to be a therapy session, but it was.

"Jesus Christ," he said when I told him about Samantha. "What the fuck."

After my second beer, Gary offered to roll a joint. I happily accepted. The three of us, emotionally raw and exhausted, smoked until we were laughing so hard June was snorting, and Gary was making spot-on impressions of Mother and what she used to say when she caught him using pot. "I will NOT be reduced to a lifestyle that involves this type of behavior." He had her facial expressions down pat, classic eye roll, disapproving tongue in cheek, the works.

For the first time in my whole existence, I felt understood.

As I was leaving, Gary told me to come by any time and scribbled their phone number on the back of a store receipt.

"Call us soon," June pleaded. "It was so good to see you, honey."

"Yeah, thanks for dropping by," Gary said on my way down the sidewalk. As I put the van in gear, I gave him one last look before driving away. He gave me a tight-lipped smile and the peace sign. June waved like I was on a parade float.

Pretty much the only thing I hadn't told them was about my failed marriage with Jimmy and the fact that I was homeless and living inside an abandoned dead man's house. And when I got there, I was instantly disheartened and cold. I started a fire after wrapping my new clothes in a plastic bag away from the smoke. The coyotes were out and howling. I felt strange. Numb from beer and pot and family. Details from the evening kept me awake that night, and gaining any hope for the future only made me nervous.

There was one more emotion I felt. I had, perhaps, forgotten how it felt. Maybe because I hadn't felt it in a long time. Maybe I had never felt it.

Relief.

Chapter 11

The next day I drove into town and scanned the classified for jobs – this time aiming to be less picky: I was sick and tired of living like a pioneer, and I craved something solid to stand my feet on. Somewhere safe to lay my head at night.

Once again, there were mostly jobs I could never get, but I did run across a floral shop looking for a delivery driver. No experience required. State driver's license only. I could provide at least that. It was called Dobson's Floral, downtown on Laurel Avenue. I knew of it because directly across the street from it was Michael's old preschool we sent him to after Samantha died. I remember driving him there a few times, when Mother would force me to get out of the house and be involved, and all of the other moms were all happy and chatting and focused on their morning routines. I strolled in like a zombie in a housecoat, a ghost of my former self, not sure what I was doing or who I even was anymore. I remember those moms looking at me with pity, whispering to each other, "that's the mother of the dead baby."

Dobson's Floral was a cute, antiquated shop downtown with dark green and white striped canopies over the big, tinted windows facing the street. The inside of the shop smelled like a funeral but looked almost heavenly with its big floral displays and bright colors mixed along with their perfume. It felt like a peaceful place, the energy was calm.

Eloise Dobson was a slight woman with smoker lines and short, bleach-blonde hair with wispy bangs swept casually across her brow. She reminded me of a much-older version of Twiggy, the model from the 70's whose trendy looks Mother had once tried to impersonate. A lit Salem bobbed between her lips as she spoke. "So tell me about yourself," she said, taking a long pull and blowing out a thick, steady stream toward the ceiling.

I felt like Anelle on Steel Magnolias when Truvy asks Anelle about her life, and she doesn't want to talk about all the shit she just left behind somewhere. Well, the truth is I don't know if I'm married or not. I managed the basics, quite literally a monologue of what she'd already read on my application. Then added, "I'm newly divorced," for flair, to stress my need for the job. She looked me up and down, sizing me up, and handed me a yellow shirt and khaki smock, identical to the one she was wearing.

"These may be a little snug," she said. "I can order bigger if we need to. Can you start tomorrow morning?"

"Oh gosh, yes," I gushed, seriously thankful. "Thank you so much, really." When she smiled at me, it was almost like I had known her for years, like she was an old friend I had forgotten about; drifted away from. I thanked her repeatedly on my way out, all the while wondering why she was so familiar, but far too taken away with my new job to care.

On the way home I decided not to tell anyone about the job until I'd given it a trial run, the last thing I wanted was to be in a position to be forced to admit failure of some kind. When I got home there was a message blinking on the machine. Beep. "Drucilla, it's your Mother. I'm having dinner for us all on Saturday evening. Six o'clock. See you then." Beep.

Rarely in my life had Mother called and invited me over as a guest: I could see more and more how much her relationship was consistently changing her, possibly chipping some ice away from her heart. Every so often I think back to those times when I was little, before she married Daddy and became a monster competitor in the race to achieve the most prominent place in the social networking of Burgess, Indiana.

I would often think of her sweeping the kitchen in shorts back in the kitchen at Grandma and Grandpa Rose's house, singing along to her records as she did, occasionally pulling me up to dance and sing along, like a mother-daughter duet. I remember her laughing at funny movies and crying at sad ones, taking care of me when I was sick and painting my nails. My memories of life with Mother back then are reminders of the only time I felt truly loved. Far away somewhere I believe that Mother still exists, and I just wish I could find her again – only it was almost like she just didn't want to be found.

***

The next morning I was up at four, unable to sleep. My anxiety about starting a new job had crept in and swallowed me whole. I sat on the edge of the bed and stared at the yellow shirt and smock hanging on their white plastic hangers and staring at me like ghosts. The shirt was the exact shade of yellow of Sam's dress. The ghosts were now mocking me. I put on my favorite jeans – then the shirt. It was about three sizes too small, I struggled to even get it on. When I finally did, I looked in the mirror and was distracted by the deep, black abyss where the shirt was stretched like a latex glove over my navel. I started ripping it off, got stuck inside and panicked and ripped the side seam to free myself. I started to wonder if it would crawl across the floor and back up onto its hanger in its victory over me.

I spent most of the morning watching Eloise make orders, or "floral support," as she liked to call it, for the deliveries I would be making later in the day. She sifted through a stack of pink, paper receipts and showed me which vases get used for which order.

Intricately painted ceramic pots and gem-colored vases for the big spenders, and cheap plastic look-alikes for the rest. "The cheaters pay the most," she said that morning. "I can get a cool hundred off a guilty man any day. Two if he wants to keep the mistress, too." She snipped a red tulip's stem. I thought about Daddy, wondered if he'd ever called Eloise and ordered flowers for Mother and Rita; if guilty money had ever passed between them.

The delivery truck was the size of a ship and Pepto-pink. I was embarrassed just standing next to it. Eloise's son, Patrick, loaded the back of the van and was clearly too shy to speak. He worked with his head down, quietly, and barely looked up when Eloise introduced us that morning. "He's not weird or anything," she said after. "Just quiet." Fine by me. Great, even. But if you have to explain that someone isn't weird, it sort of makes you wonder.

It took an abnormally long time for me to park the van at Ridgecrest Nursing Home, where I made my first delivery. It was the same nursing home where Carla used to work, and I wondered if Bea was there now, too, or even still alive at this point.

The distinct smell of urine punched me square in the nose as soon as the sliding doors unsealed for my entrance. I stuck my nose in a lily and walked fast toward the nurses' station, where I left the flowers, and then ran like I was on fire to escape the smell and stares of old creepy elders in wheelchairs and drugged-out dispositions.

I'm sure those nurses would make sure Mrs. Betty Warnall would get her birthday bouquet, in a plastic vase. "Happy 85th birthday, Mama!" the card had read. Yeah right. More like, "Happy 85th birthday, enjoy pissing your own pants and dying alone in a shithole."

Isn't life wonderful?

The second delivery was to Mrs. Palmer, the guidance counselor at Burgess High. She worked there even way back when I was in school, she'd given me pamphlets on teen pregnancy and offered hollow hugs; she even offered to break the news to my parents, if I needed her to. Did I feel safe telling my parents such news? Did I feel like any danger might arise from the conversation?

She didn't seem to quite grasp why I felt so scared, like being pregnant in high school was a common, everyday occurrence — which, I suppose, might have been for her, given her line of work. Her office was always filled with thugs or loners, the types of kids with drugstore hair colors and black nail polish, or the poor kids whose clothes' smell told you how their homes were heated. I'd even cried to Mrs. Palmer when Daddy burned my uniforms. I remember her face, her expression. I remember her not really knowing what to say. She'd been caught off guard, same as me.

Mrs. Palmer always wore long flowy skirts and smelled like pot, and that day was no exception. She was delighted by the flowers, her glassy eyes lit up like Christmas lights at her roses and the single bobbing balloon attached to it, which I was about ready to stab with the pencil behind her ear. She did not recognize me, or didn't seem to; a fact that both offended and relieved me – but mostly relieved me.

My last deliveries of the day were all death-related: a few to grieving relatives and tons to Higgenbotham's Funeral Home, casket spray included. The smell was almost too much, I had to roll the windows down until I saw petals starting to flutter around from the breeze. I hated that smell of those funeral flowers – the carnations and mums mostly. Their particular, indistinguishable, sickly sweet smell of death hung in the air for years. Eloise told me they use carnations and mums to cover up any smells from the bodies – a fact that disturbed me deeply and put me in a sour mood.

I hated that funeral home, too. Hated the undertaker for what he'd let me see. The man who had prepared my daughter and father's bodies for burial was now standing beside me at the back of my pink van, unloading someone else's family's condolences. The flowers, the smell, his face, were all too much. I cried all the way back to the shop, and by the time I got there and looked at myself in the rearview, I looked like I had actually attended the funeral.

"What's the matter?" Eloise prodded, when I came in red-faced and puffy-eyed.

"Nothing, I'm fine! Just give me a minute. Excuse me." I walked down the hall to the bathroom and washed my face, tried to gather my bearings. When I came back out, she was sweeping stems and leaves and ribbon pieces into a pile. "Any more deliveries right now?" I asked.

"No, not yet. It'll be about a half hour," she said, staring obviously at me. "Can you help me with these roses?" she said. I helped her move the roses from the fridge to the table, all of the pink ones we had in stock. "It was the funeral home delivery wasn't it?" she asked, intrusively, so much so that I was completely dumbfounded; caught off guard. "Nobody likes the funeral home deliveries," she continued.

"What? No! I'm fine, really. I'm fine. What else can I do to help?"

She started separating the roses into piles. "Did you know the Jameson's?" she asked.

"No, I didn't."

"Hell of a thing that happened," she said, shaking her head sympathetically. "Teenage girl coming home from a party, driver lost control, and she wasn't wearing a seatbelt. Beautiful girl. Good kid, too."

"My God, that's awful," I said, thinking about that girl's poor mother.

"Yup. Anyways, her favorite color was pink, so everything's gotta be pink," she said. We're gonna be drowning in pink for days."

Great. I caught myself starting to feel sorry for myself, but then I looked at those pink roses and remembered that someone else's kid was dead, too.

"You'll be making daily deliveries to Higgenbotham's. You okay with that?" she said, seriously.

"Of course."

"Alright then! Remind me to order more of that light pink ribbon, will ya?" she said, stabbing a stem into a brick of green foam. "Death," she said, sighing loudly. "Takes you places you never wanna go, doesn't it?"

***

Upset and shaken from the day, I decided to visit Gary and June for comfort. A familiar face; someone to talk to.

The Deaths

I hated what my life had become, and my attempts to get to know Gary and June would inevitably end up having to tell them about my life. My life wasn't even about living anymore; it was about surviving. I knew if I told them where and how I was living, they would take pity on me. That's the last thing I wanted, pity. I wanted something new, a fresh start with my real family, people more like myself and less like Mother and Daddy.

But regardless how ashamed I was of myself and my shitty life, I had no one else to lean on, and Gary was the only person in this world who still had his second chance; everyone else had repeatedly hurt me, but maybe Gary would be different. He had to be. I needed him to be different. My mother had wanted a lamb, but raised a wolf instead. And, a wolf is always a wolf; even when it's caged. Maybe Gary would love the wolf in me no one else ever had.

After finishing my breakfast and imagining both the best and worst possible scenarios of what could happen during our second visit, I drove over to Shelbyville and was disappointed when I didn't see Gary's Bronco in the drive. Hoping for June, I pulled in and parked. She was out on the porch before I'd finished parking, smiling from ear to ear. "Drue! I'm so happy to see you. Come in, come in. How have you been? You just missed Gary, well, um, your dad. But he shouldn't be but an hour at the most, just a business deal."

"A business deal? What kind of business is he in?"

Her mouth opened slightly as she started to speak, but then saw her redirect. "Cars. He flips cars. Buys 'em cheap, does a little fixing up, sells them for profit. He's real good at it. Very well trusted in the business," she said, nodding her head, convincingly. Her finger tapped her knee in the awkward silence between us. "So what do you do, back in Burgess?"

"Well," I said, "I just started a new job. Just this week, actually." I told her about the shop.

"Oh yeah? I know that place. We ordered Grandma's funeral flowers from there when she died a couple years ago. She was from Burgess. Hey, I just remembered, I have something to show you." She disappeared through a doorway for several seconds and came back smiling at a small polaroid. She took one last look, and handed it to me.

"Look, she said, beaming. "It's us!"

And it sure was: the photo was obviously taken the same day as the photo I had of Gary and I. I had on that same outfit, and the same kitchen was in the background. "That's the only time I ever got to meet you," she said. "I was so happy, too. You were just so beautiful and sweet. An absolute doll."

"Wow, June, that is so kind of you to say. Thank you, really. Thank you."

"Oh, don't thank me, honey. I didn't do anything to be thanked for. I was just happy to meet my niece. And when you came back, I swear, I was like… I even told Gary... it was like a blessing. Like a slap from the universe. 'Course Gary was nervous that you wouldn't like him. He's got real bad problems with feelings. Never has been one to express them, I guess is… What I mean is, I don't know. Can I get you a beer? It's five o'clock somewhere, am I right?"

She turned on the radio on the end table. The Eagles were playing. "God, I love this fucking song," she said, turning up the volume and singing. And I've got a peaceful, easy feeling… "I'll be right back," she said, heading to the kitchen for our beers. I stared at the photo in disbelief at the difference between June then and when the photo was taken. I mean, of course over twenty years had passed, sure. In the photo, she looked exactly like Jaclyn Smith in her prime, in her Charlie's Angels phase. Now she looked old and almost haggard; like she'd really been through it, like she knew what real suffering was, too. And somehow, I had an automatic respect for her for that, for quite possibly being similar to someone like me.

When she returned, she handed me an opened beer and plopped down in the orange chair across from me. "Sorry again that

Gary isn't here to see you," she said, lighting up a cigarette. "He is always real busy. Just has his hand in everything, I guess. He's always been that way, Gary has. I know he'd just love to see you, though." She took a long swig of beer, belched quietly, looking lost in thought.

"No worries," I said politely. "It was sort of a surprise visit, it's not like he even knows I'm here," I continued, convincing both her and myself. She blinked slowly and smiled.

"Thats right, Sugar," she said. "'Cause if he did, I tell you Drue, he'd be thrilled. Really. If he doesn't show up soon, I can make some calls and try to let him know you're here."

"So," I said, trying to break the awkward silence that followed. "Are your parents still around?" I asked. "My real grandparents?"

Her face fell flat. She took another drink of beer and stared out at a memory only visible to her. "No," she said. "They're dead."

Bingo, I thought. I knew that she knew loss, too.

"I'm so sorry," I said. "I didn't know."

"Of course not," she said, smiling sympathetically. "Don't worry about it, it was a long time ago. It's just something I really don't like talking about." Silence. June twirled the strings of a hole in her blue jeans.

"I completely understand," I said. When you've had to grieve for a lost loved one, the last thing you want to try to do is remember. I'd felt that way a million times.

"Actually," she said, interrupting my flashbacks from Daddy and Samantha, "you have a right to know about your own family, am I right? That was selfish of me, I'm sorry."

"No, please," I said, holding up my hand to stop her. "No need. Another time, okay? Just tell me about my father. What was… What is he like?"

"Your father? Gary was a hellion!" she laughed. "Still is! Absolute hell on wheels, that one. Head is harder than stone. You tell him to do something, he will do the exact opposite. He's always been that way," she smiled at herself, giggled a little. "This one time? When we were little kids? Gary got mad at Mama and Dad for not getting him a BB gun for Christmas. He wanted it so bad, begged for months. It was just like that movie; you know, the one with the kid in the bunny suit?"

"A Christmas Story?" I said.

"A Christmas Story! Yes, that one. He was just like that little kid about that damn gun. But Mama and Dad knew he'd get into trouble, see? So, they didn't get it, got him a bike instead. Well, after Christmas dinner, he broke into Dad's gun cabinet and pulled out a rifle, and loaded it. He walked right out to the front yard and blew both back tires outta Dad's truck. Loud as shit, neighbors came out and everything."

"Oh shit," I said.

"Yeah, it was always somethin' with Gary, the little shit. Couldn't have been more than ten or so; raising hell since grade school, that one."

Oblivious to my slight horror at the tire shooting at ten, she continued to amaze me.

"This other time? In high school? Gary grew his hair out long for the first time. Well, the school said he couldn't have long hair, said he was breaking the dress code rules. Well after he left the principal's office after being suspended for continuing to wear it long, instead of leaving, he went into the boys bathroom, lit a cigarette, and threw it in the trash. It caught fire, we had to evacuate the school. Cops were there looking for Gary, whole big deal. Shit was wild!"

"Sounds like he was quite a troublemaker," I said, fake laughing.

"Yeah, I guess you could say that." She fumbled with the strings of the hole in her jeans. "I think Gary was just misunderstood, really. Mama and Dad were pretty hard on him, and I think that's where a lot of his anger came from." She lit a cigarette, while I sat on the edge of my seat hoping she would keep talking; keep filling in my blanks.

"Gary is just wild at heart; a free spirit. But Mama and Dad didn't like that: they wanted him to be a military man like our dad, but Gary isn't built for that, he can't follow all those rules. Any rule you make, Gary will break it just to say he did. He wanted to be a mechanic and that was final. And that's exactly what he did."

"So what about you? What did they want you to do?" I asked.

"Me? Marry rich!" She laughed so hard I could see all her fillings. "But, of course I didn't. Met a guy named Paco when I was nineteen – yes, I named the dog after him, anyway, I fell in love with Paco and his love of simple things. We left for Mexico one day without telling anyone and lived on the beach for almost a year. Best time of my life. Learned a lot about life out on that Mexican sand. Still miss it, sometimes. She stared out into her memories, taking long pulls from her cigarette."

"Well, what happened," I asked, curious.

"He started selling dope; got mixed up with the wrong crowd. He's in prison now, I heard he got twenty years for drugs. Broke my heart. I tried to stay close to him, but I couldn't make it on my own. Hey. Gary should be back by now. I'm gonna call Marv and see if he's seen him. Just a sec."

She disappeared through the swinging doors to the kitchen.

When she came back, the radio was playing an old Elvis song for the whole "Ladies Who Lunch" segment the DJ wouldn't stop yammering about while I was trying to listen to June tell me about Gary as a child. June came back almost instantly. "I called over at Marv's. That's Gary's best friend. Said he just left, should be home any minute now."

"Awesome," I said, getting excited. "So, were you in love with Paco?"

She slapped the wind, "Oh, god yes," she said. "Paco was my soulmate, if you believe in that sort of thing. Truth be told, I wanted to grow old with him on that hot Mexican sand."

"Well, what happened? If you don't mind my asking?"

Her face fell, tone darkened. "Paco had a thing for the beast; his only flaw." I guess she saw my face confused. " Heroin," she clarified.

"Oh," I said, taken aback... "Gotcha."

"Yeah, he started hanging out with some pretty serious people. Got too involved; lost some money and even had a hit out on him at one point. Then he tried to sell to some tourists to make up for the lost cash to make it back quick – which normally didn't happen – and got busted. Twenty-five years. Never saw him again. Had no choice but to come back home, broke and addicted to heroin. Heartbroken. It was torture."

"Jesus," I said, concerned. "I am so sorry, June."

"Yeah. Thank you. Ancient history, though. All's good now." She cleared her throat, stroking the top of Paco's head. "My folks, they wouldn't have anything to do with me; didn't give a shit one way or another, if I lived or died. If they did, they never let it show. Had no place to go. Slept on a friend's couch for a while; spent some time on the streets after that. Hey, I'm getting a little nervous talking about Paco, you mind if I roll one up?" she asked.

"No, not at all," I said.

"Great, thanks," she said, pulling her tray from underneath the orange chair. "So anyway, I had nowhere to go, got myself in a really bad way. Finally got in touch with my brother, and he let me stay with him, thank God."

"Wow," I said. "How long ago was that?"

She took a long pull from the joint, and thought out loud. "Oh, let's see. Year? Year and a half, maybe? Not long enough!" she laughed.

I was baffled that this was a recent occurrence, she had to be in her late forties, or at least she looked it. I guess it surprised me that she was recently a homeless drug addict. I thought she was talking about her younger days. I could see it in her a little, but not really. She passed me the joint, but that time I didn't smoke; I wanted to be myself and alert when my dad showed up.

After another half hour or so of talking about June's very colorful history, June got the munchies and decided to make us some sandwiches. I sat there and looked around, searching for character clues within my eyeline. I found myself staring at a small painting of an old Indian man with the saddest look on his face. There was blood on his chest, a wound. Then, outside the window, movement caught my eye. It was the Bronco. The Astro was parked in the street, so the driveway was clear. But, instead of pulling in, he slowed down to a rolling stop, then shifted back into gear and drove away.

***

When June came back from the kitchen, we sat and ate while I pretended to be okay while listening to her tell me about a man she met on the streets who could read fortunes that told her she was going to meet someone special. "I guess he meant you," she said. I was too embarrassed to tell her about Gary, so I just played along for as long as I could; untl being there became unbearable.

"No, don't go!" June kept saying. "You barely touched your food! Gary will be so upset that he missed you!"

It wasn't until that exact moment, like a punch in the gut, that I felt a sense of longing for my mother. She'd been right all along; Gary didn't want either one of us, and he never did.

She was right. That's what stung; that's what got me. It got me thinking, and made me wonder: What else had she been right about?

And just like that, I shifted away from Gary and onto Mother, and the guilt I had for visiting him instead of trusting what she had told me shattered my own personal belief system and made me question again every mistake I'd ever made.

While I was rightfully avoiding Mother, like when Daddy was alive, it seemed to be much more manageable. It even felt justified. Necessary. But now that he's gone, was she someone else?

Her old self? Before him? Was she, since Daddy passed, even fucking okay?

How selfish I had been. How completely blind I had been to the needs of another grieving woman. I'd cussed her for things out of her control. I'd acted like an ass. It was myself I should have been mad at for Duane getting Michael. That was my fault. A sense of shame fell over me again and didn't leave.

I criticized her judgment in her marriage to Daddy even though now I can see that she was just doing what she could to keep her head above water. As an adult, I can understand that. I couldn't understand it then, though. When it mattered.

I should have been there for her, and I knew it. The days and weeks after the funeral are the absolute worst; when everyone else goes on with their life, and you are stuck in a house somewhere trying to hold the broken pieces of your own. You sit there, sick and crying, trying to decide what it is you are supposed to do next. Even showering or changing clothes was a chore, when simply moving from one room to another brought with it new memories to cry for.

I should have stayed around to clear the chaotic air between us, but I chose to run instead. It had been over two years since Daddy died, and all I'd done was run. Maybe if I would have stayed to face the music, I wouldn't have ended up so lost. So alone. So instead, I had nothing but sadness and regret for all of the days and nights I'd spent alone at the dead man's house instead of with my grieving Mother. Maybe I needed Mother and Daddy both back then, no matter how they expressed their grief. Maybe they had seemed so strong because that's what I needed; because that was what Michael needed. But I couldn't see that then. I was blind with grief and anger. Completely blind. Even my own thoughts had felt foreign, like they weren't even my own, but the true reality of their nature lived in my head rent-free.

***

The next several months at work were torture; getting to know the ropes and learning how to interact with people again became an odd chore I had to practice. Accepting Gary's attempt to escape me again was difficult. And, I hated the daily deliveries to the funeral home; *Bob the Undertaker* smiled like a psycho, carrying in the larger sprays for me; like he hadn't just been handling a corpse. Working and driving around delivering flowers to the residents of the same city that interacted with Mother was a constant ringing in the back of my head; and I feared secretly that one day I would run into her, or someone she was close with. And that's exactly what happened.

I had a long day; multiple funerals and two wedding showers. Near the end of the day, we had an order for a huge bouquet of orange crush roses to be delivered to Mrs. Patsy Rose, 1717 Seminary Street.

My heart dropped between my knees. "I can't go there," I told Eloise in a panic. "I can't make that order, I can't go there!" Before I knew it, I was crying; in a full-blown panic attack, unable to catch my breath long enough to explain to her the problem. After several minutes on the floor with the cold rag from Eloise, I finally said it. "That's my mother."

Eloise looked at me sympathetically, wiped wet hair from my face. "I am assuming you two aren't close?" When I looked at her, she smiled. "I understand," she said. "Trust me, I get it. Not a day in my life went by that I didn't butt heads with mine. I'll get Patrick to deliver it, or I'll do it myself. Not for today anyway; wants it tomorrow before noon."

Later, after we closed and were cleaning up, she asked me what happened. I told her nicely that it was just too much to talk about; and that I wasn't really ready to. She obliged, and went on to tell me stories about her own mother: who once left her abandoned at a train station to go on a date with a married, wealthy man. She said when the authorities reunited them, the mother admitted to Eloise that she'd done it on purpose; that the man she planned to marry did not want to raise another man's child. "She said she thought it would be best for me," she laughed. "Which I guess, looking back, maybe it would've been."

I was amazed at how candid and raw Eloise was when speaking about her childhood, and her mother specifically. She was usually so seemingly stoic; rough and tough; like it might take a lot to get her down. She did get a little fired up telling me about her Daddy, and how he used to slap her mother around and then laugh about it, like a bully. "He's in hell where he belongs," she said.

"Cold hearted bastard."

***

Back at the dead man's house for the night, I marveled at Eloise's childhood, and how she ended up being so seemingly "normal." She herself had experienced heartache, and a lot of it, but she was able to move on as well: put the past in the past; which was something I'd never been able to do. Mother had done a lot of shitty things, but she never abandoned me, especially not for a man. I guess that had to mean something. I'd left my own child, too; but for very different reasons. The main one being my inability to move forward in a life that has no meaning. I found it impossible to want to love someone or something again because I know just how fucking easily it can be gone. There's too much uncertainty for me here. Nothing seemed to really matter that much at all.

I hated the night. I wish it didn't exist. It was the night that flooded me with memories of people I'd loved long ago along with every mistake I'd ever made; like movie projector reels of a life once lived that played over and over in my head. Any attempt to escape them seemed to be in vain, and always no matter what I was subject to remember – I tried to do as I heard from the doctor on the radio. I tried a picture of the last time I was happy. She said "bring the moment back to consciousness." I tried every night before bed; somehow I'd begun to believe that if I could just figure it out, and bring myself back to that moment, it could somehow be a key to free me from all I had endured.

Finally, one night after months and months and even years of heartache, I did it. I remembered the last time I felt happy, and the memory cut like a knife.

An unexpected recollection that brought me right back to the weeks right after Samantha was born. It was Mother and Daddy's anniversary – January – things seemed somewhat stable, so they decided to take the night off to celebrate. They had been married for 21 years. I remember Samantha was calm, and awake.

Michael was sitting in my lap eating an oatmeal cookie Mother made that afternoon.

There's an old lullaby I used to sing to Michael that he absolutely loved, and while we sat and watched Samantha he asked me to sing it. No one was around; Johnnie was taking a break to give us some privacy, so I did it. I sang. Sam was wearing a pink and white polka dot sleeper. While we sat, she looked around, but not with really any focus. But when I sang, like I had already tried to tell Dr. Raspberry, she looked at me. Her legs kicked.

I tried to call Johnnie from the other room but she'd gone outside to smoke so I just sat there holding Michael and watching Sam singing what I thought of as their favorite song. The Little Blue Man. And for just those 10 or 15 minutes, all I felt was love. Real, authentic, love. Unconditionally. In that moment, I felt happy, I had hope in seeing her respond to me. Michael still knew and loved me then. No one was around to spoil it. We were a family that day. At that point, it was the happiest I've ever been. And I've been chasing that high ever since.

I imagined what mother would do if I showed up at her doorstep with her orange crush roses. Would she peek through the blinds, see me, and pretend no one was home? Would she answer the door, knock the roses aside and embrace me for all the years we've missed? I didn't even know any more; couldn't picture who she might've turned into after Daddy died. And in the cracked bathroom mirror at the dead man's house, I studied myself. My hair was greasy and wilted, and my clothes hadn't been washed in over a week. I was amazed at how far I had let myself go, even working in the public. My mother would be appalled if she saw me at that moment. At that house.

Before I knew it I was at the laundromat washing all of my clothes and bedding. While it dried, I drove over to the Loves truckstop and took a shower. I brushed my hair until it dried, straight and clean. With nothing to really lose, I decided to make that delivery if it killed me; and if I was lucky, it would. I'd been alone and isolated for so long that I yearned for a real human connection, and I wanted at least one of those connections to be with Michael, and Mother was the first step. I had grown weary of running in place searching for a kind of security and safety I wasn't even sure existed.

The next morning I showed up to work early and ready. I told Eloise first thing that I would be making the delivery. I didn't allow any time to change my mind; and what I found inside that old house on Seminary Street was unlike anything I could've ever imagined. The whole interaction played out like a scene from a movie with a happy ending. I broke down and cried the moment I saw her face; her coral lips; her black, native hair perfectly maintained as it always had been. I apologized over and over for leaving, for always causing problems. Mother held my hand and began wiping tears away as they came.

"I'm not mad at you Drucilla," she said, smiling. "I forgave you long ago. There's no need to ever apologize." She squeezed my hand and told me she understands grief and love and being a mother and a woman can be the hardest things in the world to endure and that losing a child is indescribable – and that she would never judge anyone on how they handle something so awful. Her words were like salve on a wound, an old one. A nasty infected, emotional wound.

We sat at the dining table and had coffee while she filled me in on how Michael had been doing since the last time I saw him. Something in the way she spoke made me excited, and made me feel like she was excited, too; like she was relieved to have me back. She pulled a snapshot from under an apple fridge magnet, and he was wearing a blue cap and gown. She slid it across the table. "This is him at eighth grade graduation, isn't he precious? Such a good boy, a real gentleman."

I was nauseous looking at the picture; could only think that I'd missed another one of many milestone events in his life. I wondered if, while he smiled for those pictures, he might've been wondering where I was. I hadn't let that thought seep in too much before that moment, I'd avoided that guilt at all costs, but then suddenly, there it all was, staring back at me. He had grown so much, I couldn't believe it. He looked so much like Duane, but in his eyes, I could see me, too. And it broke my heart that I'd been gone away so long.

After a lot of small talk, I asked Mother if she thought Michael would want to see me.

"Well, of course," she said. "Why wouldn't he?" She asked, baffled.

"Because I've been gone a long time, Mother. What if he's mad at me?"

"Oh hush that; kids are resilient. He's missed you. I'm sure of it."

Kids are resilient. No, they are not.

And in the spirit of keeping things light, she said, "Let's just be thankful that he has a chance to know you better now, so let's just focus on the good things for now, okay? Okay." She walked over to the orange crush roses and took a peek at a card. Blushed. "My goodness," she said. What a sweetheart," she gushed.

"Who?" I asked. I hadn't even thought to read the card. Mac. A man I've been seeing. Oh, Drucilla; he's just everything I ever wanted. A good man. A loving man. It's like it's finally my turn to be blessed." She hung the card by Michael's picture.

Not once did I ever think for a second that Mother would've been dating again. Never. And while I wanted to hear more about Michael, she kept the conversation focused on Mac, how much they love each other, what they did on the weekends, how they met. It was like talking to someone else completely; never had she been so candid about her personal life. She spoke so quickly and happily that I was still confused and taken aback.

"What?" She said, looking at me funny. "Why are you making that face? Aren't you happy for me?"

"Of course, I'm happy for you Mother."

"Good. Thank you. That's all I want. For us all to be happy again. I can't wait for you to meet Mac!"

She sighed and sat back down at the table. "So, how's Jimmy?" she asked. My stomach turned at the mention of his name.

"Jimmy and I are divorced," I said flatly. I'd rather not discuss it if that's all right."

"You knew when you married him that he wasn't right for you. But we are all guilty of that, aren't we? How about you come by tomorrow night for dinner, or you can meet Mac? See Michael?"

***

The next day, I arrived at Mother's at six sharp. I was scared if I came any earlier that I might run the risk of seeing Duane drop Michael off.

I wore the same outfit I'd worn to meet Gary, but I tried hard not to remember the last time I wore it. Mother would be sick if she even thought I had gone to see Gary. Oddly, my secret meeting with Gary and June, even though it wasn't ideal, gave me some sort of petty satisfaction in knowing I'd done it.

Drucilla, you're late," Mother said. "Come in. Michael and Mac are waiting in the dining room."

I knew I wasn't light by normal standards, but I didn't argue when I suddenly remembered who I was up against. Apologizing, I followed her all the way to the table where two complete strangers sat looking at me, each with their own unique expression. Mac looked exactly like John Wayne and smiled and shook my hand.

Michael, now almost unrecognizable, even from the Polaroid on Mother's fridge, barely looked at me. Almost a man, he sat and scowled instead of getting up to hug me. I was heartbroken and immediately defensive. Why didn't Mother correct his behavior? Had she told him what all I've been through? All of the fucked up shit I've been dealing with? All of the horrible shit God had thrown in my direction?

I smiled at him and sat quietly after our awkward introduction from Mother, who went immediately from that to the menu she prepared for our meal ahead.

For a good half hour, mother asked me all sorts of questions about what I'd been up to, all of which I had made up lies for to cover the truth. If she knew I lived in an abandoned house and had no real life whatsoever, no running water, no clean clothes, or basic human necessities – she would just die right then and there. The only truth I told was about my job, and even in regards to that, I'd lied about how long I had actually been working there. With my story of lies about my life, I constructed a pretty decent role for myself: after Jimmy and I divorced because he was cheating on me, I whispered to mother while Michael had excused himself to the restroom, I moved out and rented a house in Fern Valley 12 miles away and worked for a while as a bank teller while taking business classes at night for a few years. "Delivering flowers oddly pays more than the bank, so I said to myself, Drew you've got bills and tuition to pay. Doesn't matter how much you love working there and that you're almost moved up to branch manager – it was time to move on! You gotta go where the money is." I said.

Eloise had better perks, too, I explained. When it was quiet for too long., I couldn't tell if Mother was buying it or not; but Mac was and continued to ask random shit in an effort to make conversation, so I just had to keep going.

By the time our meal ended, I felt like I had just been on the witness stand. Michael had said nothing at all to me but was cordial and jovial with both Mother and Mac as if they were good friends or something. Which, I guess, technically, they were.

Right after her mother served her famous strawberry pie, we heard a *honk* outside. "Oh, there's Duane," Mother announced. "Michael honey, let me wrap this up for you to take; say goodbye, and I'll be right back."

"Bye," he said to me through a pursed lip half-smile then went in for a hug with Mac. "Later, Macaroni," he said. "Love you."

My blood boiled consistently for months after that.

Chapter 12

After Michael was gone and Mac had retreated to the couch to watch MASH, I told Mother – point blank – while we were cleaning the dishes, that my feelings were hurt about my whole interaction with Michael. Or lack thereof. "He acts like I'm just some random stranger instead of his mother."

She got fired up easily, her demeanor quickly darkened. "Well, what did you expect, Drucilla? You've been gone for years. He doesn't know you. Hell, none of us do anymore. Business school? Really?"Her sarcastic tone only enraged me.

"Why didn't you stick up for me when I was gone why not explain why I had to go?"

She'd gotten upset already, though; and interrupted me before I finished my thought. She ripped off her rubber gloves and threw them in the empty sink. "Because I didn't know why you were really gone. You didn't have to be. And I was too busy raising your son to make up excuses for you. Even Duane got himself together, we all did. Everyone but *you*." Her eyes had narrowed and she'd inched closer in a way that scared me.

"The relationship you have with Michael is your fault. Not mine, not Dwane's. What happens from this point forward depends on you."

From then on out, I played the part I was given, although I felt strongly that it was important that they at least told Michael I didn't abandon him, but I wasn't allowed to push the issue.

"You have no right to alter his life in any way." Mother had said, probably a message from Duane. But I felt that, somehow, I could win Michael back. Prove how much I loved, and still do, love him. And then when he's older, we can have a talk and then he would understand what all I had endured.

*****

Not long after that dinner, I was at home asleep at the dead man's house when I was startled awake by men's voices and shining flashlights in my face. Outside, the patrol car lights were flashing.

"Ma'am? Ma'am?" The officer kept saying. "Are you aware that this is private property?"

They didn't arrest me. It was two male officers; both young, both nice. Both pitied me; and I was ashamed. They each helped me to haul all of my belongings to the van, and helped me load it. They gave me information for two homeless shelters in Burgess, and the pastor for the Baptist Church who was known to help those in need.

I didn't need a homeless shelter; I didn't know what I needed. I had been working for Eloise for almost a year, had thousands of dollars saved up from living in a house without rent or bills. The sad part about it, to me, was having to leave it. I'd grown attached to it and didn't know why, and I found myself grieving for that old house of pain.

To this day, I still think of it; the safety and anonymous seclusion and infinite privacy – or so I thought. Without me there, the dead man's ghost would be alone again. I remembered a time after Samantha died when I had mentioned to Mother the possibility of suicide.

"If you want to burn in hell for eternity, be my guest. You need to find something else to do with your life; quit moping around. It's been months. Michael needs you."

People don't understand suicide, in my opinion. Does the Bible say you go to hell, or do people just assume that? I had a hard time imagining a god that would damn someone to hell for eternity for that. It just didn't make sense. All of the fucked up shit people do in this world, and they get damned for exiting early? That's not who they say God is, so which is He?

No one seems to know that, either.

With the money I had saved up, a whopping $6000, I rented a small house on Apple Street, bought a bed, a couch, a few tables, and a TV set. But I spent most of my time in the backyard on my lime green fold out chair, missing the dead man's house and maybe even his spirit.

I felt alone and useless, Michael didn't even need me anymore. Didn't even want me. I had to change that. There had to be a way to make him remember. He just needed to bring out all of our old, happy memories back to consciousness. It was possible. "And if you have no fond memories to cling to," the radio doctor had said, "You must create them."

Hours turned into days, and days to seasons and so on, and each day was so similar I could hardly distinguish one from the next. Michael was not far away from turning sixteen, and with each passing day he seemed to hate me more and more. I don't know if it was the classic teenager syndrome you always hear parents complaining about, or if it was due to some deeper, much more subliminal messaging he didn't even know he was sending. He "tolerated me." He didn't treat me like a parent. Looking back now, he treated me like a sibling. An equal by rights. It was an odd, unsettling pattern that was unfolding, and I didn't like it. I didn't like Michael talking to me like I was a big sister. I was much more than that.

What bothered me the most was that I felt that I somehow deserved this, that I was living out my penance. Paying the piper. So I took it. Same as I did my whole life. After all, what the hell could I actually do about it? Nothing. And so things continued.

***

On my drive home from work one day during that time, I noticed that someone on my street was selling a black jeep. Not just any old jeep, this one was old but restored: shiny black and had thick, monstrous tires that looked capable of taking on any terrain. The sign on the windshield said eighteen hundred. Suddenly, I had a brief epiphany: I could buy the truck for Michael for his sixteenth birthday. He would have no choice but to acknowledge me then. I could picture him excited and smiling, wrapping his arms around me in cheerful delight, eager for the keys to take it for a spin. Maybe he would ask me to come along. Maybe not.

But still – maybe.

The next day, on my lunch break, I skipped my sandwich and made my way down to First National to withdraw fourteen hundred dollars from my savings account for the jeep, which was what I had bargained the owner down to. When I was done, I had a bank receipt that showed my once-handsome account now had four dollars and sixty-two cents – but as long as Michael was happy, then it was more than worth it in my opinion.

A couple of weeks before his actual birthday, Mother had invited me over for dinner with Mac and her. Michael was "over at a playmate's," she said, so I thought it would be the perfect time to tell her my plan. So, I did.

"Oh, Drucilla, honey. I really wish you would have asked first," she said regretfully. I'd already planned on giving him Gerald's old truck." My heart skipped at the casual mention of his name, and for a moment, I caught myself trying to remember the last time I had heard it.

"You want to give him Daddy's truck?" I said, bewildered.

"Yes. I thought it would be something really special," she said, smiling over at Mac. She coned the cherry of her cigarette in the ashtray, then looked up at me. "They were so close," she said to me with a sympathetic smile, like she had forgotten who her audience was.

"But I already bought the fucking jeep, Mother," I said, without meaning to, but I was suddenly so pissed that it just rolled out to reach her. I was livid, and her coyness about my reaction only fueled my rage. When I looked over at Mac, he was looking down in his lap, twirling the edge of his napkin in his fingers. Mother gave me the look, the one that meant *tighten up right fucking now*. The look that said *don't you dare embarrass me, Drucilla.*

I wanted to flip the table. Almost did.

"What am I supposed to do then?" I asked her angrily.

"Well, maybe you can get your money back or something," she said, taking a long drag. "Or put it up for sale in the Tribune. Marjorie Nelson won't charge you a cent to post it in the classifieds if you tell her I sent you."

"No. I'm not doing that. I bought my son a jeep for his birthday, and I'm giving it to him." She looked offended, and she looked pissed. And she was. So was I.

"Why are you making this into such an issue? You were the one who bought it without even mentioning it first. I could have told you months ago what I planned to do with Gerald's truck." Mac cleared his throat, slid his chair back, and excused himself.

"You think Michael wants to drive around with his grandfather's ghost, smelling his old cigarette smoke and shifting the same fucking gears? No, he doesn't, I'll assure you that. No one would." I said sarcastically, adding a little half-laugh for flair.

Her eyes were wide and wild now, aggressive. It only fueled my rage.

"Stop being so goddamned morbid, Drucilla. It's not up for discussion anyway, so you will just have to find some way to deal with it, won't you?"

***

After that night, I didn't see Mother until the day of Michael's birthday. She'd tried her best to be nonchalant after the fight, maybe even felt bad (I doubt it), but she did reach out to invite me to brunch and called another time, leaving a message on the machine to tell me to be there for cake and ice cream at six sharp.

I worked all day long, my nerves were frayed and worn like an old weathered rope end. Eloise was appalled at Mother, too; said she thought it was selfish to try to take a milestone moment away from any mother. I agreed. Every day, I had to look at that jeep, my empty bank account balance, my aching, empty heart. No outlet, though. No place to release, no way to leak out even the smallest bit of pressure. I felt trapped and useless, an irrelevant component of some much larger mission.

I contemplated whether or not to go, thought Michael might even be happier if I wasn't there. But I also knew very well the backlash from Mother I would receive and never live down, so I sucked it up and got dressed and walked outside.

When I got to the jeep, I felt a tug on my heartstrings. I had played out this Jeep gifting scenario in my head a million times, maybe more, and the thought that I would never get to see that play out was something that I suddenly didn't feel I could take. I stood there looking at it, knowing I needed to get into my own damn car and drive over to Mother's to smile and eat cake and make a big deal about the reveal of Daddy's old Chevy. But no matter what, I couldn't do it. I just couldn't fucking do it.

When I pulled in at Seminary street, it was already a quarter til seven, and they were all standing out at Daddy's truck parked in front of the garage. It was so eerie pulling in behind it, like I'd just driven back in time. Mother's face was priceless. Mac looked scared. I got out smiling cheerfully, tossed Michael the keys when I approached. "Happy birthday, Michael! I said. "She's all yours! What do you think?"

Shock and surprise covered his face. "What? Seriously?"

"Of course!" I said. "I wanted to buy you your first car," I paused, and looked over at Mother. "So I did." Mother walked over and stood beside me acting like everything was okay, then she led me away by pinching the inside of my arm to guide me away like she used to do when I was a little girl.

"Are you out of your goddamn mind?" she said. "What the fuck are you trying to prove here?"

I was in tears at this point, about to tell her exactly what I was trying to prove, what my plan had been when I heard a car horn two quick beeps coming down the street. Mother and I both stopped to look. It was Duane in the old shit-brown-sparkle fucking car with a red balloon bobbing on a string from the antenna, the windows down and loud music playing on the stereo, his big, goofy smile shining like a yellowed star.

"Jesus Christ," Mother whispered to herself.

Duane got out and reenacted my previous performance. We all just stood there confused, nobody saying anything for what seemed like forever. Duane hadn't been around in months, he saw Michael maybe one or two times a year. My blood started boiling. I could feel it in my veins.

Then, suddenly, I snapped. I snatched the Corvette's keys out of Duane's hand, climbed quickly into the driver's seat, and revved the engine. Smoke was everywhere. I peeled out in reverse and then blasted down Seminary Street as fast and recklessly as possible. When I looked in the rearview, I saw Duane running on foot behind me, waving his arms. I gassed it and left him in a cloud of his own smoke, and burned up every drop of gas in the freshly-full tank. I don't know exactly where Duane Myers got his audacity from, but it was truly baffling.

I made quick turns throughout the little old neighborhoods in Burgess, not really sure what to do. I felt scared yet exhilarated, beaten down but fiery and somehow right in all my wrongness. I hadn't felt that good in years. I took Calvert Avenue out to 77 and got on the interstate, where I really opened the motor and drank of its intoxicating power. I felt the road in my knuckles, the wind in my face; and for that little bit, that very small window of time, I felt justified. *Free*. I felt like never stopping, just driving and driving and driving until I eventually disappeared into thin air, like Marty on Back to the Future, only in my movie I would never be seen or heard from ever again. I would be gone.

***

When dusk arrived, I was miles from Burgess, a good forty or fifty at least, and I had the radio blasting, and I sang along to every song as I bobbed and weaved through traffic. When I got tired of the clusters of cars slowing down my speed, breaking sourced inertia, I took an unknown exit and let the engine roar down a dark country highway. I cannot even recall what exit I took or where I was, but it was so peaceful and serene out there in the darkness, in the still quiet of the night, the big bright moon offering its silvery beams for its shine. The air was thick and sweet with the season, the sky a starry spectacular and it was then that I realized I couldn't really remember the last time I had actually sat down and looked at the stars. Felt the wind blow or anything that resembles being in nature.

When I was a kid, I remember playing outside all the time and helping Mother prune the roses and water the plants. It was some of my best, most important memories of Mother. Even if we were out there with our gloves and floppy old lady hats and pruning shears working together but not saying much outside of the work, it was still what I considered to be precious moments I spent with her when I felt like we were on the same team for once. On some level, I missed that; and I hadn't felt in so long I grew weary trying to remember. Everywhere I looked, the big silver moon lit up the treetops against the hills. Even amongst all the chaos, I was somehow relieved to have still been able to recognize its beauty.

After hours and hours of driving, I ran out of gas about five or six miles outside Burgess city limits, where I trekked the rest of the way on foot. I didn't go to Mother's, I didn't contact Duane about the car, or concern myself with the fact that Burgess PD might be looking for me. I just walked home in the wee hours of the morning, the sun just starting to form the lavender morning sky, and crawled into bed and went to sleep. Slept the sleep of the dead. I called in sick to work and slept all day with the phone off the hook. I deadbolted the door, closed all the shades, and kept the TV going in the background to make things feel normal and less hard-pressed, a tactic I'd long been using in replacement of actual human interaction.

After three days of isolation, I finally showed up to work, knowing Eloise would be in a bind without me. Though it had not been any sort of pattern for me to miss several days at work, I had strep throat once, and when I was well enough to come back to work, we were horribly behind and getting complaints for late deliveries from Patrick. She refused to hire extra help, claiming she couldn't afford it. I guess you could say I was happy to at least have some value at work. Eloise needed me. Even if nobody else did, she and Patrick did. Dobson's Floral did.

I got a letter in the mail from Duane with a bill for a replacement tire after finding the car abandoned and flat on his way to work. I didn't pay, and I didn't respond. He could drive that damn car up his ass! Flat tire or otherwise. Stupid, selfish bastard.

Mother didn't call or reach out that I know of – there were no messages at work and no one had stopped by. That stung a little, then I got pissed off again. What a bitch, she is. How could someone be so cold? After a while I started to feel guilty, knew I had embarrassed her in front of Mac, something I always did that she hated. I sent her half a dozen English roses, left them on the porch by the front door, but never heard anything back.

And then suddenly, somehow, over time, I grew bitter and resentful of our whole arrangement. And for the rest of that season in my life, I acted like a crazed hormonal teenager, throwing fits and tantrums and becoming increasingly more aware every time I spoke to Michael that while I was gone, not one person had gone to bat for me. All of that shit I went through, just poof – vanished from everyone's minds. The poor kid probably thinks I just didn't care about him. Why wouldn't they want to clarify that for him? For me? Why did I always end up with the shitty end of the stick?

I drew my strength from my new sense of justice. This would include clarifying anything Michael's heard about me other than the truth from my very own lips and withdrawing any former attempt to be Mother's submissive child simply to avoid embarrassment in front of Mac. Like I gave one shit about what Mac thought. Or anyone else. Like his opinion was more important. I've lived my whole life with my head in a noose, and no one seems to care. If Michael only knew, if he just knew how much I always loved and missed him – why I had to be away – maybe he wouldn't hate me so much. Maybe we could have a normal relationship with normal conversations under normal circumstances. But how do you explain to a child that everyone was just too shitty and incapable of being around someone who was just sad. Shattered. Write me off; here's a fucked up life now you deal with it.

I started pissing my mother off on purpose by agreeing to brunches and dinners and then pulling a no-show. She hated that; it was one of her biggest pet peeves. After my absence, I would drop by the next day or the day after as if nothing had happened. I knew she wanted to scold me for it, completely roast me for such blatant disrespect, only she couldn't. Because of Mac. So she wore her mask and played along, only dropping mild hints of disgust, like slamming my plate down in front of me at dinner and eyeing me with the stare of death through her thick mascara-coated lashes. "The Look," as I called it as a kid. I tried to avoid eye contact if I could manage, and it worked famously.

On the days Michael was there, the only time I actually got to see him, the dynamic was always really awkward. I didn't have privileges, so I couldn't take him off alone and be his mom for chrissake, couldn't come right out and tell him or show him how much I loved him, maybe explain any questions or misunderstandings he had about me or my absence. My hands were tied. I could just picture Duane being the saint in his side of the story, and that made me absolutely sick.

Any chance I got alone with him – which wasn't much – I'd pry and ask questions to see just what they said about me during all those years. Once, Mac and Mother were sitting out back drinking sweet tea in the summer sun, the locusts screaming at top volume. Michael and I were in the living room finishing Jaws 2 when I finally got the nerve to talk. There had already been a good half hour of awkward silence, so I didn't really fear I had much to lose at the time. I began, crossing my hands on my legs in a conversational way. "So Michael, I know I was gone for a long time, and I just wanted to talk to you about that for a minute. Is that all right?"

"I guess so. All right."

"Okay, well, I was just wondering if anyone ever explained why I was gone or if you ever asked? Maybe you were too young to remember me at all," I managed, suddenly terrified of what he might say. He looked at me with a wrinkled brow.

"Yeah, I remember you," he said. "I remember you. I remember Samantha and her nurse. What was her name? Johnnie?"

" Johnny," I said, nauseous at his strong, astute recollection.

"Yeah, Johnnie. She was cool." He shifted in his seat, I was starting to feel uncomfortable.

"I never really knew why you weren't around, honestly. It was just ordinary life for a while; I just never really questioned it, I guess," he said.

"You never questioned it?" I said

"No."

"Well, has anyone ever said anything about me?"

"No, not really. I think I remember something about you being sick way back when I was really little, but nothing much after that. Dad told me you were sick."

Dad. Fucking Duane. Fire burned red inside my veins and in my face red, and I could feel it.

"Sick how?" I asked.

"Beats me."

It took everything I had not to ask Mother about it; I didn't for about a year. I was scared that if I mentioned it, she would know I got that info from Michael, and then she might have Duane keep him away from me, just like before. What's new, just shit on Drue, she can take it. Hell, she's a goddamn professional. "Will take shit for crumbs" is what my panhandler sign would read.

Another time, we went to the church parking lot with fold-out chairs and bottled soda to watch the Methodist Church's grand spectacular firework show that ended up being an annoying nuisance instead of a welcome distraction. Mother and Mac were off socializing with other churchgoers and I asked Michael all he remembered about me back then before I left.

"I don't mean to make you uncomfortable," I assured him. "It's just that you're my son, and I'm your mother. I'm curious."

He looked away from the bursting stars and looked me straight in the eyes but didn't speak. Then he looked back at the booming sky and said, "I don't remember that much about you, to be honest. Even back then. I mean… I was a little kid. I remember you were sad. I remember you crying a lot. I don't know, I guess that's about it. Well, and I remember the wreck."

"The wreck?" I asked, confused.

"The time you crashed into Dad's truck on the road when I was in the backseat."

My heart sank, I couldn't speak, I couldn't move. Life had ended for me in that moment.

He was so little. I thought for sure that there was no way he could remember that. In fact, I'd become so certain of it that I confronted Duane about it by calling him at work.

"Duane Myers," he answered in a businesslike manner. Made me furious to hear his voice. That's the only reason I called him; I knew if I saw him, I'd kill him with my bare fucking hands.

"What kind of sick piece of shit turns a sign against his mother?" I asked.

"Drue, why are you calling me? I have nothing to say to you," he said.

"You told Michael I hit you with my car, didn't you? Tried to make me out to be crazy or something. Like you were some big hero dad. Mister perfect. Did you bother to tell him why I did that, Duane? Huh? Or were you too big of a pansy to admit that you were a piece of shit, that you were running from us?"

Click.

I didn't even care that he hung up, at least I got my point across. He'd have no choice but to accept the fact that I knew there was some kind of agenda for everyone to be against me while I stood alone. Years away from who they were now. But somehow, still not far from where I was. For me, it was the same year I laughed, the same year I lost the baby, the same year my husband left me for someone else. To raise a son alone. To bury a child alone. To live alone with those thoughts in those memories that never escape me, not even for a moment, not even while I slept.

If I reach back far enough in my memory, I can remember two times that Duane had promised me the world and a hundred times that he said he loved me when he didn't. There is not one single wedding vow that he abided by, and not one single happy moment was made in his presence. He tricked me. That's what he did. I thought my escape from home had been almost perfectly executed. I'd gotten pregnant, married, and got out of that goddamn house on Seminary Street. But then, Dwayne ended up being an abysmal failure in every respect, and so I found myself back in hell with a toddler and a fetus in my belly that would never see her first birthday.

Duane gets to live happily ever after with our son and his new wife while I suffer the loss of everyone who's ever entered my life. Was it a curse? Old sins cast long shadows, the Pastor mentioned at the burial right before the final prayer. Maybe he was right. Duane had cursed us, and it cost me everything.

A day or so later, I received a phone call from Mother, who scolded me on what an embarrassment it was, and a shame for one, to have called Duane in that regard. At work. On a rant on Tuesday morning. I had no right. Normal people don't act like this, she added.

I told her that abnormal reactions are normal in abnormal circumstances. I argued my defense and then hung up in her ear. Satisfied.

I didn't see or hear from anyone for over a month. After that fight, trying to process Mother's words became impossible. Work became impossible. Between deliveries, instead of helping Eloise, I'd drive out to the dead man's house, park in the road, and walk up to the haunting structure. And inside, I saw familiar chaos and smelled the musty old scent of freedom and peace. Of understanding. My old, anonymous existence, tortured and haunted by my demons who demanded the pain I was experiencing be deeply felt. Eloise noticed a shift in my affect; I suppose that was unavoidable. As my boss and the closest thing I had to a friend, she went to great measures to make sure I wasn't going too far under. I suppose she was trying to keep me from killing myself, but I had already proven that I was too weak to even do that.

What I couldn't understand was, with complete freedom, I couldn't just run away someplace new and start over. Why not try to forget the past and move on? Isn't that what other people did? What do other people do in my position, or better yet, is there a way to prevent getting there at all?

Instead of a beachside escape, a cozy apartment in the city, or even a townhouse somewhere in the suburbs, I chose to live in the house of a dead man like an animal, with no modern luxuries whatsoever. I guess, technically, there was the guilt. It was the secret corpse I carried, something in the back of my mind that I could never seem to escape. In my heart, I believed that if I were to move on, live in luxury, and laugh and smile while making new friends and eating new things, and making new memories, my baby would really die. If I didn't think of her and live in her memory, would she be forgotten? Would I forget her smile, her smell, her glassy eyes? Would her spirit slip away for me somehow? Would I ever forget how much she meant to me, or better yet, how can I make sense of her being dead? I got inside myself again. The hauntings of emotion played me like a sadistic puppeteer until I either cried or vomited.

Sometimes both.

I kept to myself and tried to keep going, regardless. Things were that way for a while; a long time.

And then, one sunny day in May, I got a call at work. Mother had left a message with Eloise for me to call her. My heart pounded, and blood banged inside my head. She answered on the first ring.

"Mac is dead." She said. Then she cried, then she let go of a scream that I can still feel in my bones.

Chapter 13

Mac left behind two sons and a daughter, four grandchildren, and my visibly broken, shattered mother. She never smiled again. She stopped going to church. Then she quit the garden club. The Junior League was long forgotten. There were no more fancy brunches, no more Sunday dinners and smiles made by Mac. In his death, he had taken with him every living part of her she had left. She became nothing but a shell of her old self: unknowable, unrecognizable. And the worse she became, the more fear crept up and choked me.

She stopped going to the salon and let the strands of salt grow in with the pepper. Her nails were – for the first time in my life – unpolished and unmanicured. She cared about nothing. Nothing. She became listless and languorous; started sleeping through the day and staying up all night, fretting alone. I worried about her increasingly erratic behavior, mostly the result of her panic attacks that had started, which, at their worst, looked a lot like hysteria.

When springtime rolled back around again, and Michael was set to graduate from high school on the twenty-sixth of May, Mother surprised us both when she said she was going to the "goddamn commencement ceremony." All day long that day at work, I worried, more than usual even, about how she would fare in a familiar, crowded auditorium with people she knew and who knew her. She hadn't been out since Mac died, and even a quiet evening at home with her was taxing.

Michael kept trying to dissuade her from going, going over and over the reasoning behind it. When I agreed with him, she got pissed at both of us and, as usual, told us we could go to hell and went anyway. We ended up having to leave before Michael's name was even called. Mother's panic began to rise once the lights dimmed and the principal began his speech. Mother said she couldn't breathe. It wasn't until that moment, seeing Michael in his Burgess-green cap and gown and Mother in her oxygen cannula, that I was struck with our actual reality like a lightning bolt through my bones; shaking up old memories and awakening ancient emotions I'd longed to forget. I did my best to pack them up in my emotional suitcase with the rest and focus on helping Mother.

After a year of this, I finally got her to go to a doctor to treat her depression and anxiety. It was a battle. She had no interest in admitting fear or grief, no matter how visibly it was destroying her, little by little, day by grueling day. Her panic attacks had gotten so out of control that she couldn't breathe without oxygen. She had to quit smoking, which was infuriating and impossible. She smoked with patches on while chewing nicotine gum. Nothing we tried worked, and Mother was too emotionally gone to care about anything physical.

She just didn't want to talk about it. After a lot of coaxing and filling in the blanks for Dr. Rance, he prescribed her a mild antidepressant and Valium, and it was an Olympic event to get her to take the fucking Valium. She hated pills, all of them. Complained of every possible side effect, claimed the Valium made her feel "drugged" without seeming to grasp the point of it. I was so desperate for her wellness that I would become livid, always leaving her with a more frustrated and hopeless disposition than I did upon arrival.

One evening, during an after-work drop-in to check on her (which she loathed), I couldn't get her to answer the door. We had already been fighting about her medicine and my "becoming intrusive" since Mac died. I rang and rang the doorbell; nothing. Beat on the hardwood door; nada. My heart was between my knees, and I was about to run next door to have Mrs. Lamb call 911 when I finally heard a relieving thud from the front door's heavy deadbolt. She opened the door just wide enough to see her sad, sunken eyes peering out at me through her tattered, half-glued eyelashes: her once always-pristine trademark.

"I'm not a fucking invalid," she hissed inside the house, sitting back at her nest at the dining table. She was drinking red wine and chain smoking; a box of Melba toast, the only thing she seemed to eat, was sitting by her Parliaments and full prescription bottles.

"Are you sure you are okay, Mother? I can come stay a while and help out."

"I'm fine. I'll be fine!" she said sharply. Then she yelled again, "I am not a fucking invalid. Stop looking at me like that. Stay out of my goddamn business!" She slammed her hands down hard on the table, the same as Jimmy had done that last fight, spilling the wine and scaring me shitless. She stood back up straight, took a long, hard pull off her cigarette, gazed up at the ceiling, blew it out hard. "I wonder if life smokes after it fucks me," she said.

The more miserable she became, the more impossible she became. Her almost-combative noncompliance was more than I could take, and her not taking the medication was a daily battle that I couldn't quite grasp. Why not take them and at least try to escape, if you can? Though, at the end of the day, there was no pill to bring people back from the dead, and I knew that as well as she did.

***

The Deaths

In May of the following year, Michael moved into the city, which left me making random midnight drive-bys to check on Mother, as Michael would sometimes do because she always kept the phone off the hook – something we fought about often. I would always wake up in a panic, knowing she was over there going nuts with grief, and I couldn't just simply dial her and make the fear stop. I had to panic constantly. There was never a moment of ease that I didn't worry about her. I knew she didn't need to be left alone, but when I offered to move in and help care for her, she acted as if I had enrolled her in a nursing home and ordered the heavy tranqs.

One day, near Valentine's Day, I came home from work exhausted from the extra work of the holiday. Valentine's Day was our busiest day of the year, even more so than Mother's Day. Orders had been flooding in and going out all week long as we stocked and restocked roses and baby's breath and love-colored ribbons and sweet cards and chocolate hearts.

It was past dinner time when I got home, and all I wanted to do was sleep. I flipped on the television and tried to settle into an old rerun of Designing Women to doze off to. The longer I sat, the more nervous I became. I couldn't focus on the show, and I couldn't fall asleep. Something just felt off.

I tried to call Mother but got a fast, busy signal from the phone being off the hook – not unusual. I called Michael to see if he'd heard from her, but I got no answer. I put my jeans back on started up the jeep, and headed over to Seminary Street. By the time I reached the house, I was suddenly flooded with a sense of dread and fear.

I found her sitting on the edge of her bed, half-dressed, bound by her breathlessness. Her lips were blue. She was pale as a mushroom. She couldn't even speak.

Mother was admitted to St. Vincent's for evaluation and treatment of a panic attack that left her breathless; her chronic COPD only made her fits worse. But on that visit, we found out that the shortness of breath she had been experiencing was not completely anxiety related; nor the COPD. She had cancer growing in her lungs; which eventually ended in her demise, as well as the demise of anything real I had ever known or any purpose I thought I would ever have on this plane. Everything that existed before had been merely fiction, some temporary nothing that left me with an intense, unwavering sense of meaninglessness.

Dr. Rapaport, Mother's oncologist, suggested a rough course of treatment that only made her sicker and never showed any results we wanted. They had all been mere attempts at hope we all desperately needed but didn't get. I no longer understood what life meant nor what good could ever come of it: I saw all aspects of life as short and temporary, little blasts of pain and fury that filled me with both severe paranoia, fear, and paralyzing, subdued complacency regarding my weakness against its force.

"Sadness settles in the lungs," Eloise said after I told her the news. And I guess she was right.

I hated seeing her that way, hated seeing that fucking cannula in her nose, hated seeing her gasping and panting in private, hated hearing her cry about her life… I began to see Mother for what she really was; a victim at best, who had seemingly lived a life of nothingness and died with the same shit. She'd been so disappointed by life, so let down, completely drowned in heartache. Now, she found herself living on borrowed time.

The need for air, to gasp and choke for it with no satisfaction, was satanic torture. Evil, vile, hideous things no one should see. To see your Mother like that was something different altogether; something that is hard to shape with words, that makes you question life, or reality – God even. Those things do something to a person that can never be undone, can never be unseen; forgotten.

It's odd the things you remember about watching someone die: the way they used to be, their smile, values, and beliefs. Things you loved about them, and things you didn't. Things you'll miss, but never the things you won't. When someone is dying, everything wrong they've done gets put somewhere else, out of sight and out of mind. They are a saint now, those who are fighting death.

Several months or so after Mother's illness, I was sloughing through a day at work.

I was so stressed out I didn't even know if I could survive it. Severely exhausted and stretched too thin, my nerves were shot. I was helping Patrick load up the van when I heard the sound of barking dogs nearby.

In the lot across the street was a pickup truck with a wire cage and a sign, "Puppies for Sale." I was drawn to them instantly, and I decided to walk over and take a look before I started my deliveries, and in the bed of that truck were five of the most beautiful, precious little stark-white puppies I had ever seen. They had long, silky, angelic hair and little pudgy noses.

"Full-breed Maltese, fifty even," the owner said, chewing on a cigar butt. "All male except the one with the bow," he continued. One kept biting my shirt sleeve, wanting to play. I picked him up, looked at him, and noticed he only had one eye.

The man saw me looking at it. "That's Gimpy," he said. "He's free for whoever wants him. He ain't worth nothing with that eye missing." He waved a dirty finger around his own.

"I'll take him," I said without another thought.

I named him Monster. He loved cheese, snuggles on the couch, rawhide bones, and me.

The Deaths

At night, after I'd finished with work and making sure Mother was alright, we would settle into a single blob on the couch and watch old sitcom reruns; whatever was playing, we didn't care. For those couple hours each day, I felt a glimmer of happiness and my first sense of unconditional love. It was the first time I felt my love be reciprocated. He would always end up on my chest, snuggled up against my neck to sleep. After a few minutes, my rapid, anxious breathing would synchronize with Monster's own relaxed, slow-burning rapture.

I didn't tell Mother about Monster, she hated animals for the most part. We never had dogs because they tore up the yard and dug up flower beds. When I was in grade school, I found a baby kitten in the alley and wanted to keep it, but Mother made me give it to Mrs. Lamb because she already had cats, and she told me to remember that "people who have cats smell like people who have cats."

But one day, on a whim, I brought him with me to check on her. He fit perfectly inside my canvas shoulder bag, and he was pretty good about staying inside it when he went places with me. When we got to Mother's that day, she didn't answer the door, and I had to use my key to get inside.

She was in the kitchen leaning forward and stabilizing herself on the countertop, breathless, completely winded. I helped her over to the dining table and, sat her down, went to get her inhaler from her bedside table, where I found a wastebasket full of bloody tissue that the doctor said would likely happen. Monster was asleep in his bag on the couch when I started a breathing treatment and made her take a Valium.

When I finally got her stable and taking longer breaths, I made my way around the house, picking up half-empty coffee mugs and Melba toast cellophane wrappers. I changed the liners in all of the wastebaskets. Then suddenly, out of nowhere, I heard Mother shriek, a weird scream of sorts that scared me shitless, and when I made it back to the dining room, I saw her holding Monster in the air, admiring him like a newborn baby. She had a look of bewilderment on her face.

"That's Monster," I said, relieved. "Because of the one eye."

She looked back at him, laughed at the name, and embraced him. I had seen a lot of things, but this was not one of them.

"That is so damn precious I can't stand it! Is he mine? Oh my God, I love him, I love him!" Her excitement sent her into a coughing spell, but she recovered quickly that time. I was godsmacked; didn't know what to say. She was kissing Monster all over his face, smiling her old smile that I hadn't seen since Mac died.

There was no option.

"He's all yours!" I said through my tears.

"Oh, thank you, Drucilla," she said between coughs. "What a precious thing! I'm in love." Then she smiled again, only this time at me.

The only thing holding my heart together was her smile.

***

The next several months went by as quickly as springtime lightning flashes, but I still felt every strike. Monster had been like a little puppy Jesus; had pulled Mother and I both out of the trenches, breathed in a bit of extra life and a source of comfort.

Though Mother's demeanor had significantly improved, her health did not. The radiation therapy we tried didn't work, and it only made things worse. She looked like death. I knew it was close; I could feel it.

It was exhausting, waiting for death. Seeing Mother cough relentlessly and gasp for breath made my own chest feel tight, made me second guess every cigarette I smoked, and sometimes prevented me from smoking altogether. Mother's illness made my own life feel rushed and chaotic, which it was; but in a really dark sense. I felt like I was trying to do everything blindfolded, like her cancer had completely blocked my vision, and I was just blindly trying to get through each day, depending solely on a consistent routine as a guide.

From each moment to the next, I couldn't decide where my focus should be. I would be at work but be worried about Mother. I would be with Mother and worry about Michael, who finally started calling Mother on a regular basis and even came by once while I was at work. I personally hadn't heard from him in months.

I had questions for Mother swimming around in my heart, things I wanted to know before it was too late, but every time I had the chance to ask, I would be too scared – Mother hated shit like that – talking about personal feelings or anything like that. Not her real feelings, anyway. But honestly, I was also scared I would find out something else I'd have to recover from. God only knows what she could be withholding. Sky's the limit. I decided it was best to just let things be; to never learn your truth.

In the months before Mother's death, I can think of only one good memory to speak of. Surrounded by mounds of chaos, illness, bullshit, death, and life: there was this one little nugget of gold that I'll always cherish, and one nugget of gold is worth more than a heap of silver.

The Deaths

It was a Saturday afternoon, and I had brought Mother a salad from the deli and a few groceries. We made small talk, and she tried to eat, but couldn't. After a while, we retreated to the living room to watch the evening news, her daily shit. I listened to a plastic-haired man talk for what seemed like forever about a tragic automobile pile-up on the interstate, then excused myself and went outside for a smoke break. I walked around to the back of the house and sat under the pergola, where I could smell the honeysuckle bushes and be upwind enough to smoke the little pinner joint I brought with me to calm my nerves and ease my burning, nauseous stomach.

Halfway through, it started to rain. The earthy, rainy smell of the storm made me sad. I used to love that smell, but now it made me sad like everything else. Nothing brought me joy anymore. I felt dead inside.

I ran back into the house before I got completely soaked. Back inside the den with Mother, I sat stoned and somber, pictures of the accident still flashing across the TV screen, Mother's thin face lit up blue by the screen.

"Does it really help?" she said.

"What?"

"Marijuana. Does it help you feel better?" she asked casually as if drugs were a usual topic of conversation. Typically she would've smelled it on me and said nothing and would later act passive-aggressive to let me know she disapproved or that she was pissed. And I would continue to not care and do it anyway, and then she would resent me for it, and so on. But this was a different time, different situation altogether. And magic happened that one crazy night on Seminary Street, and it was the beginning of one of the very best and worst times of my life mixed together.

"Yes. It does. Don't start shit with me about it, either. I will leave, I swear to God."

She interrupted – spoke over me. "I'd like to try it," she said, so casually I thought I hadn't heard her clearly. "I can't smoke it, but I know you can eat it. I did grow up in the sixties, you know."

I tried to picture Mother in a hippie headband and GoGo boots, sipping on the end of a joint, but couldn't bring it forth.

I drove to Apple Street in shock, couldn't believe I was picking up weed and eggs for my mother. My mother. And Jesus Christ, if anyone needed it, it was her. I left the car running while I went inside, grabbed the coffee tin I kept my stash in, and the carton of eggs from the fridge. On my way back to Seminary Street, my stomach was fluttering from butterflies; I had no idea what was going to happen or what to expect. But I knew that marijuana was safer than chemo or cancer, and I decided that the worst that could happen would be that she got hungry or got to sleep. Winner winner, chicken dinner.

Within the hour, the air in the room was thick with our laughter. We talked about things Daddy used to do: hacking up the Easter ham, nailing the Christmas tree in place using 2x4s and huge, long screws that he drilled through the polished wood floor when its plastic stand lost a leg. We talked about things Michael used to say and do when he was little, when we were still a somewhat normal family before everyone either died or left in shame. When people still smiled, talked about things like the weather or war: the one overseas, not the one we were living through. I reminded her of how he used to say "appy douche," and "telehopter," and somersault all through the house, filling it with the innocent laughter of my child: sounds I forgot I missed.

Then, Mother started talking about when she first met Daddy, her eyes red and glassy from pot and tears from our laughter. "I was so smitten," she said. "Gerald was so handsome and charming," she said, addressing the flowers on the coffee table. "And he loved me," she continued. She bit the inside of her cheek, her brow wrinkled. I could see her shift back into her sadness; her happy tears became dark like the sting of death, and then she looked again like how death makes you look. Miserable. Trapped. Hopeless. She cleared her throat and began again.

"He loved me until he died," she said. A tear rolled down her cheek. "He was so bitter," she continued, to my surprise. "Nothing I did worked, nothing made him happy, nothing was ever good enough. Then he died... Then Mac died, too, the love of my life. Now it's my turn, I guess."

We sat in silence for several minutes, crying together. I held her fragile body like a child, soaked up her tears and her grief inside me, cried both with and for her, angry at God and life and everything that came with it. She fell asleep not long after, a still, eerie slumber that gave me a glimpse of what was coming. I covered her with an afghan, sat nuzzled at her feet, and thought about all of the secrets Mother had told me that night, things she had never told anyone.

I marveled at how similar our feelings were, our fears. I found it incredibly sad that so many years were lost, so many beautiful possibilities that passed by because of the inherent need to withhold, to seem perfect. Toxic vanity stole healing from us all. Death took even more. Left us all in shambles, wrecked individually and together, grieving the same griefs separately but somehow tethered.

All week long Mother's words swam around my mind like hungry goldfish. How she had been shunned: disrespected. Shut out.

Unloved. Alone. I knew these feelings well, but I never considered that anyone else might feel the same way, least of all Mother, who always shone like a new penny and made everyone wear their best smile, regardless of the circumstances. Or Daddy even. I couldn't even picture him in a position to be pitied, and now, looking back, I wonder if that's why his heart exploded in his forties. Anger, resentment, loss of soul. Death takes all and leaves you wondering what the fuck just happened, and what the hell am I supposed to do next?

The next night, I got brave and asked more questions.

I wanted to know more, was yearning to uncover some hidden truth that might set us both free; some neon sign to some cure that would shrink her cancer and heal her body and our hearts, a sweeping of light throughout our darkened souls.

I asked her about growing up, about Grandma and Grandpa Rose and their lives. She spoke of her simple upbringing on a country road in the foothills of Indiana, a place where she felt stifled and trapped. "There were no people around, ever," she said. "Mom hated company. Daddy did, too, honestly. They were just very quiet people. Simple. But they were good people. Kind and generous."

Her eyes stared out to see a memory, and I wished I could see what she was seeing.

"When I graduated, I left and never looked back," she said. "I met Gary, and I wanted to live." She rubbed her left arm up and down, up and down. "'Course I regretted that later in life; after they died." She looked at me accusingly with her eyes narrowed, her head tilted to the side. "You never really appreciate people until they're dead and gone," she said. "Until it's too late. Life is peculiar to me in that way."

"Can you tell me about Gary?" I said bluntly, out of the blue; unable to hold it in another second. I could see her harden against the question. Her demeanor darkened, the energy in the room shifted dramatically south, and tension filled up the atmosphere around us.

"Drue, I don't want to do this. I'm not well."

"I have no one left to ask, Mother."

She sighed, disgusted. Sat quietly in thought for a long time before she spoke. "He was my first love," she said. "When I met him, it was just a feeling I had. I knew he was the one, and I was certain he felt the same way. I moved into the city with him, had no clue about the world, I was only eighteen." She grabbed a tissue from the box on the end table. Dabbed each eye quickly. Blew her nose. I sat there on the edge of my seat, privately dying inside, praying she would keep talking.

"'Course, when I found out I was pregnant, I was elated; over the moon. Thought he would feel the same way. He didn't. The night I told him, he acted weird. Said he was happy but didn't act like it. The next morning, he left for work, and I never saw him again. When I met Gerald, I hired a lawyer who contacted him somehow; got him to sign over his rights to you so Gerald could adopt you. I never saw or spoke to him. All my life after that, I felt like everything I did was wrong, every move I made. And I guess it was. Everything turned to shit."

Chapter 14

Alone in the house on Seminary Street, after my mother's death, memories swam around inside me like ghosts. I wanted to turn and run; never look back. Since Mother's death I had been completely unable to make sense of anything, and I wasn't sure there was even a point to life at all. If all we do is die, then what's the point of even living? To suffer and be miserable and fear the inevitable? Where's the honor in that?

Opening the front door was like opening a portal to the past; the smells of meals cooked long ago mixed with Mother's gardenia potpourri was pretty much more than I could take. The vast emptiness of the house felt unnatural: death was all around, thick in the air at that old house. But even still, there were parts that were still bathed in Mother's presence: old newspapers on the table with pill bottles and several inhalers. A single, stained coffee mug in the sink.

Her clothes, her perfume, her robe draped across her dressing chair that still smelled like her and waited for a day that would never come. The longer I held that robe and cried, the more I realized how even objects themselves can have souls, and that with Mother gone and everyone else, too. I felt that perhaps my own soul had died right along with them. Only my body remained here;

broken and useless, empty and void, just taking up space. Breathing unnecessary air.

I'd gotten stuck inside myself again, where it is always dark and raining fear, where I'd prayed like Noah for the floods to cease, or at least to be anywhere calm, bright, and peaceful, where the sun wasn't covered up with ghosts. I felt myself becoming more bitter every day, and working at the house shoveling away memories that stung. I'd become morose and angry at the same time. I was still no closer to understanding life or death than I was when Sam died, and I wasn't sure I would be able to stick around long enough to find out if there was something I was missing, or had missed, that might be a link – a missing puzzle piece to end all confusion and suffering, a bright light of hope from somewhere unexpected – a gem, perhaps. An oracle. Only now, I no longer cared. I didn't want to think or talk about anything. Didn't want to be alive. I was done. Toast.

Michael hadn't called since the funeral, hadn't returned my calls or messages about cleaning out the house. My heart was broken already, but that still hurt like hell. He had basically ignored me at the funeral and, after, spent his time loitering around Duane – who I couldn't believe had shown up. I didn't know Duane Myers had any respect to pay anyone. I felt shunned – embarrassingly so, like I was some lone drifter instead of the daughter of the deceased. I didn't write thank you notes for flowers or casseroles or condolences. I threw everything in the dumpster. Fancy old lady casserole dishes shattered on the metal dumpster floor and made the neighborhood dogs bark.

In the year after Mother's death, my focus shifted from life to death and stayed there. I began to have anxious thoughts about ordinary things, and I looked for death around every corner; anything could trigger it. Accidents, illness, fate, age. One single solitary act can kill you graveyard-dead. This reality struck me then as something extremely hard to swallow, and made me question God. I didn't want to, but I did. I couldn't help it. It was all too much. Why had everything always been so bad? Why were we cursed? What do I do now?

Eloise kept riding my ass about my lifestyle since Mother died; my lack of effort, my flat, careless affect intertwined with bouts of nervous, paranoid fits of rage. I finally gave in and went to the clinic to see Dr. Barbour, whom I had known since I was a kid from church. He diagnosed my grief and provided necessary prescriptions to treat it, which all made me dizzy and sick, enough so that I would oftentimes have to call in sick to work.

Eloise was concerned about my job performance and my lack of progress in healing so many months after Mother died. She blamed my loneliness on solitude and my grief on anger. "You need Jesus, honey. We all do," she'd say.

It pissed me off when she did that – acted like I was a nonbeliever. Some empty-hearted atheist or some shit. Even though I had told her on multiple occasions that I grew up in church, sat in those oak pews every time the damn doors were open. Sat among powderey-necked women catching all the high notes of the hymns, and men in sport coats who were really just wondering about numbers on some scoreboard somewhere.

Afterward, they would all gather to eat lunch and sin – talk shit about each other and others, stuff their fat faces and forget all about God – whom they didn't appear to be worshiping in the first place. Growing up for me, church was like a pageant. You acted a certain way, looked a certain way, and said certain things. You smiled, shook hands, and sang. You pretended to read those scriptures; hear the prayer. Then you left and went right back to being the same sorry asshole you were when you sat down in that red seated pew.

I believed in God, knew he took as well as gave. I knew God very well, and I was terrified of Him. More than anyone, I think.

I dug out the boxes I'd collected for donation into the living room. There must've been at least 20 or 25 big boxes plus a solid 10 or more trash bags filled with clothes and memories. I started with the clothes. I went back through all the closets and gathered up all the hangers I had left bare. It took a full day, but I hung up every piece of clothing in the bags, separated them out – mothers, daddies, Michael's, Samantha's, and mine.

I dedicated a room to each person, starting with Daddy's old suits that still smelled like his Old Spice aftershave years after his death. I threw up twice and had to lie down once, but I managed to separate his work clothes from his dress clothes, including the navy pinstripe he had worn to Samantha's funeral. Her tribute was still in the pocket of his lapel, folded like an accordion.

All of Daddy's work clothes were still starched: his button-up polos, and his standard Levi 501s. Their armpits were severely discolored with sweat, big, huge, yellowish brown circles. I couldn't believe no one had ever noticed that before. Could've been a sign of heart disease? What if that could've saved his life? Could a minor mess like that result in someone dying? If so, what all had I missed?

The peculiar thing, I suppose to some, was that I didn't hang the clothes back into the closet. Instead, I brought down a box of strong wood nails and covered the walls with them. In the master bedroom, mothers' expensive dresses and blazers and skirts and smocks covered the room like moss. While making my mother's room, I found a dress I remembered her wearing to my baptism, to church, to meetings at City Hall. It was a vintage Chanel, and she adored it. But I distinctly remember that she wore her black onyx beaded necklace every time she wore the outfit. She claimed it was its perfect accessory. I found the beads inside her jewelry box and hung them around the top of the hanger.

Her sweaters were the hardest, because of the smells.

I took one off the hanger and cabinet beside me in bed; The green one with white lace embroidery around the neckline. She always wore it during the holidays. I buried my face in it to sleep and would often drift off to some old memory tied to the smells that lingered and its threads. Something about being surrounded by walls of past worn garments of my parents made me feel safer, like they were there, surrounding me… I wanted them to make me feel safe. I don't know why, or, then again, maybe I did.

Instead of bunching up scarves, necklaces, sunglasses, or any other accessory, I hung them all up separately. Mother required more space than anyone, so I made my bedroom into her accessory room. She would've loved that. She deserved a big, walk-in closet like she always wanted. Well, I guess I did what I could as far as that goes. Although I know she would never be around to enjoy it. She would never see all of the care and thought I put into her rooms. I kept a bowl of her favorite Gardenia potpourri from Joanne's Fabrics. I bought a whole large case of it to avoid multiple trips to refill it. I also kept a bowl in each bathroom, just like she did.

Inside a black zip-up garment bag of which there were two, I found her funeral dresses. There were several, and I recognized them immediately. In another – special occasion outfits for weddings, baptisms, and awards ceremonies. The only thing that stood out was the champagne-colored silk formal she'd worn at my wedding. The fabric was soft and familiar in my hand. I put it in the bed, too, and would rub the end of its sleeve against my cheek for comfort.

She was wearing that dress when she gave me the emerald earrings and warned me not to marry Duane. I knew she was right; she usually was. Why did I work so hard to disobey her? Why did I constantly torture her with her mistakes? And in my mother's room, I sat a brown metal fold-out chair right in the middle. I sat there and remembered her; every detail of her face, her hair, her smell, her frail hands. The same hands that used to wipe away tears when I was little when I was too young to appreciate it, when I was too young to realize that one day, she might be gone, too.

I was baffled at how I – someone so fixated and stabbed in the soul at the fragility of life, could be so blind...

But Mother – she was an enigma: different from others on every level. She was strong. She was confident. She knew what she was doing, for Christ's sake, and I never trusted her and gave her the benefit of the doubt like a loving daughter would have. I just did what I did best: fuck shit up. 'Cause regret, make irreparable damage in relationships with people I am supposed to love and who are supposed to love me back.

I wasn't strong enough physically or emotionally to complete a new room for several months after I finished mother's. The weight of the memory sat on my chest and showed me things I hadn't noticed before, and before I knew it, I had a mental list of about 1000 regrets and conversations I wish I'd been able to have with her, things I never had the nerve enough to say. Questions I was too afraid to ask and apologies that would sit in my throat and rot like meat in the sun.

It was early fall, September maybe, when I finished Mother's room. When the holidays came, I decided to pull out all of our old Christmas decorations. I moved my TV stand over to the corner and put up a 10-foot-tall artificial tree that Mother must've purchased after Daddy's death, because all my life, that man never allowed an artificial plastic tree to represent Christ Almighty. The tree was pre-lit with soft, twinkling white lights. I preferred the colored lights – like we used to use back in the old days – so I found several strands and wrapped each one carefully around the tree with delicate detail, and worked until I was satisfied with the lights' nostalgic glow. I used yards of red and gold tinsel around the doorways and on the mantle, and I hung all of the stockings found in the box. Everyone's was in there – Mother had saved them all.

Sam's fuzzy pink and white stocking from her first and only Christmas, my green velvet one with my name in gold, the thick quilted Nutcracker monstrosity she made for Michael.

Mother's antique ceramic nativity scene pieces were each carefully and purposely wrapped in bubble wrap for safety. A gift from her grandmother. She seemed to look forward to the holidays only to see that display set up glowing in holiday twinkle, in the season of Christ himself. Seeing baby Jesus and the hay lying in that manger, really put things in perspective, she told me many times…

I never knew what she meant. I still don't. But, I put the scene out just the way she liked it, and I lit a candle in her memory and sat it by the display.

The ornaments were a variety of both new and old. Babies' first Christmas, handmade gems from Michael's elementary school days, popsicle sticks, sleighs, fake plastic snow globes, and pipe cleaner candy canes twisted into stripes. Then, Mother's old crystal icicle ornaments added her flare and her elegant tone. Daddy loved the handmade traditional things, while Mother preferred a more modern, unique approach. After careful planning and consideration, I created a beautiful, equal balance of both. I admired it for days, my eyes glassy and dazed from tears and lack of sleep. I did not use any decorations outside. They were all for me. Plus, I didn't want anyone to see me hanging lights in the snow with wilted hair and my blue gown and pink bathrobe that I wore like a dirty, stained uniform. Speaking of uniforms, I hung Daddy's old marine gear and war memorabilia in the parlor and dedicated a section of our living room shelves to his years of service and sacrifice. It was a reminder that, at one time, my daddy did good things that helped the whole country, me included. It was more than Gary did – June told me he never served. Coward. Textbook pansy-ass coward.

About a year went by, and it stayed Christmas year-round on Seminary Street. Mother's old maid of Marion winter dishes sat on the table, their snowy winter scene giving the table an icy chill, but was warmed by the cream-colored candles in mother's antique crystal candlestick holders she bought when I was a kid. I even pushed Michael's old wooden high chair up in his old spot at the table, the one between Mother and me.

Some nights, I'd fry myself an egg and sit at one of those empty seats, and instantly regret all of the times I've sat there before and complained about the food, the company. Or when I would bring up something politically liberal to piss Daddy off and set the tone, the stage of the same old scene. The one I used to prove he was the bad one, not me. It was a game I played recklessly and constantly, and it hadn't occurred to me until that moment that maybe that's why he died so early. Maybe that's why everyone had died so early – I had simply killed them. I had caused enough stress, enough chaotic tension, that it killed my family and their legacy. It killed any chance of me ever having one myself. I added those regrets in the journal I kept that proved that I had indeed contributed to such a painful past, a painful present, and future.

Then, I decided to work on the kids' rooms.

Michael's things, I found, were the most surprising. The cleaning lady had only accumulated items from the rooms downstairs, not the attic, so everything seemed to be current and/or old enough to be out of touch with what I would remember. Because of that, I had very few of his items that brought me any comfort. Most of it looked to be from elementary and middle school times: yearbooks, baseball card collections, ninja turtle action figures, Tee Ball trophies, and group candid shots with all the players wearing big caps with their ears bent over. I found old report cards with grades that would've made Mother proud – or did, I guess, while he was in her care. With a box of thumbtacks, I hung each one proudly beside the other and finished off the paper collage with photos taken from the family album and a few I had found in his things, even one with Duane in it.

In that picture, Duane and Michael were squatting in front of a pond, holding several perches on the line, and smiling at the camera. It was an old photo, browned with age and curled up on the edges. Michael looked to be six or seven. Couldn't have been more than seven.

Then it struck me like lightning: Duane had been there. Duane. He'd come back, and become a father. But then an even bigger truth revealed itself and came with such a wave of revelation that I could hardly stand to even think it, but there was no escaping the fact that Duane had never even really left at all. I did.

I'd become Gary Berryman in an instant, without even knowing it. I'd become the very thing I hated most, and that was a pill I choked and choked on and never was able to swallow. The realization felt like some pre-ordained death on earth that doesn't end. The kind you just have to live through, no matter what, like a grossly eternal torture of the soul. Unpardonable, and with every tear that came after that, I knew I deserved it. Karma had come to collect her dues, and I gave myself willingly.

Hidden under a box of Samantha's crib set and a pile of old winter coats was a three-drawer filing cabinet with every recorded memento imaginable. I'd forgotten what a stickler Daddy had been about paperwork, and I suppose that's part of what made him such a good businessman. And, clearly, he taught Mother to continue after his death. On every log of checks, Mother's blue ink signature took over the monthly statements the day she died, and all of the insurance papers and death certificates were neatly filed in a folder marked "Gerald."

I found the titles for Mother's car and Daddy's truck and even titles for vehicles I've never seen, probably one that they drove when I was too young to remember. I found bank statements, water bills, electric bills, and the deed to the house. I found two thick folders of medical papers from Samantha I didn't understand, numbers and words strung together in a fit cord of trash that would only be in the bad way. Among those folders were hundreds of thousands of dollars in medical bills for things I couldn't even pronounce addressed to me. And all her life or death, it never occurred to me that we'd had to pay to watch her suffer and die.

In a folder marked "old," I found a Polaroid of Daddy in his marine outfit, smiling at what I assume was a gift for his service. A shiny, new car. I say this because of his uniform, his face, and the hand-painted congratulatory banner hanging on someone's porch in the background. He looks so happy. It had his name written on the back, with the date of January 5, 1959. It alarmed me, after doing the math, that not even 25 years had passed between that fall photo in his death. In his eyes, there was no trace of fear, no hatred. No signs of early heart disease or sterility. Just pure, smiling ignorance.

He had no idea what was coming. I was ever come with an overwhelming empathy for him all of a sudden, and that was the first time I had ever felt that for him. Even at his funeral, I didn't pity him. What an awful person I am. Did I even cry? I could barely process his death, but I knew for sure that until that day on Seminary Street, I had never grieved him. But that day, for whatever reason, I did. He did more for me than my own father had. He had at least done *something*. Been there. Helped out. Supported Mother and me. And what had I done in return? I killed him. That's what I did. Drove him to an early death with my life, with my dead baby's life, with every choice I ever made. My very existence robbed my daddy of ever having a normal life. My mother too. My children. I catapulted them to their demise the second daddy adopted me.

I never found the adoption papers, which I'll look for diligently for hours. And after a moment, I wondered if I'd become an orphan again.

Like any logical person would, I tacked Daddy's photo on the parlor wall and the title to the car right beside it. I liked the way it looked, like I had made another stride in remembering who Daddy was, who Mother was, and who they would've been. I liked to think I was paying tribute to them with the memorial I had made. It was the very least I could do.

From there, I decided to keep going. I found the blueprints from the original planning of the house itself and tacked them on the wall beside the couch. Decided to arrange a variety of photos of it completed for reference. Mother and Daddy had designed that house together; and Daddy had built it. It wasn't the happiest place on earth; it certainly wasn't fucking Disneyland; but still, it was the only real home I had ever had, and I ran away from it for as long as I could; I held out till life pushed me right back through that front door to open me up again, to make my wounds fresh again. Poke and prod at my vulnerabilities. My weaknesses.

After I made sure the photo and title looked just right, I gave it a thick coat of varnish and went back to the memories for more. I felt suddenly and profoundly artistic, and my efforts to memorialize a life unlived became my only passion, my obsession. I worked tirelessly for two and a half years to get it just right. I would do this to make them proud – even if they couldn't see it, at least I would know before my own death that I had gone back through time and realized my part in the play. Until I saw the gas I threw it on the big fires, and how I'd also started some fires myself, only for someone else to have to put out. Some burned for so long that there was nothing left, but at night, when I tried to sleep, a spark would come back to me and send me down another foot deeper into my own grave.

After displaying the title and accompanying photo, I decided to keep it up, and after days and days of work, I carefully and successfully displayed every paper inside the filing cabinet. After I finished organizing the papers based on their particular category, I gave the walls a coat of varnish, too, to give them that more permanent feel. I liked the way the paint would slightly blur and gloss my creations, giving it an artistic, nostalgic vibe. For days, I had to keep the windows open to live with the residual fumes. After I completed the walls of each room, all I had left was furniture, dishes, and Mother's decor.

In a futile attempt to make the house feel less abstract from what I've always known it to be, I carefully moved every piece of furniture back to its original place. The only thing I couldn't put back were Mother's paintings, since I have the walls covered in our memories. So, I took them up to the attic, where I found even more heartbreaking remnants of our family.

The most painful – was the crib. The crib both of my children had slept in, the one Michael cut his teeth on, the one that held Samantha until she took her last breath. Touching the wood, fingering tiny teeth marks sent shivers down my spine. It was an instant time warp that sucked me back into the days we waited for the inevitable. The one thing I wasn't able to handle correctly – the death of my daughter. I could hear her in my memory. I could hear Michael's sweet voice asking me questions I couldn't answer: Will my baby get better? Was my baby going to live with us forever? Why does my baby need doctors? Why can't I hold my baby?

Out back, Mother's roses and hydrangeas grew wild, even without my tending. The very same bushes I'd had to scale as a teenager to sneak out and ruin my life with Duane.

By the time I finished the inside of the house, there was not one square inch of wall showing. I even had the crown molding varnished with receipts for old water heaters and other appliances Mother and Daddy had purchased through the years. The hallways, bathrooms, and bedrooms were covered in the clothes my family had worn when they could breathe and talk, and the longer I sat with them, the longer I lived in the midst of their past, and the more the clothes became like ghosts; possibly somehow supernaturally filled with their spirit, or their soul, or whatever it is that supposed to be eternal.

And, I honored their ghosts out of respect for them that I never had or never gave, when they were here. I lit candles. I spoke to them; apologized. Played their favorite records, watched their favorite TV programs with the volume turned all the way up so they could hear it no matter what, even if it was too loud. Mother hated it when Daddy ran the volume too high, but he was half deaf in one year since childhood, so it was just the way it was. Having the volume up high was essentially more accurate, so I based the final decision on that.

The Deaths

On Sundays, I made a meal like Mother always did. "It's tradition, Drucilla," she would say when I scoffed about having to sit at the table with the family or any guest that came instead of snacking on Cheetos in my room watching Sunday reruns on my portable Console. There were – of course – no guests at my dinner, but that never stopped me. In the box of kitchen things, I had found Mother's favorite cookbook which she had added her own recipes to – some from magazines, some from newspapers, and some in her beautiful penmanship written on white index cards. Over the course of a year or so, I made every recipe, every single dish, at least a couple of times apiece. Beef Wellington, chicken Parm, golumpki with rice. Mother had always been a fabulous cook – everyone thought so. That's why she had so many events at our house. Everyone seemed to always be eating and complementing her food, especially on Sunday.

Sometimes I ate what I cooked, but usually I just didn't have the appetite for it; especially if I needed something that startled up a memory or emotion I wasn't able to handle well. I made everyone up late like usual, set the table, like the dinner candles, and then after an hour or so, I'd scrape all the food in the trash. Sometimes, I did the dishes right away, but usually, I'd let them sit for days, weeks, even, until the smaller side of mold would force me to do it against my will.

Someone recently asked me if I ever felt lonely during those years on Seminary Street, but to be quite honest, I was never really alone. I had grief; I had shame; I had enough guilt to fill the universe – and the results of all of those were pretty much enough to keep someone's mind busy at all times. To have had company – of any kind – would've disturbed me. I wouldn't have had the tolerance for it.

Michael wanted nothing to do with me whatsoever. He moved to the city, but he didn't call or invite me to the wedding or any other event. When I read the announcement in the paper that they still delivered faithfully each week and Daddy's name, I called Duane's house to complain about it, but he told me that Michael wanted nothing to do with me at this point and to please stop calling. What bothered me the most about that conversation was how Duane spoke to me. It seemed that he pitied me, felt sorry for me, and that enraged me. I called him every name in the book, told him everything was his fault, that he started a family and never finished it. He hung up in my ear. When I called back, there was a fast busy signal for days, like he'd taken it off the hook.

On the anniversaries of each of the deaths, I put new flowers on the graves. On birthdays, I would buy some inexpensive little gifts that wouldn't cost too much but would also signify something special and memorable. For instance, for Sam's last birthday, I bought her a Minnie Mouse doll and placed it right beside her headstone; I told her I loved her. On Mother's birthday, I gave her a porcelain angel figurine holding a red heart. Mother hated sentimental shit for the most part; but I still like to think that she would've appreciated the gesture. For Michael's birthday, I would send a card to Duane's house with a handwritten note and a $20 bill inside. I would always include my phone number in case he had forgotten it. Forgotten me. To this day, I don't know if he ever got them.

For Christmas one year, I found a rare coin that I thought would go with Daddy's extensive collection. I put it inside a thick plastic case and, against my better judgment, set it beside the fresh poinsettia and put it on his grave. But, when I went back a few days later, someone had stolen it. The sheer disrespect of someone so awful disturbed me. Stealing from the dead. What an abysmal loser. It absolutely infuriated me to the point it was all I could think about.

After that, I set a trap. I took a random Canadian dime, put it in the same type of case as the other. Put it on the grave in the exact same spot. I parked in the lot across the street and hid in the woods behind the cemetery. I brought Daddy's 357 magnum, fully loaded, in case they came back. Anyone who committed such disrespect would pay, period. For three days and nights, I camped, locked and loaded, Ready for the thief. But no one ever came for it.

Gary had a space in the house, but it was a small one. That single solitary picture I'd held on all my life hanging on the refrigerator with a magnet for mothers old bank. I used a black marker pen to draw an evil-looking mustache and devil words – a reminder of who he was to me. Every day I see that photo at least 10 times, and every time I think, what a real piece of fucking shit. I tried not to think about him or June; they're fake welcome and they're fake invitations. How dare Gary mock my mother. Sacrilege!

I did not make a room for myself. I wanted nothing of my former self to be remembered – much less memorialized. Everything I'd ever done wrong was already hung on the walls anyway, soaked into the memories of the people who had no choice but to give up on me long ago.

During the end of the span of time in which I created a relic of all that had been and not been, I developed a taste for red wine, just like Mother did when her nerves got bad and stayed that way. However, I didn't develop a taste for wine in the actual sense; what I did was develop a momentary reprieve – a brief shift in perspective. I liked the fact that, if I drank enough, hours would go by that I wouldn't even have to remember. I'd also grown used to easy deliveries from Marco's Pizza. I ordered a large hamburger pizza, a thin crust, and a supreme calzone every time.

Thanks to Marco's pizza, I gained eighty-one pounds in less than two years. I always paid by leaving the money under the mat, and the employees always had clear instructions to leave the order on the porch table beside the front door and go. Don't ever ring the doorbell, I told them about 100 times. Always left a sizable tip to avoid bullshit from the drivers. They all obeyed. No matter how sick of the food I got, it was the easiest meal to acquire without an interaction of some sort.

The pictures of Gary I found in the attic brought with them an odd feeling of no longer being rightly angry at him because I was guilty of the same parental crimes. However, there were still unsettled feelings. He looks so happy with me in the pictures. What changed? Was it me? Mother? Why do you go Gary? I knew why I left, but I never understood Gary's motive. I hung those pictures in the bathroom with the one singular shot I took by the mirror. I looked at them multiple times a day, wondering why he couldn't just stick around and make it work.

One night, deep into a couple of bottles of Merlot, I did the unthinkable and gave Gary a call. June answered, so I hung up. I didn't want to hear more excuses from her. I wanted to speak to my father. The funny thing is – I had no idea what I would say. I suppose I'd let the wine steer the direction of the conversation. But then, moments later, the phone rang. I let the machine pick up as always;

I've been screening my calls since Mother died, and her old friends would keep calling to offer condolences I didn't want to keep hearing. If it wasn't Michael or Marco's pizza, I'd have the damn phone disconnected altogether. I wasn't really interested in life enough to have a phone, but on the off chance Michael called, at least he could leave a message, and I could easily call back.

Beep. "It's June," a familiar voice said. "My caller ID showed your info when you called. Sorry, we got disconnected. Give me a callback, please. Miss you!" Beep.

Caller ID. A new feature, or fairly new, that clearly everyone had me. Fuck. Embarrassed and regretful, I put the phone off the hook and left it there for at least a week, maybe more. But, no matter how hard I tried, I did still want to speak with Gary. I did still have paternal feelings to bury. Those damn photos had erupted a volcano of emotion inside me, and I had nowhere else to expel that energy but onto him. No one else has made it out alive. Why him? Why, the most irresponsible, the most emotionally harming person?

After a while, my courage came back and enveloped me, and inside a bottle of wine, I sought to make things right. There were no other choices. At that moment, justice was my only goal. I had nothing to lose and no one to live for. I looked at the clock. It was 10:07 AM. I picked up the receiver and dialed. He answered this time after about 10 rings, right when I was about to hang up. Instead of a formal answer, he opened with a question. "Drue, is that you?"

"Yes."

"Junebug said you called a while back, how are you?"

"I'm fine," I lied. "It's just that when I was going through Mother's things I found some old photos I've never seen before. I just wondered if you might want to come by and look at them with me? Maybe talk for a while? Catch up?"

"Sure," he said, with a slight hint of hesitation. "Yeah, of course, I'd like that."

He was busy then, he said, but he'd be by later that same day. I'm not even sure what I did to pass the time; I don't remember being either excited or scared, and I don't recall any preparations to make myself or the house suitable for company. No one but me had crossed the threshold in the three years since Mother died – but I didn't care. I no longer felt the urge to impress anyone, even Gary, and the thought of cleaning or showering seemed a task far beyond my incapable state.

I was surprised when I saw the Bronco pull up. For some reason, I didn't understand, he brought June along with him. I guess he didn't want to be alone with me. Probably didn't want to be there with me at all. I watched them walk up through the peephole. Gary finished his cigarette and stamped it in the yard before ringing the bell. I watched them and waited a minute before opening the door. I didn't want them to think I'd been standing there waiting, watching.

When I did open the door, I was greeted by familiar faces looking at me like I had grown extra limbs instead of putting on a few pounds. My memory had grown weak and delusional by that time, so it was hard to tell if either of them had changed at all. They both looked healthy and suntanned, smiling and wearing clean clothes and shoes. It wasn't until seeing Gary's bright white T-shirt that I noticed my own had turned into a dingy yellow. There were pizza sauce stains around the collar. I ignored my own filth and invited them inside, led them into the parlor, and invited them to sit across from me on the couch. I sat in Mother's corner chair, my mind reeling with feelings of the past and present, demons I've wrestled with my entire life. I tried to speak, but nothing would come out. They were both focused on the walls, still covered in memories, and they both seemed to be in a state of a sort of shock. It was Gary, surprisingly, who broke the awkward silence.

"So what's all this?" he asked, his finger waving at them now dusty, archaic-feeling memorabilia.

I answered honestly and without hesitation. "This is my Daddy's room." They both looked at me with confused faces. "Not you," I added, laughing halfheartedly. "The one who actually raised me." June stood up nervously and walked over to a photo of Daddy varnished on the wall, but Gary just kept looking at me like he was trying to figure out my thoughts.

Clearly, he didn't get it. "Was this him?" June interrupted, pointing at Daddy by his war car, smiling that naïve ignorance that haunted me.

"Yes. Just after he got home from war, he was a real hero," I added. Gary got up, walked over, and looked. "See, here are his medals and some of the other things he earned. Do you wanna see my mother's room?"

They exchanged looks. "Sure!" June said happily. "Go ahead and give us the tour. It's a beautiful home, Drucilla." The mention of my own name, for some reason, made me flinch like Mother had whispered it to me through June's lips.

In the long hallway to Mother's room, I showed them pictures from the family picture album. They covered the walls top to bottom, until the last few feet, when I ran out. When we reached the kids' room, I announced it proudly. "This is my kids' room. Both of them."

"Oh?" June said. "Does anyone live here with you, Drucilla?"

I laughed at her question and giggled. "No, who else in the world would live here with me? Everyone's gone!"

They said nothing, and followed me into the bedroom, and I flipped on the light. And all its glassy glory were any remnants I had left of either one of my children. "Drue, why are all of these papers here on these two walls? And why is the window covered in foil?"

"So the baby can sleep. The papers up there are her medical records, first day to her last. If you read them starting over there, you can see her decline. I must've missed something, but I'm still working on figuring it out. It's still a mystery to me."

"Figuring out what, Drue?" Gary asked.

"Well, lots of things, Gary," I said sheepishly. "I've got to make sense of something, right? Otherwise, what's the point?"

"The point of what?" Gary said. June was looking at Samantha's post-Mortem shot dabbing her eyes with a sleeve of her T-shirt.

"Of everything Gary. Any fucking thing." Gary put his hands in his pockets and closed up around the kids' things, so I led them down to Mother's room.

"Wow, it… It smells so good in here," June said.

"Thanks, it's my Mother's favorite. Gardenia. You can only get it at Joann's Fabrics. Mother used to get mad at Daddy for buying the wrong kind when she sent them on errands for last-minute things. 'That other crap smells like a funeral home, Gerald!' she'd say. He would roll his eyes and head out to the garage to avoid any more interaction." June smiled lightly.

Inside Mother's room, Gary removed his hands from his pockets, ran one through his hair, and scratched the back of his head. He looked nervous, uncomfortable. He kept glancing over at June while I tried to reminisce with them about the items that hung on the wall. And although June seemed to be genuinely interested in what I was saying, I caught her glancing over at him, too. Since they seemed overwhelmed by my past, I led them into the kitchen to put on a pot of coffee.

It had simply slipped my mind that it had been weeks inside and even used the kitchen other than the refrigerator. There was a rotting rosemary chicken on the stove and a solid 8 to 10 pizza boxes on the counter. Maybe more. The sink was filled with dishes from who knows when, and I had no cream or sugar to serve with the coffee. Neither of them took a single sip of their black Folgers, even after I repeatedly apologized for the inconvenience.

I moved six or eight stacks of Daddy's newspapers from the table and joined them. I remember feeling foggy and strange, sitting there with them. Also, I felt slightly exposed and disappointed at the lack of positive feedback about all of the work I'd put into the house. I felt no appreciation or respect from Gary whatsoever. That made me angry, and honestly, a little defensive.

"So, Drucilla," June said sweetly. "What do you do? Are you still working? Are you still a florist?"

"I was never a florist," I corrected her. "I delivered flowers. Big difference." I lit my cigarette. "But now I do nothing but remember." She looked at Gary like she pitied me. I hated that – being pitied. I don't need their pity. I'm fine. Too late for pity now, now I don't need it. Does me no good.

"So, you said you had some pictures you wanted me to see," Gary said. "Was that all of those you've hung up?" he asked.

"No, those aren't the ones, I'll be right back," I said. I left the kitchen and went to get the pictures I discovered that had to me, indicated more involvement at the beginning than I thought, and I was hoping he could shed some light on that for me.

When I came back into the kitchen, June asked if she could use the phone. "I've left a dog with a friend so I could come here. I just need to make sure everything is good," she said.

"Of course," I said. "Phone's in Daddy's room." She smiled politely and left the room to make her call, leaving Gary and me alone.

"Wow, look at us!" He said in a fake-sounding voice, like he was mocking me. "Drue, you were always so happy," he said. Everything I said made you laugh, but I think it was just a beard because you were way too young to know what I was saying. I studied his face for signs of insincerity but found none.

He spoke about this Sears family portrait of the three of us: Gary, Mother, and myself, all smiling happily and in sync with what appeared to be an almost-laugh, what I would give to know what had brought us all such joy. Was it a skilled cameraman who was good with kids? Or Were we all just genuinely happy to be together? What the fuck happened? Where did that version of us go? Did he secretly hate us? Was he, under some moral obligation from Mother, just tricking us? Smiling for pictures and showing up to see me buy me a toy and then bail, like a Barbie dream house would replace him? Magically make me forget his existence?

With June and Gary both back at the table, I asked them what my mother really felt about him being a mother. Gary started telling me how excited Mother was to be a parent and that she even had names picked out before she told anyone she was expecting.

Then, I heard a knock at the door. "Who is that?" I said. Frightened and paranoid, I grabbed the pistol I kept loaded in the cabinet by the exit to the backyard and hid it in my shorts on my hip. Gary and June both looked at me in fear.

"What's going on? Gary?" I said, seeing an officer barge towards me. I screamed while officers filled the house. While one chased me out the back, Gary was right behind him, pleading with me to stop running. I remember stopping, turning around and looking Gary in the eyes, and raising the gun. The officer standing between us suddenly, and without warning, tackled me down into the grass, firing a shot into my left thigh. My senses shifted into another reality, and everything I could see swirled into nothingness and faded into black.

Chapter 15

The next time I woke up, I was surrounded by the color white. Not the light of heaven but the halogen glow of a hospital ward. I was in tremendous, nauseating pain. There were tubes in my nose and throat. A nurse came in immediately and praised my waking up. I was a lot less enthusiastic than she was.

"Where am I?" I asked her.

"St. Vincent's hospital, honey. How is your pain; are you feeling alright? The doctor is coming shortly to talk with you, and you got Dr. Weber, and he's the best doctor here. You'll love him."

I became furious and sick to death of my nurses' obtuse optimism. "Why can't I move my arms and legs? What the fuck is this?"

"Restraints, dear," she said cooly. "You're on suicide watch. You shot yourself, dear. And from what I hear if that officer hadn't tackled you, we wouldn't be here to have this conversation. But you still got yourself, right here on the left side, see? Try not to move so much, or you'll bust a stitch. Dr. Weber is on his way; here's some pain relief. I'm putting it right here in your IV, okay dear? Any minute now, you'll be feeling better. Any minute now."

Within seconds, my thoughts seemed to flicker, and the bright fluorescent lights down to a milky twilight, and I saw the flickering thoughts run smoothly throughout and within each other, until nothing at all made sense anymore.

In my morphine dreams, I felt like a lighter version of myself, like I hadn't even lived my old life before like I wouldn't even know who my mother was if someone had asked me. I felt a sort of strange, cosmic relief from somewhere outside myself. In my morphine dreams, I don't recall feeling the least bit of fear – or confusion, for that matter – no matter how unusual my circumstances became in this new dreamscape. It was the most peaceful I've ever felt, there inside my own dreams. Possibly the first time I've ever experienced it. For whatever reason, in those morphine dreams, I was free.

I spent several weeks healing in our private room at St. Vincent's because of wound care, and was then moved to the psychiatric wing. During my initial mandatory six months, I saw at least half a dozen different psychiatrists and got nowhere but heavily medicated. I'd become so consumed by my illness that I would sometimes dissociate and not remember my combative, violent behavior. A state of psychosis is how Dr. Franke – my first doctor – described it. With every doctor I saw, I had two new diagnoses added to my chart. But still, there was no relief for my confused, neurotic state.

Dr. Franke was tall and handsome, and he knew it. He was arrogant and misogynistic, like a crooked politician and thought I was crazy before he even heard me out. Before he even heard my whole story. In our sessions, he gave me the impression that he was not listening nor interested in what I had to say. He upped my Haldol and added Lithium for a "chemical imbalance," he said was happening inside my brain.

He asked mostly questions about my childhood but refused to answer any questions I had. While I gave my answers to his private questions, I would catch him tapping his pen against his pad, looking at his watch, and sighing while passing me tissues if I started to cry. I loathed Dr. Franke. He would also take phone calls during our sessions, and allow his secretary to interrupt us to give him phone messages.

In our last session, I told him I thought he was a fraud. He started listening then. I called him a quack, Dr. Cuckoo Nuts. In front of several staff members, I shouted at him to stop using patient's time to take calls from girlfriends to meet for lunch dates. "You have a newborn son!" I shouted. All information I'd learned from the constant interruptions. I suppose he thought I was too crazy to pay attention. For the rest of my stay, I never saw Dr. Franke again, not even in passing.

Dr. Kiminski came next: an older gentleman with a bad lip and worse allergies. He was always sniffing, snorting, or honking snot into his handkerchiefs, which were actually thin, cheap bandanas. I was fascinated by his mispronunciation of ordinary words; his hesitation before beginning a sentence made me nervous. After our second month, I declared him useless.

Dr. Kiminski added Borderline Personality disorder to my list of mental illnesses. He sat there in his frumpy grandpa sweater vest with a runny nose and told me that I simply had a problem with authority and adhering to rules. My "rebellious acts," were what got me into such a mess. My selfish need to live in a world without consequences. It was he who finally took me off of lithium, but in its place, he added two more.

After that, I went on a psychological strike. Nothing or no one could get me to speak. I'd muted myself from the inside, and no one could get me to break. They took away privilege after privilege in an effort to shake me – but nothing worked. Eventually, I also stopped eating and drinking. This only got me into a lot of trouble because if you start to act in ways that affect your physical health, the staff has no choice but to have their way. If a family member came to see a patient who was starved and dehydrated, there could be a lawsuit. Physical health was more important than mental health because of that very reason.

After being sedated with fluids and a feeding tube, the strike was over. They then passed me on to Dr. Ruger, where I got Generalized Anxiety Disorder and Panic Disorder with Agoraphobia added to my chart. He also added back Bipolar Disorder and put me back on Lithium, against my emphatic reservations. He put me on so much Lithium that my liver enzymes started to go haywire, and he had to switch me to something else. I can't even recall which drug it was at that time. But I do know that in it, I found no relief.

After making my way through the entire list of psychiatric providers at St. Vincent's, I was preparing to be transferred to another facility. I was moved to my own room with no other patients around me that I could see or even hear.

While I waited for transfer, I saw a counselor who was making the rounds in the temp unit, which appeared to only consist of me and one other. He was an old man, at least late seventies, and he kept an unlit tobacco pipe in his mouth, even when he spoke. His white-grey hair was always messy like he had just woken up, and he always wore the same brown suit with brown wingtip shoes. He kept a very serious tone and expression when he spoke. His name was

Dr. Weber, he told me, in a dialect I couldn't quite establish. Nonetheless, his first question is what caught my true attention.

"Drucilla, can you tell me – in your own words – why you are here?"

I watched him for signs of apathy, but found none. "Apparently, I have behavioral issues," I snapped.

"Yes, I read that," he said, sifting through my chart before closing it again and setting it to the side. He crossed his legs and rested his hands on his knee. "But what I'm asking is *why* do you think you ended up here at St. Vincent's?" His question disarmed my sarcastic guns, and they were fully loaded. I felt my defenses weaken. No one had ever asked me that. They had just told me why. He peered over his glasses with raised eyebrows, waiting for my answer.

"I lost my family. They're all gone," I said quietly. "And now I'm left with only ghosts." This time I didn't cry. I felt stoic and numb. A hopeless feeling hung around my neck like a thick, tightly wrapped scarf. The words just kept coming and coming until I had nothing left to say. He never interrupted me, not once. For at least ten or fifteen solid minutes, I babbled, gave life to every indiscretion I'd never been able to swallow and spoke of a grief I had, so far, not been able to comprehend. And when I was finished, he cleared his throat, and blinked quickly several times before speaking. "I see," he said. "Duality is a very clear issue at hand, Mrs. Myers. And that," he said, leaning forward to look more seriously at me, "will be your obstacle."

Dr. Weber took me on as a patient, and I ended up staying at St. Vincent's under his counsel for longer than I would like to admit. Soon into my treatment with him, I felt I could open up, and I began having longer, more in-depth conversations about what really bothered me. We'd gone through most of my childhood while Dr. Weber nodded and took notes. By the time I started full care, we were deep into my marriage with Duane.

One day, he asked me what it was that attracted me to Duane in the first place, and I couldn't even fake an answer. He asked me why I wanted so badly for the marriage to work. I answered honestly. I told him the pregnancy was what made us get married, and that my wanting to get away from my parents was what drove me the most. I still had hope then, I reminded him. "It was very short-lived optimism."

"Yes, I understand that," Dr. Weber said. But what I want to know is why you dated him in the first place. Did he have any qualities at first that you liked?"

I knew Dr. Weber wouldn't let it go, so I formed the best answer I could. "He was laid-back. Quiet. Meek."

"Would you say that those qualities were absent in your father? In Gerald?"

The question eluded me. "Yes."

"So your initial relationship was built on safety, not love."

"Yes."

"And what were your hopes for getting into this marriage?"

"Happiness. Peace, maybe," I said, laughing sarcastically. "Yeah, right."

"You do know those are the same thing, right?" he said. "Peace and happiness. People try to make them different, but they're actually the same. Happiness is, by definition, a state of peace."

I made a joke, asking if I could have some of whatever the hell he was smoking, but he didn't laugh. He hated it when I joked. "Your humor is a mask," he was fond of saying.

"You haven't known peace yet, Drucilla. When you've tasted it, you'll spend your entire life trying to get it back. Your body wants peace, your mind wants peace, your soul needs peace. Only then will you feel real, authentic joy."

One session after that, I was humbled but willing.

"How does Michael feel about Duane accepting him as his own but not Samantha?"

I was riddled with anxiety about the question. But as hard as it was to do, I admitted my mistake to him. "That was a lie. I made that up."

"What would drive you to make up such a lie?" He asked.

"To make Duane look like the piece of shit he was."

"And in what ways, in your opinion, is Duane a piece of shit? What was his biggest offense?"

I couldn't answer for several weeks. But with Dr. Weber, he always came back to those questions later. Every time I thought I'd come up with a reason, it would be crushed and replaced with a more professional, medical perspective.

Months later, Dr. Weber helped me to understand that I had hated Duane simply because he didn't love me and that I caused more harm than good to everyone trying to keep our marriage afloat, especially when he made it very clear that he was done.

Those were hard truths to swallow, but thanks to Haldol twice a day, I swallowed.

Doctor Weber was good at his job.

"And what were you doing, do you think, in your marriage with Jimmy?"

"I wanted to start over, like Duane."

"Do you view the deaths as punishment, Drucilla?"

"Yes I do."

"And who is the one that is doing the punishing?"

"I don't know. God, I guess."

"And was God punishing you, or them, when they died?"

"I don't know. Me, I guess; maybe both."

"And why would God want to punish you, Drucilla?"

"I don't know."

"Think."

"I said I don't know."

At my three-month mark, Dr. Weber asked me to write a letter to my mother. I refused at first, but as things typically went with Dr. Weber, I ended up having to write the damn letter anyway.

It was one of the hardest things I've ever done. Truth came out that I didn't know how I felt, and I instantly knew why Doctor Weber had insisted on the exercise.

Mother,

There are parts of me I didn't bury properly. I don't even know what's wrong with me anymore; it just seems pointless to even keep going. It always has. I'm not a corpse, yet still, I rot. Always dying, never dead.

I tried so hard, you know that, right? I tried so fucking hard.

I was so consumed in darkness that I couldn't see anymore. Somehow, I had forgotten that other people lost Samantha, too. Somehow, I forgot when Daddy died, that you lost your husband. I had forgotten that when Duane stepped up and took Michael in my absence that you lost him, too. I know why you were so broken after Mac, I know how you felt, because that's how I feel right now, Mother.

I should've been better to you, I should've been a better daughter. A better mother. A better wife. I'm sorry that your life was miserable and that it was cut so short. I'm sorry you had to suffer, I'm sorry for causing you suffering in ways that I am only now beginning to understand.

Way too late to count.

I'm crazy, sitting here writing a letter to no one. Mother, sometimes I can still smell you. Sometimes, I feel like you were right beside me, and then sometimes, I feel like you were never really here at all. Are you alive on the other side? Are you holding Samantha in one hand and Daddy's hand in the other while you sing praises to the Lord? It's hard to believe that's the case. It's hard to believe in anything anymore, for that matter. I don't know where you are, but I hope with all of my heart that you at least have peace now.

Wherever you are. Wherever you all are. If I could've traded places with you, Mother, I would have. I hope you know that, and I hope you know that you deserved better. You deserved life, not death. Your absence haunts me every moment of every day. I love you.

Love, Drucilla.

I gave Dr. Weber the letter, but he didn't address it until a few sessions later. "In the letter to your mother," he began, "You mention being consumed in darkness. Are you familiar with the term? Darkness?"

"Pretty sure I am," I smarted off. "It's all I've ever known." Dr. Weber got up, walked over to a bookcase in the far corner behind his desk, pulled out a standard English dictionary, walked over and handed it to me. "Look it up."

"Seriously? I just said I know what darkness is."

"Look it up," he said louder.

"Darkness: the partial or total absence of light."

"Alright, that makes sense, right? Easy enough. Now look up light."

I sighed in disgust at whatever this little game was. He knew I hated shit like that. It made me feel childish. I shuffled my way through the musty pages. "What does it say?" he asked.

"Light. One: The natural agent that stimulates sight and makes things visible."

"Okay. What else?"

"Two: an expression in someone's eyes indicating a particular emotion or mood."

"Keep going."

"Three: understanding of a problem or mystery; enlightenment."

"Perfect," he said, almost smiling. "Now, if we connected those definitions, then wouldn't it read that light is the natural understanding of a problem or mystery that stimulates sight and makes things visible?"

"It would seem so. Yes."

"So, could it be safe to assume that your being consumed in darkness stemmed from a lack of understanding? A lack of knowledge and reason and understanding? Of enlightenment? Your beliefs have been challenged, so you question the source of those beliefs. This is not uncommon. About ninety percent of my patients are suffering a spiritual crisis; they've developed a neurosis from the source of meaninglessness of life. And once you consider life meaningless; you'll soon lose your soul to the world, and then death won't matter. And a person's death should matter, Drucilla."

The conversation lived inside me for weeks, months; like an open, pulsating heart, bringing with it a kind of new perspective. But the truths I became aware of made me anxious and regretful – as aware now, and that made me worry and feel paranoid.

"You need to build your foundation," Dr. Weber emphasized. "You need to find your own truth."

He took me to a room across the hall, adjacent to his office one day and invited me inside. I went in and saw mahogany bookcases from floor to ceiling. There were more books than I thought one person could own, even a doctor. "You said you did some reading before, right? Out at the abandoned house?"

"The dead man's house," I corrected him.

"Right. The dead man's house. I was just curious if you had read or studied any sort of philosophy or psychology or religion?"

"Dr. Weber, I didn't retain much information back then. I tried, but I just couldn't understand."

"Well, here's your chance to save yourself. Find at least one truth you can truly believe in, and start there. Jung, Kant, Nietzche, Lao Tzu are all excellent recommendations. I feel it would do you well to study these. A great many minds have come before you with similar problems and questions; the good ones wrote about it."

In the corner of the room was a sitting chair and table; a gorgeous Tiffany lamp illuminated its stained glass shade across the entire room. It was dim, calm, and beautiful. "When you find something that makes you stir in here," he covered his heart with his hands. Start there." He smiled politely and backed slowly out of the room while I fumbled through his books.

"In the vast majority of my patients," he said quietly, "I sense an insecurity and unease that comes from a loss of faith. A loss of the quintessential requisites of personal religious experience… Alright, I'll leave you to it, then."

Over the course of the next year, I read my way through The Handbook of Psychological Change: The Black Books by Carl Gustav Jung. Most of his work I soaked up like a dry sponge and read multiple times. Man and His Symbols, Memories, Dreams, and Reflections, and then more plain books like A Therapist's View of Psychotherapy, and I even managed to make it through the DSM (Diagnostic and Statistical Manual of Mental Disorders). I read Psychology of the Unconscious, Aion, and The Secret of the Golden Flower.

When I became overwhelmed with information, I switched over to fiction, read a selection of novels, some first editions, and sat amazed at the tragedy of someone else's life. I read The Bell Jar, Girl Interrupted, and Catcher and the Rye. I read The Great Gatsby and cried for a fictional man who just wanted to be loved.

Dr. Weber emphatically expressed the importance of reading books by writers who had similar questions; who wrote of similar themes that I might relate to. I was to understand, first and foremost, that I was not alone; and that there were others who questioned what we are doing, and why. There are others who don't understand a God that allowed such worldly horrors such as death. Tragedy. The bitter taste of resentment mixed with fear, with no release valve. It just stays inside and swirls throughout my thoughts and keeps me tied to The Deaths. Keeps me stuck in disbelief, depleted of all hope, and struggling to make it through my days.

Reading was not only interesting, but it also provided a welcome reprieve from reality. I began to visit the library daily for a good portion of the day. I came to these philosophers, psychiatrists, and theologians for help. Dr. Weber mentioned that one of my main issues to be resolved was the fact that I'd taken The Deaths personally as if I'd been punished horribly for something I didn't do and, therefore, couldn't fix. This, he said, created my fear of the Punisher. And who was the Punisher? God? Satan? Surely not God, right? But even if the culprit had been Satan, why had God allowed him victory over me? Over my daughter? My parents? To me, at the bottom of my soul, I found little difference between the two entities.

When you experience death at a young age, or especially that of a child – it changes you. You'll question everything you have ever known, comb through every possibility trying to figure out where they've gone..and why. You'll take it personally, just like I did, and feel like you've been singled out. When you stop caring about what's left behind, like a lot of people do, they just don't quite seem to understand the magnitude of emptiness, how the memories sit like a heavy box on my chest, when I try to remember too much, I will find that I can no longer breathe the air around me.

It's easy to lose grip on reality when everything you've ever been taught keeps proving to be more of a lie. How can you prepare to battle the enemy if the enemy is always in control? What was I fighting for? I would say that most run. Some hide. Same as me. We struggle to do ordinary things under tortuous mindsets soaked in timeless, never-ending memories of the life we lived before we lost them. You leave people behind to try and hide, like I did with Mother and Michael, and that made me realize that if Samantha had been allowed to live, I most likely would have failed her, too.

In my lifetime, I struggled with being somewhat nihilistic with an emphasis on my fear of God, which created in me a fear of life itself. I was terrified by what was allowed to happen under such a loving, omnipotent Being with the all-seeing eye.

The fear had become debilitating enough for me that I saw no real point whatsoever in participating in the mundane tasks of everyday life: showering, laundry, eating or drinking. I saw no point in participating in what was only temporary distractions from the fact that nothing matters. You'll die anyway.

All my life, I had feared evil. I'd unconsciously run from it like it was something coming to devour me whole while I did nothing, powerless against it, while God watched and did no more than I. I found myself constantly looking over my shoulder, waiting for the next shoe to drop, just as my Mother had.

Chapter 16

"So, what are you studying now?" Dr. Weber asked me, pointing to the book in my lap.

"The Soul," I said, proudly. He smiled, pleased with my answer. In our last session, he went into great detail for me. He expressed his thoughts on the human soul, which is not subject to the laws of space or time. He made it clear to me that my madness was simply my soul suffering the life I was living, the life I had lived – not the things that happened to me.

"In this regard," he said. "You can still be saved." I'll never forget how seriously Dr. Weber spoke about the soul. Even more than when he spoke about death.

"Knowing about the soul and its mysteries, you can free yourself from the fascination which makes you suffer. But most people – most people do anything, no matter how absurd, to avoid facing their own souls. But if you can put in the work like we are doing here, and if you learn about yourself and eventually discover more or less who you are, you also learn about God and who He is. Religious civilization has proved hollow to a terrifying degree; it is all veneer. The inner man has remained untouched. His soul is out of key with his external beliefs. In his soul, man has not kept pace with external developments."

He shifted in his seat, crossed the opposite leg. He was gaining momentum, and I was waiting. "I'm convinced wholeheartedly," he continued, "that this is a conflict that lies among most people. I also believe it creates an internal struggle in all mankind, a soul death in full action that causes all sorts of horrible events. A man whose soul is dying is a very sick man. In turn, he loses himself. He has no truth of his own to stand on. A man with no truth becomes a man with no morals. Call him the Devil if you shall, but any soul in dissociation with the self will result in death."

***

On a muggy April afternoon, on the day of my 46th birthday, I sat alone in the courtyard reading Jung on Psychological Types when Gloria, the nurse in my unit, came out with a strange expression on her face. Gloria had known me since I arrived, and so I could see by her face that something was off.

"Drue," she said quietly. "You have a visitor, but there's no one on your list." My heart jumped around inside my chest.

"A visitor? Who is it?"

"A man. Gary. Gary Berryman."

Dr. Weber and I had discussed this scenario – or one similar – in several of our past sessions. He wanted to know how I would feel the next time I saw my father. My response? "I'll never see my father again."

I filled out the necessary forms to allow Gary a visitation, and the nurse brought him over to the visitor's center where I sat, waiting, for what… I didn't know. I was surprised he was alone; my first thought was that something had happened to June, but then again, I wouldn't necessarily have been on their call list after our last interaction.

I was sitting on one of the two chairs when he walked in. He looked exactly the same as the last time I had seen him. He had his cap cupped in his hands as he inched slowly toward me like he was paying respects to my corpse in a casket.

Neither of us knew how to act, what to feel. What to say. There was an air of shame looming between us, like a fog. The atmosphere became almost unbreathable.

"Thank you so much for seeing me, Drue. I'm so sorry for the sudden visit. I hope you're doing okay." In my mind, I had rehearsed this scene over and over, despite telling Dr. Weber that I was certain I would never see him again, that he had been done with me before I was even born.

"Lots of parents regret things they do in their youth. Or in pain," the doctor had said.

"Not Gary," I'd assured him.

But then, all of a sudden, there he was.

"Of course," I said, responding to Gary after a moment of silence, suddenly aware and embarrassed by my beige nuthouse patient scrubs. "How are you? How's June?"

"June? June's great. Yeah, everything is good; it's just that lately, I've really been feeling like I needed to come and talk to you. See you face to face; clear the air."

I said nothing, and we both sat there in silence for several, long moments.

"I hope you don't hold anything against me for getting you some help that day. I panicked. June panicked. I didn't know what else to do." He started to cry. He wiped his tears with his fist and kept talking. "I keep replaying everything in my head over and over, trying to think of what I could have or should have done differently. But I was scared. I was scared for you. I'm a coward, and I always have been," he said, with tears streaming down both cheeks. "I woke up this morning knowing it was your birthday and you were alone because of me, and I couldn't take it anymore. I knew if I didn't see you face to face and tell you that I'm sorry, I would never sleep again. I had to come here and look you in the eyes and tell you that."

As he spoke, my heart bled at every seam. Deep within my chest, a tension released. I could breathe. It was as if the blood had seeped down into my soul and given a nourishing drink to a long-traveled companion who – as Dr. Weber put it – had dried up like an earthworm on pavement.

But until that day, I don't think I'd ever felt that part of my soul. Only pain had come out before, but now there was a sensation of love where brokenness used to be, where abandonment had lived inside and haunted me.

In my next few sessions, Dr. Weber helped me to understand that Gary's getting help for me was an act of love, just like any father would have done, and that his visit to apologize for any wrongdoing was a humble, sincere act of love. Love is a sacrifice, Dr. Weber was fond of saying. "Real, authentic love is a sacrifice, Drucilla. And an experience of God also requires a sacrifice."

"Why does an experience of God require a sacrifice?" I asked.

"Good question. Very astute. Allow me to elaborate.

"It's been my experience that only those who hit rock bottom have any chance to have an act of God displayed or any sort of spiritual experience. If you are one who has repressed or repented too much – if you have not hit rock bottom fully human and flawed, it could prevent you from ever experiencing the true gift of Divine grace. But, through my studies of early Christian writings, I have gained a deep and undeniable impression of how dreadfully serious an experience of God is."

He continued this lesson the following week.

"It does not seem to fit God's purpose to exempt man from conflict and hence from evil. Without error and sin, there is no experience of grace – that is – no union of god and man. The point of this is that only in darkness can you see the light. If you believe in a life without suffering and conflict, you are robbing yourself of reality and the workings of the soul of our universe. You will stumble hard during your conflicts, become bitter that you have them, and then blame God and become a lost, bitter soul. A man who dies long before his physical death. Then, in your dark slumber, you'll curse God for all you've done to yourself. You'll become bitter instead of understanding that conflict is necessary for one to grow and, most importantly, that the conflict was, in fact, a product of his own making, or possibly someone else's, because we all have the gift of free will."

I sat, stunned, unable to speak.

"So then, does it make sense to you, Drucilla, that in order to experience the light of God, one must experience darkness and suffering?"

"It does now."

"And so it is," he smiled. "Mistakes arise from sinning, and mistakes are – after all – the very foundations of truth. If man does not know what a thing is, at least he will know what it is not. If we should continually repent and repress all sinful behavior, one must repress a great deal of natural human emotion. Habitual repression of the emotions is dangerous. It can even endanger life. A person would do well to learn this before reaching old age."

I thought of Mother and Daddy; both dead before their time, and I wondered to myself if they had fallen victim to repression's deadly knife. I thought of all the times I saw Mother smile, laugh and host those brunches even though she'd been crying earlier that morning or just the night before.

I thought of Daddy in his Sunday suit, passing the offering plate down rows of baptists, holding secret affairs in a chest that was unable to bear the weight of secrecy or of an unlived life. "Shame is a soul-eating emotion," Dr. Weber always said. And I suppose he was right about that.

But Samantha… there was no repression there. There had been nothing; she never even had a chance. My therapy sessions had gotten me no closer to understanding that specific loss, the loss of a child, and how this life could be livable after having experienced it. When I presented the question to Dr. Weber, I was hesitant and nervous about his reply. I was scared that if he couldn't form a suitable answer, that it might keep me at St. Vincent's forever.

The question had remained unanswered for me by pastors, priests, books, and people alike. The question, I believe, plagued people privately, even if they have never experienced it: chances are they know someone who has. The thought is enough to make a man put his faith in almost anything that stands a chance of saving him from such horror. That conversation between Dr. Weber and I lives, to this day, in my mind like it was burned into my soul by God Himself. His words ran like a vital electricity through my veins.

"What is the reason for the death of a child?" He had a curious look on his face. I could tell he was waiting for this challenge, for this question to be addressed.

"The birth of a human is pregnant with meaning; why not death?" he said, crossing his legs.

"So you think Samantha's death is meaningful?"

"It certainly seems so, doesn't it? Seems to me that Samantha's death was extremely meaningful. The meaning is the gold in the dark, Drucilla. The light. Was Christ not God's child? The decisive question here is whether we are related to something infinite or not. One does not become enlightened by imagining figures of light but by making the darkness conscious. What one can make conscious and face directly and heal as an adult frees one from an unconscious bondage to the past."

It took months of further discussion coupled with my own self-analysis to come to the understanding that the only meaning that can come from the birth and death of a child is the experience of the most cosmic depths of love. There is knowledge and wisdom that come from such experiences, should you seek it. And that wisdom is of primal importance and should never be forgotten if you wish to make it on this earth, and that is that God enters through the wound.

And that's when it struck me: if bad things are necessary to understand anything good, then is "evil" a demonic force or a necessary one?

It takes sadness to know happiness, noise to appreciate silence, and absence to appreciate presence. That is what makes life so confusing and paradoxical. It takes chaos to value stillness, clouds to appreciate the sun, and death to appreciate life. This I came to understand as the paradox of both love and life, as well as the ambiguity of God.

Moments become memories, and people, unfortunately, become painful lessons, all because a certain level of darkness is needed in order to see the stars.

I finally began to understand God and the workings of universal law. And that which you understand, you don't fear.

***

The next day, I saw a cardinal in the courtyard. It came right up close; I held my breath and remained still so I wouldn't scare it off. It looked at me, hopped two steps closer to me, turned its head to the side and looked again. Then suddenly, there was her red flash flying and fluttering back out into the wild.

At that exact moment, I knew it was time to go home.

Chapter 17

I left St. Vincent's on a golden Autumn afternoon in September. Gary had planned to pick me up, but I told him I'd rather walk. What I didn't tell him was that I wanted to be alone when I was released back into reality in case my reception was too emotional or triggering. It was hard to believe three years had passed since the accident; it was hard to believe that it had been three years since I'd seen the house on Seminary Street: the scene of all real and subconscious crimes.

It was Gary and June who cleaned the house for me; well, them and the professional crew they had to eventually hire. A lot of the sheetrock had to be replaced, and the entire inside needed to be sanded, scraped, and repainted. June asked me privately if I'd like them to donate the clothes from the walls or any furniture or other memories. I told her *no*, that I wanted no reminders of my illness or the years leading up to it outside the house. But most of all, I didn't want to bump into someone at the grocery store wearing my mother's blouse. I was nervous to see the house again, but at least I knew it wouldn't be the same as the day I left it.

On my walk home, I passed by Burgess High. The football players were on the field training. On the side by the bleachers, cheerleaders laughed and yelled and practiced their routine. I thought of my twirling days, the thrill of Friday night lights and the adrenaline of school spirit in full swing. Sadly, everything after my twirling years is tied to a memory with Duane that I'd rather not remember at all. Most people would probably kill to relive their old high school days. I, on the other hand, would rather die.

I passed the bank where Daddy kissed the lady in my fever-ridden haze, cursing our relationship and any chance of ever reconciling our differences while he was still alive. I felt a great sorrow for him now: as an adult, I understand what unhappiness feels like, and I also understand the desperate acts to feel alive again.

When I walked past the Brookstone Apartments, I recalled how proud Daddy had been to get the bid and how he beamed with pride anytime we passed by them on our way to church each Sunday. I felt sad that his life was cut short like rest and that he never got to truly be who he was on the inside. It gave me a sense of his inherited pride to see what he had built; and helped me to heal anything he had ever unknowingly dismantled.

I was flabbergasted when I passed by the Hi-way 77 Motel – which was now a Holiday Inn Express. Nothing of the former foundation remained: it was now a two-story, brick hotel with cars buzzing around its giant parking lot that stretched over where the old graveyard used to be for discarded motel furniture from Don and Lorraine. The only recognizable feature on the entire property was the stone fountain in the center of the courtyard. Had it not been for that fountain, I might have questioned if the motel had ever really been there at all as if I'd created it in my mind to escape reality. But then, across the street, was the gas station where I ate my deli burritos and stale chicken strips, scraps from the day, like a stray dog.

I thought about Jimmy. I'd already decided years prior that all I had done to him was wrong, and I prayed and hoped that he found what he was looking for. I hope he had a loving, beautiful wife with a dozen kids and dogs. I hoped he found love, and most of all, I hoped he never remembered the details of our sad, unusual relationship.

When I made it downtown, I walked past the courthouse and the DMV, and from there, I could see the green and white striped canopies of Dobson's Floral. I thought of Eloise and Patrick, and wondered if they were even still around. I was reminded, suddenly, of how awful I'd treated Eloise at the end: unanswered doorbell rings, rotted casseroles made with love, flowers I left on the porch, unaccepted. I always hoped she knew it had nothing to do with her; I hoped she understood that I just… couldn't.

Our old neighborhood was the same as it always had been: big old oak trees and perfectly manicured lawns and beautiful, historic homes. My entire body shook when I passed by the corner of Seminary and Rosebud, and when I caught sight of my house, I was almost completely panicked. But then, when I saw it, all of my panic vanished into thin air. It was as if I had traveled back in time.

While at St. Vincent's, Gary had promised he and June would clean up the house; what he didn't tell me was that he would paint, mow, edge, and revamp the entire place. He'd brought the entire property back to its regular, pristine glory. It looked like it did the day we moved in. Mother's roses, now pruned back instead of being wildly overgrown, stood like holograms of what used to be.

My hands shook while I fumbled with the keys, finally hearing the relieving thud of the deadbolt. Terrified of what I might see or smell, I pushed the door open and back into the pain. But instead of Mother's Gardenia potpourri, I smelled only the clean smell of layers of fresh white paint. Like I'd requested, everything familiar was gone.

The hardwood floors had been cleaned and polished. The windows, instead of being covered in quilts of dread, were now full of sunshine and autumn foliage of the trees in the yard. The house seemed to be lit up with an almost ethereal glow. It made me smile. I found it peculiar and unbelievable how both Daddy, and my father's hands had a part in the construction of this one house. It was a testament to how the workings of the universe are full of the love and magic I had always hoped for in life.

All three bedrooms were painted a soft beige and showed no signs of the crazy person who once resided there. The house was completely empty, just as I'd wanted. I walked into the kitchen, which was painted and polished clean as new, just like the rest of the house. The sun lit up Mother's Spanish tile floor and gave the room a soft, golden hue. I walked out the back door and looked inside the garage, which was empty, aside from my Jeep. The car was clean and waxed, and Gary had flushed and changed all fluids and put in a new battery. She started on the first try and purred like a kitten. I backed out of the driveway for the last time and drove to Gary's house in Shelbyville.

I hired Charlene from Burgess Reality to sell the house on Seminary Street. My time there was complete. Afterwards, I stopped for a burger at McDonald's and drove out to the dead man's house. There, inside the fenceline of that old familiar house, were absolutely no differences whatsoever from the day I'd left it with officers at my side. I walked over to the back of the house and took down all of the numbers and letters from the old, rusty water meter. I took it up to city hall and found out the address of the house, which sat on Red Oak Road, as well as the name and contact information of the current owners.

With Mother's "death money," which Dr. Weber corrected to "life insurance," I purchased the dead man's house and the eight acres it sat on for next to nothing and sat across from someone at the closing, who had once tried to have me arrested for squatting. The lady was old, rigid, and seemed to be thankful to have finally sold that property. I keep her face in my mind and remember that we all have homes we once loved, where memories live in the bones of the foundation but nonetheless can't keep holding onto anymore.

I bought a double-wide manufactured home and had its foundation perched on a hill on the east end of the property, overlooking the dead man's house and a large stretch of Red Oak Road and the cow pastures that surrounded it. Most people would have probably had that old house torn down, but I kept it there in its original state to remind me of the importance of death and destruction. It stands for me as a monument of my death on earth. My new house on the hill is a symbol of rebirth. The house on Seminary Street is, in this sentimental context, a symbol of my transformation between the two.

While the land was prepared for my new home, I lived with Gary and June. It was the best time of my life. Never had I felt so welcome and loved. I felt that I had finally found the other half of my family, and over time came to realize that I was much more like my father than I thought. We played spades and made margaritas; we played music loud and sang along. We laughed at funny movies, classics that he wanted me to see. We ate at restaurants and celebrated holidays, and talked about life in depths I hadn't before. And it was so refreshing to have someone listen to me without judgment and who took the time to understand how one can go crazy when the light goes out, and sometimes you need someone who really knows the depths to get your flame back up and strong again.

For my housewarming gift, once it was time to move home, Gary gifted me the Indian painting I'd stared at for hours in his living room. It was a family heirloom; the man in the painting was my thrice great grandfather. Before my illness, I barely had a family, and now I had an heirloom to pass on to my son one day. Where there once was profound grief, there was now profound love.

After three grueling years and a new chance at life, I walked into Dobson's Floral and prayed I would see Eloise. The smell of the flowers punched me right in the heart. Fortunately, I found her behind the counter with a cigarette hanging between her lips and an armful of autumn mums. When she saw me, time seemed to stop. We hugged until we cried, and honestly, it was one of the better feelings of my life.

Patrick walked up from the back cooler and smiled when he saw me. "Good to see you, Drue. We thought you had died or something."

"Patrick! Not everything needs to be discussed," she said through clenched, embarrassed teeth.

"It's okay," I laughed. "I almost did."

"She's missed you," he added with sincerity.

We spent a good hour or so catching up, and in the meantime, I helped her fill her daily orders. "So," I asked. "Are you looking for any help?" She peered at me over her glasses.

"Are you kidding me? Every girl I've hired since you has made more goddamn mistakes than deliveries."

Being back at work made me feel like a new person. Every day, I was reminded how far I'd come since the last time I drove that loud, pink van. On my way home in the evenings, I put the top down and played the stereo up high, enjoying every mile out to the dead man's house, my new and final home, my house on Red Oak Road. There, I reveled in my solitude. I read books and watched movies and took long walks and planted flowers and fed birds and wrote this book during my evening sunset meditations.

I took long baths and soaked myself wrinkled every day. I made good health a priority and began growing my own vegetables. After a while, I stopped eating meat and became a vegetarian altogether, self-sustained for a good portion of each year. I spent hours planting, picking, canning, and storing to have all I needed. I usually had enough to feed both me, Gary, and June, but it was a common joke between us that no one but me really wanted to be vegan.

One morning I had a delivery to Bob at the funeral home, plants for him, not a service. Two snake plants and the biggest ivy I'd ever seen came through our doors. I almost dropped it twice on the way in since I always refused to make two trips if I could help it. The sentiments on the cards were all congratulatory: "Congratulations on your retirement," "Happy Retirement!" and "You will be missed, take it easy!"

It was strange delivering to the front entrance. The green bulb was burning, which meant there was a body inside. I rang the bell and waited. Within moments, Bob came strolling down that long, creepy hallway, snapping off gloves into the trash before opening the door. "Well, what a surprise!" he said happily. "Here, let me help you with those, dear."

"Congrats on your retirement, Bob. I would've thought you were too young for that," I joked.

He laughed. "Yeah, it came faster than I expected. I never even learned how to golf!" he laughed.

"Well, I bet you'll be glad to be away from all of this death and sadness all the time," I said.

Bob sat the ivy on the sill. "To tell you the truth, I'm actually going to miss it," he said somberly. "I'm gonna miss helping people who struggle with these things we do here and helping them to say goodbye on their darkest day. They are almost all the same. Almost. Most people don't understand that what's left behind here is just the vessel."

"Vessel?"

"The body," he said, turning to face me. It's just the vessel that holds the spirit." He turned back to untangle the plant's strings. "Hey," he added. "Would you like to come have dinner with Maureen and I? Say Friday night, seven-ish?"

Still taking in his vessel speech, I stammered and rushed my answer. "Uh, ok sure. Sounds great."

"Perfect," he said. "Maureen will be so pleased!"

After work that afternoon, Eloise came by to have coffee and complained about Patrick not having a normal social life, a constant concern.

"He just sits there watching television like a GD geriatric!" After listening to Patrick's daily routines and habits, I finally interrupted her and told her about the dinner invitation that I was already regretting accepting.

"Go," she said, blowing steam from her coffee. "You need to meet new people."

"They aren't exactly 'new' people, Eloise. Bob has embalmed my whole family," I sneered.

"Shut up," she laughed. "You know what I mean, asshole. They're seriously great people," she added. "I've known them for years, being in this business. They lost a kid, too; did you know that?"

What the hell, I thought. "No, I didn't."

"Yup. Horrible, awful thing it was. Must've been at least twenty or more years ago. Overdose. Heroin, I think."

"Jesus," I said, truly shocked.

"She definitely had a monkey on her back," she continued. "Several stints in rehab, jail, the works. Wasn't but nineteen or twenty when it happened. Awful. Maureen was a mess, I remember. Bob, too, but Maureen had a full-blown nervous breakdown. Hospital and all." She looked at me. "You know how it goes."

She lit another cigarette. "Patrick needs a girlfriend, that's what he needs."

Later in the night, when I was alone again, curiosity overthrew me. I drove down Old Sandbanks Road and parked by an unknown family. I grabbed the flashlight I kept in the glove box and searched and searched for hours through the wet grass until I found it.

Brenda Grace Harold

August 4, 1960 - April 17, 1981

There was an oval-shaped photo of her below her name, a school portrait of a pretty blonde with a forced smile and chaos in her eyes. On the back of her stone was an etching of the night sky, a galaxy, with letters above it in laser-cut cursive.

"Your star shines brightly upon us in the darkest of hours."

Mom and Dad

Suddenly awake, I kept walking. I don't know why. I read the names and dates on every stone I passed, considered their ages, family trees, number of deaths. There were numerous families with over twenty or more plots apiece, some dating back to the 1800's. Some people I knew, most I didn't. I came across the Jameson girl I delivered for on my first day working for Eloise. Her grave was still covered in pink flowers and sentiments. A stuffed pink bunny lay on its side, wet and lonely from the rainy night. I sat it upright against a vase to keep it from falling over again and made my way down the path to the south side to continue my mindless searching.

I found the graves of Jimmy's grandparents and aunts, uncles, and cousins I never knew. I saw a new grave, a mountain of red dirt and dying flowers, still too fresh to look peaceful. I was out there for hours without stopping, doing nothing more than realizing just how common death really is; and thinking about people out there who are just like me who were also left behind to pick up the pieces of a life left unfinished. I counted one hundred eighty-four graves for infants before I stopped, and that was only halfway through the north side.

Ordinarily I would have gone over to see my own family, only this time I didn't. For the first time in my life I didn't feel that unrelenting need to read their names and wallow in my own self-pity. I was starting to feel different, and I knew it that night. I drove home with the windows down and the radio off; the wind and the bright blue moonlight my only company.

Chapter 18

When Friday came, I was nervous but excited for my dinner with Bob and Maureen.

When I made that day's funeral deliveries, he was there smiling. "See you tonight, right?"

I arrived at their house right on time, even though it was farther away than I expected. When I was a kid, they lived in the brick house behind the funeral parlor that had matching brickwork. But now they live outside of town down Triggerfish Road, which seemed inconvenient. When I mentioned it to Eloise that day at work, she said, "No one lives in that house anymore. That's where it happened. Been abandoned since the eighties."

The thought made me uneasy; heavy-hearted; vulnerable again to the sting of sudden death; the scars it leaves on your heart.

For speculative reasons about the home of an undertaker, I pictured their home to be something out of a Stephen King novel, but when I pulled up to their quaint-but-spectacular cottage-style home on Triggerfish, my tensions eased.

The yard was nothing but flora; every inch was beautifully covered. I felt like Judy Garland on the yellow brick road coming up the sidewalk. Everywhere I looked, something new was growing;

the air smelled like the flower fridge at work. I had never seen such beauty in my life. And Maureen wasn't even in the garden club. I guess some people are just as happy going unnoticed. Bob answered the door before I could knock, wearing a red Hawaiian-style shirt with big yellow flowers. He had a cup towel draped over his shoulder and a beaming smile on his face. Without his funeral suits, he was damn near unrecognizable.

"Drue! So glad you came!" he said, coming in for a hug. The smell of Italian food; basil; filled the air behind him. "Maureen made you her famous bolognese," he said, leading me through the living room toward the thickening kitchen smells. "Been in her family for generations." The inside of the house was as quaint and cozy as the outside; built-in shelves covered the walls and were filled with ceramics and snow globes and pottery and all sorts of things, like an old antique store.

The television was on but muted, and Dan Rather was speaking seriously to us about Desert Storm with his plastic hair but no voice. Explosions and tanks in dirt moved through the picture block beside his face. Maureen met us at the double swinging doors that led inside the kitchen, drying her hands on a pale pink, old-lady apron with a ruffled hemline. "Oh my 'sakes! Drue, I am so very happy to see you!" she said, as sweetly as always. She looked the same as always, floral blouse; polyester pants; tan nurse shoes. She led me to the immaculately set table and seated me at the head like a king. While Maureen scooped a heaping serving of spaghetti onto my plate, I broke the awkward silence by asking Bob what he was planning on doing with his time now that he'd retired.

"Well, I suppose," he said, wiping his mouth, "that Maureen and I will do some traveling. Running the parlor hasn't exactly offered us a lot of freedom."

"I'd love to see the East Coast," Maureen interjected. "I would really like to go and see the whales in Maine."

"That's first on our list," he said, smiling at her and patting her hand, which I had just realized was shaking.

"I've got a hobby or two that I'm interested in also," he said, changing the subject, "a few things to keep me busy. After dinner, I'll show you what I'm most interested in. Maureen, honey? Ready for pie?"

While we ate apple pie with caramel sauce, Maureen talked about her time growing up on a farm in northern Indiana until she met Bob on a random trip to the Schwartz Theater in Indianapolis. As she talked about her days milking cows and gathering eggs and feeding livestock, I found my mind drifting; wandering around the room searching for signs of grief. Or Brenda. I found it only when I excused myself to the restroom down the hall and saw a poster of a galaxy tacked on the wall opposite the bathroom door, the same one etched on Brenda's headstone. There was a red tack on one of the stars. Beside the poster was a gold-framed picture – a candid 4x6 shot of Brenda standing on a beach in a bright orange poncho, a stormy sky and dark sea in the background.

Back in the kitchen, Bob was polishing a giant silver telescope with a white cloth. Then he attached it to the tripod sitting on the floor beside him. He folded the legs and picked it up. "Come outside with me, Drue. It's a clear night, perfect for seeing the stars."

The backyard was just as brilliant and full of nature as the front. The smell of honeysuckle blew through the wind. From the pergola where we stood, I could hear Maureen washing dishes while Bob set up the tripod and focused and refocused its gigantic lens.

"Okay, okay. Here, I've got it," he said. "Look."

Through the lens, I saw a star, perfect and celestial; fiery and alive; magnificent in its bright, blazing glory. "That's my daughter," he said quietly. I held my breath, still looking at her, holding my breath and not knowing what to do or say next. It was me who broke the silence. I pulled away from the telescope.

"Your daughter?" I asked in a surprised manner as if I hadn't scoured the cemetery grounds like the FBI looking for her grave in the middle of the night.

"Yup," he said, sighing, crouching to sit on one of the wrought-iron patio chairs. "She died in '81," he said. I walked over and sat down in the chair opposite him.

"I'm so sorry; I had no idea," I lied.

"Most people don't anymore; it was a long time ago," he said. "Funny how something that happened so long ago can still feel like yesterday, you know?"

"I do know," I said. "Yes."

I sat quietly, hoping he would keep talking, which he did.

"Her name was Brenda, after Maureen's late sister. A spitfire, she was." He leaned back in the chair, lightly patting his knee, thinking from painful memories. "Really something special."

He crossed his legs, fiddled with the buttons of his shirt. "But she got mixed up in the wrong crowd; started using drugs. She'd stay gone for weeks or even months at a time; then, she'd pop up out of the blue, needing money or a quick place to crash; and then…"

Bob stopped. Swallowed a lump in his throat. Took a minute to continue.

"Then she started using heroin," he said. "And we never got her back. Died of an overdose on our bathroom floor."

"Jesus Christ, Bob; I'm so sorry," I said, meaning it.

He sighed a little, looked over at me and smiled. "Nothing to be sorry about, dear. All part of life."

We were quiet for several moments before I blurted out what I wanted to say.

Then he stood up. "Stay here, I'll be right back."

While he was gone, I tried to figure out how he landed on that star being his daughter and just what, exactly, a spiritualist was. And as I sat there alone, looking up at the black, velvet sky, I was taken aback by the brilliance of the stars. When I looked through the telescope again, I saw Brenda shining in all her glory.

"Bob, what did you mean when you said that that star is Brenda?"

He smiled. "That's where I think she is; that's where I think we go," he said. "Up in God's sky, shining for eternity."

"That's an interesting theory," I said, baffled.

"Trust me," he said. "I've seen enough death to know the energy in a dead person's spirit is indeed gone. Only energy doesn't just disappear; it's transformed. And I believe that transformation is cosmic. Pure, godly, magic."

He thumped his cigarette in the damp grass.

"Death is nothing," he said. "It's life that's hard. An old wise man once said that real life is always tragic, and those who don't know this have never lived." He lit another cigarette.

"In my business, I've seen the many ways that death gets to people. Anger, guilt, confusion. Fear. Same things Maureen and I felt when we lost Brenda. Same things I felt when my parents died, when Kennedy was shot, when wars broke out and worlds collided; when diseases ran rampant and people starved to their last breath. For most people: that's where they stay. But you, I think you're a little different; like me," he said through a pleasant grin.

"Me, different? Why? How?" I asked, confused.

"I remember you very clearly the day your daughter died. You were so young, so broken. So lost. You reminded me a little of Brenda, but you had the same look on your face as Maureen: that shattered, heartsick mother look, the one that never really goes away but changes with time."

I sat godsmacked; hanging on every word.

"But you, Drue," he continued. "You fought back. Faced death straight on; a battle of death and love. You stared it straight in the face. When you did Patsy's makeup before her viewing, I saw you turn that fear into strength and that strength into love. And when I see that, that's when I see the work of God."

"Bob, can I ask you something else?" I said, a thousand pounds lighter. "Where did you learn that? About the souls of stars?"

He smiled at me as if he was happy I'd asked the question. "I've learned a little here and a little there over the years, but I will tell you this: there is a point where astronomy collides with physics and universal law. The birth and death of a star; a supernova; begins a new life. Those points where everything merges into a single, unexplainable truth – that's when I know God is alive and well inside the mystical realm of ancient spirituality. Unscathed by the shame we've brought upon his sacrifice; his love; to worship a man of integrity instead of embodying Him. His strength, diligence, and independence; not just in his death, but in his life. We worship the dead savior on the cross instead of the one who walked this earth with a mission to save souls at any cost; souls humans had long forgotten about or given up on."

From the computer I bought for myself, I found out, in the end, that Bob had been exactly right.

Article after article proved scientifically that we are all, in fact, made of stars. When stars get to the end of their lives, they begin to enlarge and throw off their outer layers. If a star is heavy enough, it will explode in a supernova. The particles that make up our bodies have existed for billions of years, and will continue for many more. Cosmic dust created our bones, and cosmic light make up our soul. Together, they form the human experience as we know it. It created life.

I bought myself a telescope and took an astronomy class online that winter. Every night, I look at the bright diamond souls of my ancestors. And yours.

The following Monday, back at work, I made my funeral home deliveries for the morning. I rang the bell, and a strange-looking man with thick glasses and balding red hair answered, wearing a dark suit like Bob. "Flower delivery," I said.

"Oh, uh, thanks. I'll be right out," he said. It was my first trip to that funeral home where I didn't see anyone I knew, that I didn't gag on memories of the past, and that felt a hell of a lot like freedom to me.

All was well when things began to come together into my truth. Before it, I had nothing solid to cling to, nothing worthwhile to believe in. I continue to be grateful for Dr. Weber's keen, psychological observations that saved me from my private, nihilistic death.

I'd created for myself my own foundation of truth, my own foundation of life. I was, for the first time in my life, somewhat happy. There was still one of my own demons I could never tame, no matter how hard or how little I'd allowed myself to try. I couldn't, for a million different reasons, explain myself to Michael. I could never get him to love me; could never make him understand how much I loved him, no matter what my actions might have shown.

That was when I decided to put my journaling together and write this book. I'd sent several letters from St. Vincent's to Duane's address, hoping one would make its way to Michael. If one did, I hardly think it would've meant no more than a sheet of ramblings from an insane person. With the book, though, I could write it for him as a gift, my story about my own experiences in my own words. Maybe I could save him, or at least try to save him from learning about life the hard way, like I did. Maybe, somehow, I could write away his pain, and mine.

I wrote feverishly and consistently until it was complete, until I had said all I needed to say. In that book, I gave him everything I had, hoping to make up for the things I never did.

I found his address online. He was living on Morton Street in the city if the address was correct. I tied a thin, blue ribbon around the manuscript and slipped it carefully inside a large manilla envelope, terrified of what might come of it, whose hands it may fall into, or the possibility that I may only be making things worse.

Months went by, almost a year, before I received a response. I'd all but given up when, one day, I saw the mailman's truck stir up the dirt on Red Oak Road to deliver a certified letter from Morton Street, in Indianapolis. The letter shook in my hands, and I cried at his blue, masculine penmanship. No matter what the contents of the letter were, I could at least know that he'd received the paper version of my heart. I could never explain otherwise.

I watched Michael's silver pickup truck make its way down Red Oak Road; my heart was banging around inside my chest. From behind the drapes, I tried to take deep breaths to calm myself as I watched him pull up by the dead man's house and stop for several long moments before coming up the hill into my driveway and parking beside the Jeep.

"I can't believe you're still driving that old thing," he said, smiling, walking up to greet me on the lawn.

"Hard to let go of," I said. He nodded, walked over, and gave me a hug. Not just any hug, but the kind that is years in waiting, lying dormant for that one perfect moment to come along. The kind that makes you both stand there and cry. Remember. Forget.

I'd been trying to go home my whole life, and there he stood in front of me, now a full-grown man with a thick beard and graying hair. But it didn't matter how much he'd changed or grown. I would know him blind.

I began an apology. The words were painful, like gravel in my throat. He squeezed my hand and asked me to stop. "It's okay,

Mom. You can relax now. Everything is okay. I forgave you long ago."

I thanked him, hugged him again. He looked back over his shoulder. "So that's the dead man's house?"

My heart stopped at the words. Skipped several beats before starting up again. "Yes."

"Can I see it?" I was surprised at his interest in the house. Not even Gary or June had ever asked to see it.

"Sure. Of course."

We walked down the hill and chatted about the land and made small talk about the weather. Standing on the porch, I repeated parts of the dead man's story to him, watching him actually paying attention to my words, taking in what remained.

"That the stump?" he asked, pointing to the dead man's tree, surrounded by monkey grass and yellow daffodils I'd planted the year I bought it. Michael kept his hands in his pockets, walking around slowly. Listened. "Can I see inside?"

"Of course," I walked over to the door, did the old lift-and-bump that was necessary to open that old, weathered door. The musty smell of age and time filled my nose and throat. It was nothing short of an abandoned disaster area, with broken windows and boards falling in; a caved roof, now in the back bedroom. Several of my old blankets and sweaters were still strewn about in my corner. Michael pushed through debris with the toe of his shoe.

"So, this is where you lived?" he asked me. "After Papa died and you disappeared, you lived here?" He just couldn't seem to fathom it.

"Why are you so surprised?" I asked him.

"It's just so… awful," he said. "I guess I just assumed you lived a normal life away from us."

I noticed the comforter from the motel, the one with the sunflowers molded and the one with the filth. The flowers brought me right back to that old motel, making that sunflower bed and breathing thick, bleach-filled air.

"No," I scoffed. "I never lived normally," I said. "Ever."

I haven't forgotten those years; the years of my lost and broken soul. Their memory remains strong to remind me of where I've been and, where I want to go, who I want to be. I might not have found out who I was back then, but I certainly figured out who I was not, and that's pretty much the same thing.

"Come up to the house. I made you some dinner," I said. "And I have something for you."

We ate fresh cheese, spaghetti squash and eggplant stew, and a fresh blackberry cobbler from scratch. He told me all about his life in the city, his job; and I could tell by the way he spoke, by his mannerisms and choice of words, that he was nothing at all like me. I hadn't ruined him after all; I hadn't cursed his life with my own. He was a happy, solid, well-rounded person, and the only hand I had in that was the fact that I stayed away. I didn't leave Michael because I didn't love him; I had left him because I did.

Inside a deep valley in my heart reserved only for holy matters, I felt a great deal of gratitude for my parents, and even Duane, for saving him from me. For giving him a chance – a foundation.

And finally, after years and years of torture, I started to be able to forgive myself; and when I did, it helped me to forgive others, too. Inside all of that forgiveness, I understood grace and thus felt the polarity of the true essence of God.

Ashes to ashes; dust to dust. To be a star, one must burn.

Just before Michael was leaving, I went to my bureau and opened the top drawer. I pulled out the black velvet jewelry bag and clutched it one last time. I held the bag out and he took it, slowly, cautiously, as if it were a bomb.

"These are your Nana's," I said, emptying the contents into his palm. "I wore these the day I married your father. I know you'll want to marry yourself one day, and I wanted you to have these. Nana would've wanted that, too." He smiled at me in sweet bewilderment. And just for a moment, he looked like a child again.

***

The day Michael and Gary met was a day I'll never forget. Those moments are branded across my very soul. The smiles; the handshake; the hug. The generations. Lost years finally found again and given light.

Michael had already gotten Duane's interest in old cars, so he and Gary shared that same love. Before I knew it, Gary had purchased a black '62 Mustang, and they work on it when they can. I have a photo on my mantle of the two of them smiling, arms around each other's shoulders, the Mustang shining like onyx in the background. It was a beautiful, unexpected gift. Their bond renewed my hope in what life can really be.

At the cemetery one day, changing the flowers, I stood staring at Samantha's headstone reading the words, and not being able to stand it.

The Deaths

Walk softly, my baby sleeps here.

My baby did not sleep there.

I called Bob the second I got home and ordered a new headstone. After several months, he called me when it was ready, and we all went up to see it as a family. Michael, Gary, June, and I paid respects to the people who still haunted me but were there, secretly waiting for me, just on the other side of my skin.

When it was ready, we went together down Old Sandbanks Road to the cemetery. The black, shiny granite gleamed in the sun. Her name and her dates were etched in cursive on the front of the large, statuesque square; and on the back, I'd added a different quote.

"The birth of every human is pregnant with meaning, why not death?"

Chapter 19

The understanding of death is what saved me.

My understanding.

In my life, I struggled to believe that God would allow such horror as death, and that struggle killed me many times over through my younger years. How can one beat death? No one can. Possibly understanding it, accepting it. By attempting to understand death, I, too, learned of God and life. When I thought God is fallible, it was only the human body that truly is. What I believed was a curse on my family was only my shallow belief system; my house of cards that caused years of anguish I have only now begun to dismantle. I knew only of death and had isolated myself from love for years in an effort to escape losing it again. Like I could beat the grief by hiding.

The wasted years haunt me, as I can never get that time back, but at least I learned something valuable in the process.

Alas, I know that death is not evil. It is a necessary part of life. It was only when I began my search for the light in the darkness that I was finally set free from the chains that had bound me for so long; the weeds growing through my memories.

The Deaths

When I look at the stars, I can see my family. When the sun shines on my face, I know it is God; the risen sun, who sustains all life – even mine. For us, death is a culmination of love stuck in time; for the dead, they are free and twinkling in the midnight sky. It is your job to set them free to be in peace.

Death itself is not evil, and that changed my life.

Nietzsche said that "to live is to suffer, but to survive is to find some meaning in the suffering." For me, the only meaning that can come from suffering is love.

Love brings both despair and a rapturous bewilderment that can make life seem magical and bearable again, or, maybe, for the first time. Love makes us do disgraceful things in an effort to obtain true grace. How can one experience grace if one does not sin? Love is a sacrifice. It is the highest risk with the greatest reward.

The suffering I felt with each death became my duty to them; I decided one day that I simply didn't want to forget. Every smell, every sacred moment with them, I will cherish every single day. The pain only reminds me that they were real.

Love can leave pulsating wounds on a person's soul that can only really be healed by love itself. We are attracted, like moths, to the very things that kill us. Love is frightening, but it is also vital and necessary for life. It is also life-giving and beautiful.

Everything we do is for love, and there is nothing else.

He who loves will suffer, but love is the greatest suffering of all. The darkness will always be there; night will always come. But so will the morning sun. You must learn to turn from the darkness and face the light.

The dark side of love is just as important as the light, for one does not exist without the other. As it is with all things, their opposites are just as vital.

How ambiguous God is!

You must learn to turn from the darkness and face the light. It will always be there, even if you think it's impossible. Sometimes, you really have to push yourself to see life's beauty and the irony that comes with it, like seeing wildflowers in a graveyard. And a truth that saved me, I'll never forget, was how God was just as misunderstood as the rest of us.

Never forget that you need that endless, black abyss if you ever really want to see the stars.

THE END

www.ingramcontent.com/pod-product-compliance
Lightning Source LLC
Chambersburg PA
CBHW070641310726
48982CB00001B/362